THE LAKE LIGHTS

OTHER TITLES BY WILLIAM D. BURT

The King of the Trees
Torsils in Time
The Golden Wood
The Greenstones
The Downs
Kyleah's Mirrors
The Birthing Tree

The Creation Seekers

BOOK ONE

THE LAKE LIGHTS

William D. Burt

By

WILLIAM D. BURT

Author of the "King of the Trees" series

~Published by Creation Way Books~
An imprint of KOT Books, LLC
3237 Sunset Drive
Hubbard, OR 97032

Creation Way Books
KOT Books, LLC
3237 Sunset Drive
Hubbard, OR 97032

Printed in the United States of America.

Cover and illustrations by Becky Miller.

The author is solely responsible for the design, content and editorial accuracy of this work.

ISBN 13: 978-0-9983079-0-9

ISBN 10: 0-9983079-0-4

CONTENTS

"And God created . . . every winged flying creature after its (his) kind. And God saw that it was good."
Genesis 1:21
(Literal translation from the Hebrew)

In loving memory of Dr. Donald Chittick—man of faith, man of science, and man of peace—who entered into the joy of his Master on December 4, 2016.

PROLOGUE

Gliding silently through the night, the huntress skimmed the lake's moon-silvered waters, her own reflection moon-like. Lured by the light, a trout swam to the surface, where the she-beast scooped it up and devoured it whole. Her offspring joined in the frenzied fish-fest. Voracious predators, taloned yet toothless, nameless yet having many names, they ruled the lake.

The natives who arrived later knew the beasts as the *Skookum-kallakala*. No one—especially children—ventured out at night when the Skookum-kallakala were hunting. Fish were not all they ate.

Out of the east the creatures had come. Winging upon the prevailing winds, they skirted the jagged young mountains and reeking volcanoes thrown up during the Great Flood. Harsh winters drove them across uncharted oceans and seas. In their quest for warmth, shelter and prey, they traversed wastelands of freshly laid stone where others of their kind lay entombed in their final agonies.

At length, the Skookum-kallakala reached the coast of a vast continent teeming with wildlife. Enjoying the land's abundant food and mild climate, the newcomers lacked only a suitable place to breed.

Above an inland lake valley, alternating flows of basaltic magma and an iron-rich slurry had invaded a mountain of flood-borne sediment, forming thick beds of a heavy brown ore. Much of the molten basalt spewed out of the mountain, leaving behind lava tubes and caverns—a perfect refuge from ice and snow, fire and flood.

The Skookum-kallakala had found their ideal home.

Chapter 1
RATS IN THE WALL

Whoa! Whoa, Ginny!" cried the trainer, running alongside the galloping horse. He grabbed for the reins but missed. Other shouts rang out around the Equestrian Club as a frightened blond girl with eyes as big as teacups clung desperately to her foam-flecked, runaway mount.

Ginny wasn't listening. The mare veered off the arena's well-trampled training track and onto softer ground, tore through the cattails and swamp grass fringing the placid pond beyond, and dug her hooves into the muck. The girl tumbled head over heels off the horse's back and sailed into the water.

"Jennica! Are you hurt?" cried Jon, her brother. Racing to the pond, he waded in and dragged her to shore with the help of their grandfather, a tall, rugged-looking man with a good-natured face.

The old gentleman was climbing out of the pond when he slipped in the mud and fell backwards into the water. Arms flailing, he stood up and shook himself like a wet dog.

"Don't we make a fine pair!" he told Jennica with a chuckle. "We look like a couple of drowned rats. I'd better get you home. Your mother would never forgive me if you caught a cold."

Jennica sat beside the pond, hugging her muddy legs and weeping. "Why would Ginny run away like that?" she sobbed. "I've never been mean to her, and she's always been gentle with me."

Jon sighed. He couldn't understand why his sister was so horse crazy. To him, horses were just big, smelly farm animals.

Just then, the trainer dashed up. "I'm awfully sorry, Dr. Roberts!" he panted. "I don't know what got into that tired old mare. I've never seen her so spooked. Are you three all right?"

Dr. Kendall Roberts smiled at him. "We're fine, Scully," he said. "And you can call me 'Ken.' After a change of clothes, we'll be as right as rain. Speaking of rain, I'd say we're in for more."

Charcoal clouds were gathering over the Lake Oswego Equestrian Club. One of Oregon's most upscale communities, Lake Oswego was named for the four-hundred-acre body of water stretched out like a sleeping dragon among wooded hills and million-dollar mansions. Jon hoped to visit the lake during his summer break.

Fat raindrops spattered on the pond's surface, each one raising rippling splash-rings. Jon pulled his coat over his head and sidled closer to his grandfather and little sister.

He had been looking forward to skateboarding after Jennica's riding lesson, but the rain would put a stop to his favorite outdoor activity. His Saturday was shaping up to be a complete disaster.

Scully shook his head. "To be honest, Ken, all our animals have been skittish lately. Coyotes might be to blame, but I haven't heard them howling around here." Taking Ginny's reins, he led her away.

Dribbling water, Jon and Jennica trailed their grandfather to his battered red pickup and piled in beside him. He started the engine, and it sputtered to life. Grinding the gears, he bounced along a pot-holed access road before turning onto Twin Fir Road and starting the steep, winding climb to Wembley Park Road.

"It smells terrible in here," Jon grumbled. Mingled with the wet-clothing odor and the stench of decaying pond muck was another scent that strongly reminded Jon of just-struck matches.

He tried clearing the fogged-up passenger-side window with his damp shirtsleeve. The fog quickly returned. Grandfather Roberts liked to pile fossils on the dashboard to examine them as he drove. The year before, a fern fossil had fallen into an air vent, and the pickup's defroster had never been the same since.

The wheezing pickup turned off Wembley to climb Iron Mountain's steep flank. It pulled into the driveway of a rambling, blue-gray house tucked between two winding branches of Glen Eagles Road.

As if on cue, the front door swung open and Olivia Oliver emerged wearing a yellow blouse, leather boots and blue jeans. Her rangy six feet, two inches had earned her the nickname, "Blond Amazon" in college, where she was the women's basketball team's star player. Her long, golden hair was pulled back in a ponytail, and she was carrying a trowel and a packet of sweet-pea seeds.

Seeing the slanting downpour, she wrinkled her nose and was retreating inside the house when she spotted the pickup. Confusion muddied her delicate features as she peered through the rain.

"Why are you back so soon?" she called out.

Jon rolled down the pickup window. "Hi, Mom," he said. "Jen's horse bucked her off. We all got dunked in the pond."

Olivia rushed to the truck and threw open the passenger-side door. "Are you hurt?" she asked Jennica anxiously.

Jennica bravely shook her head. Tears leaked from her eyes.

"What did I tell you, Dad?" Olivia said. "A girl Jen's height and age has no business trying to ride a full-size horse. She could have been seriously hurt, and then where would we be?"

I would have some peace and quiet, Jon uncharitably thought. He fondly recalled the first five years of his life as an only child.

"Nine years old is not too young," Dr. Roberts countered. "I started riding when I was six. Besides, Scully tells me Jen is just the right age and size to take riding lessons, and I trust his judgment. He's been teaching kids to ride for forty years. The Equestrian Club has an excellent safety record, too. Something spooked that mare and made her bolt. Believe me, it was a fluke."

"Speaking of 'flukes,'" said Olivia, "there's no telling what sorts of nasty parasites are lurking in that pond. You all need a shower."

Jon sighed as he climbed out of the pickup. To hear his mother tell it, the Equestrian Club pond was harboring leeches, the West Nile and Zika viruses, malaria and maybe some alligators, too.

After showering and changing into dry clothes, the three came out to find the dining-room table set with a platter of tuna-fish sandwiches and a pitcher of milk. Jon suddenly felt hungry.

"What on earth did you all get yourselves into?" Olivia demanded as she set out napkins, plates and cups. "The laundry room smells like a bomb went off inside." She fixed Jon with a stern, squinty-eyed look, as if he had personally bucked off his sister into the pond.

Dr. Roberts ran his fingers through a thatch of graying hair. "It's just the stinky swamp scum, Liv," he quietly told her as he and his grandchildren took their places at the dining table.

"I just hope your clothes aren't ruined," she crisply declared.

"I'm sure they'll be fine," said her father. "Let's bless this excellent lunch and dig in. Jonathan, would you do the honors?"

Jon had been glumly staring out the dining-room window. The reflection of a freckled, blue-eyed, brown-haired boy stared back. Ordinarily, that window offered quite a spectacular view south across Oswego Lake, the wooded ridges above it and into the misty reaches of the Willamette Valley. It was like sitting on top of the world.

That afternoon, though, the rain had drawn a leaden veil across the dark backdrop of dripping, solemn Douglas-fir trees below the house. Raindrops drummed incessantly on the roof and chuckled through the downspouts. *So much for skateboarding*, Jon thought.

"Jonathan?" Grandfather Roberts repeated with a raised eyebrow. His mouth curled in a faint smile that reached up to crinkle the laugh-lined corners of his hazel eyes.

"Uh, all right," said Jon. He didn't like praying in public. "Dear Lord," he began. "Thank You that Jennica is okay after falling off the horse and that Grandpa Roberts could join us today in our nice new home. Please protect Dad over in Afstanigan. Oh, and thank You for this yummy lunch that Mom made for us. Bless this food to our bodies' health and strength, and bless Mom, too. In Jesus' name, Amen."

"It's 'Afghanistan,' silly," Jennica whispered to her brother.

Jon bit his lip. He hated being corrected by his little sister, who seemed to take perverse pleasure in pointing out his mistakes.

It was bad enough when he tripped over his dyslexic tongue at school and the other kids made fun of him. To top it all off, he was left handed, making his most valiant attempts at handwriting an awkward, ink-smeared scrawl. Blushing, he bit off a chunk of tuna sandwich and washed down his humiliation with a swig of milk.

He wished the rain would stop so he could enjoy the rope swing his father had hung from the limb of an ancient oak tree in the side yard. Perched near the brink of a twenty-foot rocky cliff, the house sat on a spacious, beautifully landscaped lot with a weathered wooden deck hanging over the bluff in back.

Jon's family had moved so his mother could be closer to her teaching job at Uplands Elementary School. Not wishing to change schools, Jon and Jennica had dug in their heels, but in the end, their parents prevailed—as parents usually do.

Jon was glad they had. With its cramped, treeless yard, their old house in Beaverton offered scarcely enough space for the rickety metal swing-set that he and Jennica quickly wore out.

Looking up, Jon saw tears coursing down his mother's pale cheeks. Grandfather Roberts reached over and patted her hand.

"Liv, you don't have to do this alone. Just say the word, and I can take some of the weight off your shoulders. I'd be happy to rearrange my university schedule so I could pick up the kids from school."

"Thanks for the offer, Dad, but I can manage," Mrs. Oliver huskily replied. "It's just so lonely without Matt. He writes and calls as often as he can, but that's not the same as having him here. I know he wants to serve his country, but I wish he'd come home soon."

"We all do, Liv. We all do," said her father, helping himself to another bulging tuna-fish sandwich. "When he does return, please don't mention that I borrowed some of his clothes!"

Jon swallowed the lump in his throat. Two months earlier, Dr. Matthew Oliver had left to work in Afghanistan as a civilian contractor. Ever since then, the house had felt all hollow. Jon was thankful his father wasn't serving in a front-line combat role.

Still, he missed him terribly. After lunch, Jon saw his grandfather out the front door. Then he stole down the hallway to his father's private office. Jon knew Matthew Oliver's "man-cave" was strictly off limits to anyone and everyone—including Mrs. Oliver. For that reason, Dr. Oliver always kept his office door securely locked.

Except on one occasion. At three-thirty the Saturday morning before his father left for Afghanistan, Jon was sneaking upstairs from playing video games in the basement when he heard a scraping sound in the hallway. Peering around the corner, he saw his father straightening one of the framed family photos that hung on the wall. Then the physicist let himself into his office.

Jon waited a few minutes before trying the doorknob. It was un-locked—but nobody was inside the office. Dr. Matthew Oliver had quite suddenly and mysteriously vanished, only to reappear the next morning at the breakfast table with dark bags under his blue eyes.

Ever since then, the office door had remained firmly locked.

Now that his father was overseas, Jon decided he had waited long enough to unravel the secrets behind that closed door. His heart pounding with delicious anticipation, he studied the family photo. In the picture, his father grinned boyishly back at him, wearing his trademark crew-cut. Jon gingerly lifted the photo away from the wall. As he had suspected, a key was wedged into the picture frame's back.

Jon smiled as he used the key to unlock the door. His father was a brilliant man, but sometimes he was rather predictable.

Slipping inside, Jon quickly closed the door behind him and surveyed the spacious office. In the center of the chilly room stood a familiar, low-backed captain's chair and polished oaken desk. They had occupied a prominent place in the office at the old house, but since the move, Jon had forgotten about them.

He settled into the sturdy chair, which supposedly had once belonged to the famous Northwest explorer, Captain Robert Gray—and frowned. His father had drilled an angled hole into the left arm-rest, evidently for use as a pencil-holder. It seemed a shame to ruin such a fine piece of antique furniture by drilling a hole in it.

Jon also noted that the chair's feet were bolted to the floor. He could understand why a seafaring captain would want to anchor his chair to the deck of a heaving ship in rough seas, but why would Matthew Oliver fasten his office chair to the floor?

The desk itself was remarkably uncluttered, as was the rest of the office. Perhaps Jon's father had put most of his computers and other experimental equipment in storage somewhere. Nothing Jon could see in the room was worth keeping under lock and key.

On the wall behind the desk hung an ornate antique mirror. Into its frame was tucked a card bearing the words of Psalm 23:1—"The Lord is my shepherd; I shall not want." Dr. Oliver certainly did not want for awards. Plaques commemorating his many achievements decorated the office walls. Gazing at his father's honors and tributes, Jon basked in the presence of Dr. Matthew Oliver's humble genius.

At age thirty-eight, GyroSensors Laboratories' owner and senior engineer was already an accomplished scientist with numerous patents to his name. With the help of Dr. Ronald Ingersoll, his business partner, Dr. Oliver developed advanced guidance systems for civilian and military aircraft. Jon toyed with the lanyard that he always wore around his neck. It was attached to a memento of happier days—a key card his father had lent him for accessing GyroSensors' facilities.

"Jonathan!" Mrs. Oliver's muffled voice cut through the door, jarring Jon out of his reverie. "Where have you got to this time? Please come help us with the dishes, won't you?"

With a groan, Jon heaved himself out of the chair and left the spartan office. After locking the door behind him, he replaced the key in its special spot and joined his sister and mother in the kitchen.

Once the dishes were washed, he slipped downstairs to play video games at the console he had rigged up in the basement. He was hoping to get in a half-hour of game time before Jennica found him. His pesky little sister stuck to him like chewing gum in a shag carpet.

In the basement, a familiar burnt-matches odor stung Jon's nose and eyes. Since the laundry room sat directly above him, he decided the sharp smell must have wafted down the stairs before his arrival. After all, the basement door was usually left ajar.

The room felt like a sauna. The wall-mounted thermostat was set at fifty-five, but its thermometer read eighty-two degrees. Jon sighed. He would have to tinker with the malfunctioning device—another chore on his long to-do list. It wasn't easy being the man of the house. Still, he had made the basement his undisputed man-cave, complete with the video-game setup and a sagging couch for naps.

Peeling off his sweater, he tossed it onto the couch, which sat under the thermostat. Then he seated himself at the game table. Behind it loomed a pile of unrestored captain's chairs mixed with assorted Christmas decorations like an unstable heap of coal-mine tailings.

Ignoring the real threat of a junk avalanche, Jon was switching on the game console when he heard a scratching noise. He groaned. Jennica had already found him. So much for his precious alone-time. If only the basement door locked on the inside!

Turning around, he called out, "Just give me a few minutes at the console and then you can have a turn." No one answered. He peered up the stairs. Nothing moved in the steep, shadowy stairwell.

Scritch-scritch-scritch.

Jon jumped up and stared about, the hair on the back of his neck prickling. Who—or what—was making that noise? It seemed to be coming from a spot behind the east wall. Tiptoeing to the wall, he put his ear against it and heard a scrabbling sound. He had heard similar rustlings under the creaky wooden floor at his old house.

Whoosh! The pent-up breath escaped his lungs. *Rats.* The furry vermin were living inside the wall. Jon laughed nervously. *Get a grip,* he told himself. How could he let a few rodents spook him? If his sister ever got wind of this, he would never hear the end of it.

Jon returned to the game table, but his hands were shaking too badly to operate the controller accurately. With a sigh, he left the table and started up the stairs. Before shutting off the lights, he turned to scan the basement for signs of vermin. He saw none, though the room seemed oddly chopped off at the back, where the green sheetrock looked freshly painted next to the dingier side-wall panels.

With the flick of a switch, Jon doused the lights. He cocked his head to listen for the scratching noise one last time.

Scritch-scritch.

Chapter 2
HOUSEWARMING

The next morning, Jon's mother took the family down the valley to visit the New Hope Church. Mrs. Oliver set the car's squeaky wipers on high to sweep away the sheets of rain plastering the windshield like a hail of kamikaze jellyfish. It reminded Jon of the way his mother dashed away her not-so-secret tears whenever she was missing her husband.

The torrential rain also reminded Jon of the soggy walks he used to take with his father. When a rain squall would sweep overhead and threaten to drench them both, Mr. Oliver would point upward and say, "There are just three main weather conditions in Western Oregon: 'Raining,' 'Just Rained,' and 'About to Rain.'"

When the sky promised a shower, Jon would beg his father to bring along a "bumbrella" before they set out. Mr. Oliver would only wink at him and say, "Oregonians don't carry umbrellas. A little rain never hurt anyone. Umbrellas are for sissies and Californians."

Jon avoided reminding him that Dr. Roberts carried an umbrella.

As Jon and his sister puddle-hopped through the church parking lot, he wished his only umbrella hadn't turned inside out in a recent windstorm. At least his cap and jacket helped ward off the rain.

Jon missed his friends at their old church, but he did like Reverend Sanford, New Hope's minister—a tall, spare man with a receding hairline and a delightfully dry sense of humor. Sunday's message was entitled, "Enduring Times of Testing." Jon thought having a know-it-all pest of a sister was testing enough for anybody.

Jen's typical tormenting pokes, jabs and tickles punctuated the wet drive home. Knowing he shouldn't respond in kind, Jon steeled himself to ignore her. Still, he was sorely tempted to wrestle his sister to the car's floorboards and sit on her until she promised to behave.

When the three arrived home, Olivia opened the front door to a blast of warm, smelly air. "Jonathan Matthew Oliver!" she scolded him. "How many times have I told you to turn down the thermostat before we leave? We can't afford to heat this house like a Turkish bath while we're away. It's a waste of electricity."

When his mother used all three of his names, Jon knew he was in serious trouble. "But I did turn it down!" he protested. He was sure he had. Had all the thermostats in the house suddenly gone haywire?

His mother checked the thermostat. "Why, so you did," she said. "I apologize for accusing you. Then why is it so hot in here? And what is that awful stench? You two open your bedroom windows, and I'll open mine. We need to air out this place, rain or not."

Jon and Jennica ran into their rooms and threw open the windows. Still the smell lingered. Muttering something about "stinky pond water," their mother collected their sodden clothes from the laundry room and tossed them out onto the wet driveway.

By then the rain had subsided, and a bashful March sun was breaking through the ragged clouds. Unable to endure the stench inside, Jon escaped outside with his mother and sister.

"Let's take a walk," Jennica suggested.

Strolling up the steaming road, they passed several power poles plastered with handbills. Jon stopped to read one of the leaflets, which featured an inkjet photo of a furry animal identified as a cat, though the rain-blurred photo resembled a deformed gopher.

"$50 reward for return of Siamese cat," the poster read. "Slinky was last seen on March 2. She has a crooked tail. If you find her, please call the Stevenson family or bring to: 1723 Glen Eagles Place."

"Huh!" said Jon. He didn't recall seeing a crooked-tailed cat around the neighborhood, but he hadn't lived there very long.

"Listen to this," said his mother, who was standing on the opposite side of the power pole. "'Missing: Black poodle that answers to the name "Midnight." If found, call this number.'"

Reading lower on the same pole, Jennica said, "Here's another one. It says, 'My name is Tanner. I'm a purebred beagle. If I follow you home, call the number on my tag. My owner is offering $100 for my safe return. No questions asked.'"

"I think we should go into the pet-recovery business," quipped Mrs. Oliver. "Maybe then I could quit my teaching job."

"I thought you liked teaching kids," Jennica said with a hurt look.

Jon smirked. His naïve sister took everything people said at face value. He had once tried explaining to her the meaning of "tongue in cheek," and she had spent the afternoon in front of the bathroom mirror, poking out her cheeks with her tongue.

"I was being facetious, dear," said Mrs. Oliver. "I do enjoy teaching at Uplands. It's one of the finest elementary schools in the whole state. The staff and students there are top notch."

"What does 'facetious' mean?" Jennica asked her.

Mrs. Oliver was about to answer when doors began banging open up and down Glen Eagles. Coughing and gagging, people poured out of their homes. A familiar, foul smell filled the air.

"What's the matter?" Mrs. Oliver asked an elderly lady who was staggering down the street dressed in a blue robe and slippers.

"What's the matter?" the woman repeated shrilly. "I'll tell you what's the matter. My house is hotter than a sauna inside, and it stinks to high heaven, too. I hope it will smell better soon."

You're not the only one driven out of your home, Jon thought.

The woman continued, "A rat must have died in the crawl space. Do you know of any good exterminators I could call?"

Mrs. Oliver didn't. She glanced at Jon with a mystified look that said, *How could a dead rat heat up someone's house?*

Now that Mr. Oliver was overseas, Jon's mother was turning to him more often for help. He didn't know what to say.

"Maybe we should go home," he lamely suggested.

Excusing herself, Mrs. Oliver herded her children back down the street, where they met more dazed residents milling about. Quite a few of them were loudly voicing their opinions.

"Call the City!" one man said. "There's gas leaking from the sewers. If it explodes, it could blow us all to kingdom come."

"No, no!" said another. "It smells like a natural gas leak. Someone needs to call the gas company, and quickly, too."

Making their way through the crowd, the Olivers found Grandfather Roberts waiting outside the house, his gray hair awry. He was poking around the home's concrete foundation.

"There you are!" he said, looking relieved. "I wondered what had become of you all. It's not like you to leave the front door wide open, Liv. Is there a gas leak in the neighborhood?"

"I certainly hope not, Dad," said Olivia. "We can't afford to live in a hotel while some leaky old pipe is being repaired."

"It's awfully hot inside the house, Grandpa," said Jennica.

"And it smells like ammonia or old gym socks," Jon added. "We opened all the windows, but it still stinks in there."

Dr. Roberts sagely nodded. "It's strong enough to smell out here, too," he said. "Let's all go inside and see if we can find the source."

Warm, smelly air was still billowing out the front door as the four ducked inside. The overpowering stench immediately made Jon's eyes water. Coughing, Jennica and her mother fled back outside.

"This is no gas leak," Dr. Roberts told Jon before also escaping.

Hoping the basement had cooled off enough for him to play his video games, Jon headed downstairs. He had taken only a few steps when a blast of hot, stinking air struck him, forcing him to turn back, his lungs and eyes burning unbearably.

He rushed outside to find his family coughing and wiping their eyes. "Fire! Fire! The basement is on fire!" he wheezed.

Grandfather Roberts weakly smiled. "No, I don't think there's a fire inside. Unless I'm greatly mistaken, that smell is sulfur dioxide. It's a poisonous gas that irritates the eyes and lungs."

"But where does it come from?" Jennica asked him.

"It's released from deep underground," the professor replied. "I suspect a hot springs may have opened beneath these houses, but we won't know for sure until some tests can be run. I have a friend in the U.S. Geological Survey who may be able to help, if he's in the States right now. In the meantime, you should stay out of the house."

"That's easy for you to say, Dad," Mrs. Oliver grumped. "Where will we all sleep? I'm not about to cram everybody into a motel room with two beds and a shower. Even with cable television, we'd be at each other's throats in no time."

"You could stay at my place," said Grandfather Roberts.

Olivia snorted and tossed her head. "I appreciate the offer, Dad, but you've got only two small bedrooms and one bath. Where would you sleep? Besides, we don't want to intrude."

"You wouldn't be intruding," said Dr. Roberts genially. "And I could sleep on the couch. When your mother was alive, I spent many comfortable nights on that couch. She snored like a freight train, you know. Kept me awake for hours on end, and the neighbors, too."

"Hey!" Jon said. "I have an idea. Maybe we can sleep outside on the back deck. It would be just like camping in the woods."

Jon loved to camp, but his parents were usually too busy to take time off for a vacation. At their old house, he and his sister had to settle for camping in the back yard during the summer.

"I don't know," said his mother, rubbing her bloodshot eyes. "What if some wild animals attacked us? We live on top of a forested mountain, after all. There's no telling what sorts of creatures come out at night here—maybe even bears and mountain lions."

Grandfather Roberts winked at her. "Don't worry, Liv. Most wild animals are afraid of humans. I think Jon's suggestion is excellent. Let's see what we can find in your garage, shall we?"

A minute later, Olivia and her father emerged from the house loaded with a lightweight tent and three sleeping bags and foam mattresses. Jon's mother had turned a delicate shade of lavender. She exhaled explosively and sucked in a long, shuddering breath.

"That's better!" she gasped, dropping the sleeping bags and mattresses onto the porch. "I thought I was going to faint from holding my breath the whole time. I've never been so thankful for fresh air."

"It's still pretty bad in there," Grandfather Roberts agreed, grappling with the unwieldy tent. "Let's go around back and set up our campsite on the deck. Maybe we could convince your mother to make us some lunch. I don't know about you, but I'm starving. Breakfast was a stale doughnut and a lukewarm cup of coffee."

The four lugged their camping gear around the side of the house and up onto the deck. Jon helped his grandfather erect the tent, while Jennica and Olivia rolled out the mattresses and sleeping bags.

"There!" said Dr. Roberts, dusting off his hands on his trousers. "Now let's see what we can find to eat in your cupboards. Since we're roughing it, we should probably try to keep our meals simple."

He and his daughter darted in and out of the house, bringing out loaves of bread, jars of peanut butter and jelly, chips, dip, some grapes and apples, a jug of milk, paper plates and cups, knives and napkins. They also picked up some changes of clothing.

"I wouldn't exactly call this 'roughing it,'" said Mrs. Oliver with a smile. She was balancing a paper plate piled with chips on her knee. "Still, while the weather holds, it's nice to eat outside."

"I can't remember the last time we went camping as a family," the professor commented, chewing on a peanut butter sandwich.

Olivia grimaced. "*I* do. You took us to Spirit Lake two years after Mount St. Helens erupted. We just followed you around as you conducted your research. I was five. Ronnie was eight."

Dr. Roberts chuckled. "Yes, I remember that trip. Just before we arrived, a massive mud flow had rapidly carved a miniature 'Grand Canyon' one-hundred forty feet deep. Quite remarkable, really."

Olivia's eyes brimmed with tears. "Dad, I don't care about mud flows, canyons, or Mount St. Helens. I just would give anything to have Mom and Ronnie back with us again. I miss them."

"So do I, Liv, so do I," said her father heavily. "At least we have the hope of seeing them again in Heaven some day. I can't wait."

"Neither can I," Jon's mother sighed.

Chapter 3
THE IRON MOUNTAIN TRAIL

While the grownups chatted, Jon munched on his sandwich at the deck's back edge. Its timbers overhung the low cliff that dropped into the forest below.

Jon had never met either Grandmother Eunice or Uncle Ronnie. They had perished in a tragic car accident years before his birth.

Eunice had been driving Ronnie to a swimming lesson at the local pool when their car skidded on a patch of black ice and rolled down an embankment. Every November since that day, Grandfather Roberts had placed a bouquet of his prize late-blooming chrysanthemums at the crash site along that lonely stretch of road.

Leaning on the deck's railing, Jon gazed over the rocky escarpment. Its crumbling slopes reminded him of the accident scene, stirring up the old grief he often saw in his mother. A narrow trail hugged the cliff's base, clinging to the steep, wooded slope. A deer demurely stepped out onto the path and sniffed the air.

Jon motioned his sister over and pointed out the deer on the trail. Jennica smiled as the deer's ears twitched. Alarmed by some unseen threat, the animal bounded noisily into the underbrush.

"Grandfather! Grandfather!" Jen cried. "We just saw a deer."

Grandfather Roberts ambled up to the pair and glanced over the railing. "It doesn't surprise me," he said. "Those trees are just the kind of cover deer like. Say, since the sun has come out, how would you two like to explore that trail? You may take your lunches along if you wish. You'd better ask your mother first if it's all right with her."

With their mother's grudging permission—and only after they had promised to be back for supper—Jon and Jennica took turns changing their clothes in the deck-tent. Wearing denim shirts, blue jeans and hiking boots, they followed Dr. Roberts off the deck and through some bushes and brambles to Glen Eagles Road.

"Let's go down the hill," he suggested. "I'll bet I know where the trail begins." The three trotted along the steep, tree-lined street, hanging onto each other to help maintain their footing.

Just off the street, they came upon a circular graveled drive beside a split-level house tucked into the mountainside. Leading away from the drive, a narrow trail dove east into thickets of blackberry vines, hawthorn, ocean spray, and wild plum. Ivy-infested white oaks clung stubbornly to the steep slope below.

Left of the trailhead stood a glass-paned, wooden kiosk erected by the Friends of Iron Mountain. It housed some helpful informational literature on the trail's history and native plants in the area.

"Somebody went to a lot of trouble to blaze this path through such rocky terrain," Dr. Roberts observed as he led Jon and Jennica down the trail. "It's a pity the forest here has become so overgrown with English ivy. It's slowly choking the trees."

Over a hundred yards farther along the path, a trailside observation deck overhung the downhill slope on the right. The three clambered onto the semicircular wooden deck to read a plaque honoring the Eagle Scout who had designed and built the impressive structure.

Although a tall fir tree obscured the outlook in the center and bigleaf maples further obstructed the view on either side, the vista was still magnificent. Oswego Lake's waters sparkled through the distant trees. Beyond the lake, darkly wooded hills marched rank upon rank into the misty and mysterious southlands.

"What's that road down there at the bottom?" Jon asked his grandfather, pointing beyond the craggy slope's tree-shrouded foot.

"That's Iron Mountain Boulevard. It runs between the lake and this mountain," the old man replied. "It's quite the scenic drive."

Jon turned back to the uphill view above the path. Festooned with ferns, the cliff face was deeply indented, as if a giant had taken a bite out of the decaying hillside. Huge boulders lay jumbled at its base. At the top, some familiar timbers jutted over the cliff's edge.

"Look up there, Grandpa," Jon said. "It's our deck!"

Following his grandson's gaze, Dr. Roberts glanced up at the cliff. "Why, so it is," he said. Ambling up to the cliff's base, he climbed a few feet, removed a disc-topped, spiked object from his pocket and pushed the spike into a patch of rocky soil.

Jon and Jennica stared up at the paleontologist. "What are you doing over there?" Jon asked him. "Do you need some help? That cliff doesn't look safe to climb, even with that spiky thingy."

The professor sniffed the air. "I can smell sulfur dioxide seeping out of this cliff. Anyway, I'm just conducting a simple experiment. And this isn't a rock-climbing piton, but your mother's meat thermometer." He winked. "Please don't tell her I used it!"

He pulled up the thermometer and squinted at its glass dial. His eyes bulged. "The temperature of this soil is nearly seventy degrees," he announced. "It shouldn't be that warm at this time of the year. No wonder it feels like an oven inside your house!"

"Do you still think it's a hot springs?" Jon asked him.

Professor Roberts shook his head. "I can't say for sure. There's one more test I need to conduct, but not here. Let's move along."

Just past the observation deck, they came upon two glass-fronted interpretive signs standing opposite a wooden picnic table. The second sign read, "The Prosser Iron Mine."

Dr. Roberts tapped the sign. "This says that in 1861, large deposits of high-grade hematite ore were discovered here. Oddly enough, the iron ore was sandwiched between two basalt layers.

"That was the start of the Prosser Mine, which operated on Iron Mountain until 1878, when the Oswego Iron Company acquired it. In 1882, it was sold again, this time under the auspices of the Oregon Iron and Steel Company. The mine was closed for good in 1894."

The other sign was labeled, "Into the Bowels of the Earth." It depicted the Prosser Mine's layout as it had looked in 1893—a convoluted maze of meandering tunnels and drifts resembling the galleries of a carpenter-ant colony infesting a Douglas-fir log.

"What does this mean where the sign says, 'Area worked out'?" Jon asked his grandfather.

"That refers to the places where the miners removed all of the ore that could be safely extracted," Professor Roberts replied. "These three spots labeled 'unexplored area' were probably sections of the mine too dangerous for even experienced miners to visit."

"Why were they dangerous?" asked Jennica.

The professor shrugged. "The Prosser hasn't been properly maintained in many years. Even when it was still operating, tunnel ceilings could collapse without warning. Most mines are that way. Mining is one of the most hazardous occupations in the world."

Jon searched for signs of a tunnel entrance, but he saw only thick draperies of English ivy and poison oak festooning the crumbling hillside. He would have loved to explore those old mine galleries.

Holes in the ground had always fascinated him. At his old house, he had dug a network of burrows and caverns in a mound of dirt in the back yard. Eventually, he created so many passages that the dirt pile had collapsed, burying his armies of toy soldiers and knights.

Now he pictured himself wearing a hard hat and a miner's lamp, uncovering veins of pure gold that the original miners had overlooked in their search for iron ore. What wealth lay beneath his feet?

At Dr. Roberts' suggestion, Jon and Jennica finished their sandwiches while sitting at the picnic table. Afterwards, Jennica gestured vaguely through the trees. "What is that, Grandpa?" she asked. "It looks like an airport down there, but where are the planes?"

Nestled among thick stands of trees at the foot of Iron Mountain sat a Quonset-style white shed. A few tiny figures were milling about the spacious, grassy grounds surrounding it.

Dr. Roberts stood and peered through the trees. "That's the Equestrian Club's main stable below us. Don't you recognize it? You should know that place like the back of your hand."

"Oh, yeah, you're right," Jennica sheepishly replied. "It doesn't look the same from up here." She tugged on her brother's arm. "C'mon, Jon," she said. "Let's go home. I'm tired."

"Not yet," Jon said. "I want to look for that deer. I'm sure it must be around here somewhere. Maybe there's a whole herd."

Leaving the picnic table, Jon led his sister and grandfather down the muddy trail, single file. On either side, the three symmetrical leaves of western trillium lilies were unfurling. Most of the shrubs and trees beside the path were also waking up. Some white-flowered bushes overhung the path, perfuming the air with a musky odor.

"What are these, Grandfather?" Jennica asked him.

"Those are Indian plums," he replied. "In these parts, they are the first shrubs to leaf out in the spring. They're coming out early this year. And those other white-flowering bushes are wild currants. I'd say they are breaking their buds early, too."

"Why is that?" Jon asked him.

Grandfather Roberts rubbed his jaw. "I don't know, but I aim to find out. The plants elsewhere in Oswego aren't this far along in their development. This whole mountain poses a mystery."

Moving on, they came to some massive stone outcroppings that formed fern-draped walls on the trail's uphill side. Water trickled down their worn faces and puddled in the trail, creating slick, muddy spots. In one of those spots, Jon noticed a large, bird-like track sunken deeply in the mud. Then his sister trampled over the track.

A hawk's screeching cry shattered the heavy silence.

Farther along, groves of maple and fir dappled the ivy-shrouded forest floor with shifting shadows. Rounding a bend, the party came within sight of a cozy house sitting at the trail's end. "We had better turn around now," Dr. Roberts announced. "We mustn't trespass on private property, though the trail may still be accessible."

He gazed wistfully at the little house before turning back. "This path," he murmured, "was once the bed of a narrow-gauge railway that was used to transport the mined iron ore all the way down to the old Riverfront Park blast furnace." Grandfather Roberts loved trains.

Disappointed that no deer had yet appeared, Jon trudged back up the path after his grandfather and sister. Presently, they came to a fork in the trail. The right fork led upward—to the Glen Eagles trailhead—while the left-hand fork angled downward through the trees.

"I don't recall seeing this lower path before," said the professor.

"Me, neither," chimed in Jennica.

"We must have missed it on the way down," Jon concluded.

"Are you two game for more exploring?" their grandfather asked.

"I'm not in a hurry, and I have an idea where this leads."

Jon shrugged. "I'm in. I'd rather go down than up."

"Me, too," said Jennica. "My legs ache."

"Then down it is," said Grandfather Roberts.

The path cut diagonally along the mountainside. At one point, the trail detoured around a large fir with a steaming, brown-and-white pile at its base. Jon gave the foul mound a wide berth.

"Gross," he said. "Horse manure. My favorite."

Dr. Roberts remarked, "Members of the Equestrian Club must ride their horses along this trail." He bent down to examine the mound. "This isn't horse manure, though. It resembles bird or lizard droppings more than it does mammalian dung."

"I'll take your word for it," Jon said, gagging.

"Eww," said Jennica and held her nose.

Their grandfather's gaze traveled up the fir's furrowed trunk. "Here's something else," he said. "Do you see how the droppings have coated the trunk? Whatever left them had to have been sitting up in this tree. Maybe it was a blue heron, though I see no nests."

In spite of himself, Jon sneaked a quick peek up the tree. Above the pile, a disgusting mass of droppings had cascaded down the trunk and was slowly drying in the afternoon sun.

"Can we move along now?" Jon asked his grandfather. His stomach was riding a roller coaster that had lost its brakes.

The professor agreed, and shortly afterwards, the trail leveled out as it reached the valley floor. Through the trees, handsome horses could be seen trotting around the Equestrian Club's riding track. Beyond the track stood the gleaming white stable.

"Let's cut through the woods here," Dr. Roberts suggested. "I'd like to revisit the pond—out of scientific curiosity, of course."

"I'm really not up for another swim," Jon quipped.

"That makes two of us," Jennica agreed.

"This time, I'll be the only one getting wet," the professor assured them. "It won't take me more than a few minutes."

Hugging the trees on the track's north side, the hikers came at last to the pond. Jon's churning stomach heaved again. Scores of dead frogs and fish were floating belly-up on the water among mats of shriveled, blackened lily pads and dying cattails. Across the pond, a lone blue heron croaked plaintively and flew off.

"What happened here?" Jon asked in amazement.

Jennica daintily sneezed. She rubbed her eyes and nose. "And why does it stink like sulfur whatchamacallit?"

"I'm about to find out," said Dr. Roberts. With a determined set to his jaw, he plowed through the rotting vegetation and waded into the pond. Pulling out the meat thermometer, he plunged it twice into the water. Then he awkwardly clambered out again.

"Phew!" he said. "It does stink out there. Let's go home."

"What did you find, Grandfather?" Jon asked him.

"I'm afraid we have a very serious problem," he said. "The temperature of that pond water is about eighty-five degrees."

Chapter 4
MEASURING A MOUNTAIN

Jon's mother whistled. "Eighty-five degrees? That's almost warm enough for bath water!" Slouched in a collapsible camp chair, she was relaxing on the deck with her father and children. An anemic spring sun was setting behind scudding storm clouds. A stiff breeze sprang up, driving away the foul, sulfurous vapors.

"You're right about that, Liv," said Dr. Roberts. "The water was so warm it cooked every living thing in it. A pond that size should be around forty degrees at this time of year. I took a couple of readings to be sure my results were accurate."

"How did you take your readings?" Olivia asked him.

The professor reddened as he withdrew the meat thermometer from his pocket and handed it to his daughter. "I, ah, borrowed this," he said sheepishly. "I must say it worked nicely and held up well. It's ruggedly built—for a common kitchen gadget, that is."

"Dad! What have you done to my meat thermometer? That was a Christmas gift from Matt. You should have asked my permission first. If you've ruined it, you'll owe me another."

Jon knew his mother wasn't entirely serious. She loved to tease his grandfather whenever he "got scientific," as she put it.

Grandfather Roberts held up his hands in a gesture of mock surrender. "Peace! Peace!" he said. "Just rinse it off with soap and water, and it'll be as good as new. Besides, it was all for the sake of science, my dear daughter, all for the sake of science."

"That's what you said when you whipped up a batch of plaster in Mom's best mixing bowl!" Olivia scolded him. "I'll never forget the look on her face when you told her you were making a cast of a dinosaur footprint. We ate crunchy plaster bits with our pancakes and waffles for weeks afterwards."

Professor Roberts chuckled. "I remember that incident. Eunice was so upset, she banned me from the kitchen for life. How did she put it? 'I won't stand for a mad Welshman mucking up my bowls!' I suppose it didn't help to remind her that I was *her* 'mad Welshman.'"

"And then I went and married a mad Welshman of my own," said Olivia with a rueful laugh. "At our old house, Matt was always running messy experiments in the kitchen." A quizzical look crossed her face. "Now that I think of it, he hasn't created any more disasters or burned out my appliances since we moved here. I wonder why."

Once, Jon's father had invented a contraption that would pry the top off a frozen orange-juice can, suck out the concentrate, add water and stir out the lumps. It had worked quite well—the first time. On the second attempt, it had sprayed orange juice all over the kitchen.

"Dinosaur footprint?" said Jon hopefully. He loved dinosaurs and often got himself into trouble at school for drawing "dino" pictures when he was supposed to be studying math or history.

For Jon's birthday, his grandfather had taken him to visit his laboratory at Columbia University in Portland. The lab was crammed from floor to ceiling with dinosaur fossils of every description: petrified skulls and legs, ribs and eggs, claws and teeth, tracks and feet—even complete skeletons. Jon could have spent weeks poring over the distinguished professor's extensive collection.

He had come away from that visit with a parting gift—a genuine dinosaur fossil. "Fruitadens," Dr. Roberts had told him, "is the smallest known dinosaur from North America. It's also one of the rarest fossils ever found here. Please do be careful with it."

Jon was. He prominently displayed the fossil on his dresser, and he never, ever let Jennica touch it. He felt sorry for "Fruity," as he called the animal, which was embedded in a sandstone slab. The little reptile must have died in torment. Its head and neck were contorted, its jaws gaping in an agonized rictus that exposed its stumpy teeth.

The more teeth a dinosaur had, the better Jon liked it.

"Dinosaurs are just a bunch of boring old bones," Jennica sniffed. "You can ride a horse, but you can't ride a dinosaur."

"Who says?" Jon retorted. He wanted to remind his sister it was a horse that had bucked her into the Equestrian Club pond, but he thought the better of it. Instead, he asked his grandfather, "Do you know what made the water so warm in that pond?"

Dr. Roberts nodded. "I suspect low-level geothermal activity is heating up this mountain and the surrounding area. That would account for the earlier flowering of the plants and would also explain the distinctive smell of sulfur dioxide. I'll need to do more research first and talk with my friend in the USGS. He's a renowned volcanologist, though his views—like mine—are somewhat controversial."

A pained look pinched Mrs. Oliver's face. "Are you saying our house is going to smell like a chicken coop for the rest of our lives?"

"Then we could stay out here," said Jennica. "It's a fun place to blow bubbles!" Dipping a plastic wand into a bottle of soap solution, she coaxed a necklace of shimmering spheres into the air. They floated like fleet-winged fairies across the deck and over the forest below.

"Don't worry," Dr. Roberts said. "I'm sure whatever is happening beneath our feet will be short lived, like most minor thermal events."

"I hope you are right," Olivia replied with a sigh.

When Dr. Roberts had left for the night, Jon and his sister bedded down beside their mother in their mildewy sleeping bags. Some time later, Jon was awakened by the moon's light shining through the tent's thin nylon fabric. After crawling out of his sleeping bag, Jon poked his head outside—and gasped at the magnificent spectacle.

An enormous full moon was rising majestically above Lake Oswego, dwarfing everything around it. Spooky, spiky shadows were scudding across its pocked face. *Those are just owls*, Jon told himself, but the silhouettes were too large for any owl. Then what were they?

In the distance, glowing blobs like giant fireflies were gliding above Oswego Lake. Was he dreaming, or was the moonlight playing tricks on his eyes? Shivering, Jon ducked back inside the tent as shrill moon-screeches echoed madly around the mountain.

Before work the next morning, Mrs. Oliver took down the deck-tent and bustled around the house turning off fans and closing windows. Just as her father had predicted, the Oliver home had cooled off considerably during the night and the burnt-matches odor had subsided. Even the basement air was breathable, though still acrid.

By the time Jon and Jennica arrived home from school, the house smelled and felt almost normal. An hour later, their mother dragged in from work and flopped down on a couch in the living room.

"All these dreadfully boring after-school meetings ought to be outlawed as cruel and unusual punishment," she groaned.

After a short rest, Mrs. Oliver had just begun preparing dinner when the doorbell rang. "See who that is, won't you, Jon?" she asked. Jennica followed him as he went to the door. Dr. Roberts was standing on the porch with a stocky, bearded man wearing leather work boots, blue jeans and a Harris Tweed wool coat over a denim shirt.

"I am sorry to barge in on you like this," the professor said. "This is my friend and colleague, Dr. Graham MacKenzie. He's a volcano expert. I've asked him to have a look at our mountain. Dr. MacKenzie, these are my grandchildren, Jonathan and Jennica Oliver."

"Did someone mention volcanoes?" called Mrs. Oliver from the kitchen. She came out drying her hands on a towel and introduced herself to Dr. MacKenzie, who bowed with old-world charm.

"It's a delight t' meet ye all, Oliver clan," said Dr. MacKenzie. "We Celts must stick together, ye know. Ye favor yer grandfaither a guid bit, bairns." Jon noted the Scottish burr in the scientist's voice.

Dr. Roberts interpreted. "He means, 'You look a lot like your grandfather, children.'" The professor nudged his friend and whispered, "They've never met a native Scotsman before."

Dr. MacKenzie grinned ruefully. "Sairy—sorry."

Towering over the compact volcanologist, Mrs. Oliver asked him, "Does this mean our home is sitting right over an active volcano?"

"I won't know till I can conduct some tests," said Dr. MacKenzie. "However, I dinna believe an eruption is imminent. From what I've read o' the local history, this area hasn't experienced significant volcanic activity in hundreds o' years. I've brought some equipment wi' me to help us determine what's happening on yer mountain.

"Jon, would ye help me unpack and carry some o' my gear?" In the volcanologist's Scots brogue, "carry" came out as "keery."

"Sure, Dr. MacKenzie!" Jon replied. Slipping on his jacket and boots, he joined the scientists outside. Dr. MacKenzie's jeep was a battered, mud-spattered affair, evidently having survived several volcanic eruptions. The volcanologist took two green backpacks out of the jeep, tossing one to Jon's grandfather and putting on the other.

After the scientists had strapped on their packs, Dr. MacKenzie instructed Jon to remove two brass contraptions from the jeep's floorboards and to stash one in each man's pack. With their spigots, dishes, antennae and other odd protuberances, the devices resembled discarded spacecraft hardware.

"What are these things, anyway—space junk?" Jon asked, grunting with the effort of lifting the heavy equipment.

Dr. MacKenzie chuckled. "They're called 'tiltmeters.' If magma—molten rock—is forcin' its way up into this mountain, these meters will register the bulging that results. Two tiltmeters should be guid enough for now. I also brought along some other instruments that should help us in our investigation."

While retrieving the tiltmeters, Jon noticed a black Bible stuffed between a couple of the jeep's seats. He knew it wasn't polite to ask, but he did anyway. "Are you a Christian, Dr. MacKenzie?"

The volcanologist heartily laughed again. "That I am," he said. "Yer grandfaither tells me ye're a believer, too. Is that right, laddie?"

"Yes, sir," said Jon. He had assumed Dr. Roberts was the only scientist in the world who genuinely believed in Jesus and in a literal, six-day creation of the earth and the universe.

Grandfather Roberts beamed. "Dr. M. is the founder of an organization known as the 'Young Earth Geological Society.'"

Dr. MacKenzie winked. "That's 'Y.E.G.S.' for short. Yer grandfather here is also a charter member, by the way."

The acronym sounded rather silly, but Jon didn't dare say so. He didn't want to embarrass Dr. MacKenzie.

"Ye won't find many young-earth geologists these days," said the volcanologist, running his fingers through a shock of salt-and-pepper hair. "Still, our numbers are growin' as research confirms that old-earth chronologies are seriously flawed. But ye didn't come out here to hear me talk about my favorite subject. Let's go down to that trailhead and see what we can see."

Hoisting a shovel over his shoulder, the volcanologist followed Jon and his grandfather down the road and onto the wooded Iron Mountain trail. Leaves sighed and whispered in a cool, misty spring breeze, tugging at Jon's heart. At the observation deck, the three hikers stopped to admire the view.

Recalling what he had seen while camping on his deck, Jon said, "Last night, I saw some lights moving over the lake down there."

"You probably saw some pleasure boats running with their navigation lights on, or maybe a float plane coming in for a landing," said Dr. Roberts. "There's always traffic on the lake, even at night."

Dr. MacKenzie shot Jon a shrewd look from beneath his bushy eyebrows. "Perrhaps so, and perrhaps not," he said, lapsing into his Scottish brogue. "I'd say ye've seen the Lake Lights, laddie."

"Lake Lights?" chorused Jon and his grandfather.

"Och, I had forgotten ye just moved up here," said the volcanologist. "Folk ha' been seeing the Lake Lights for years, though they've been more active lately. I've been conducting some research on th' subject. Afore we Europeans settled this lake, which the local Clackamas Indians called *Waluga*, the natives referred to these pale lights as *Kawak-moon*, meaning 'Flying moon' in the Chinook jargon."

"That's a good description," Jon remarked.

"Recently, I ran across an older Indian name for the Lake Lights: *Skookum-kallakala*," Dr. MacKenzie added. "Roughly translated, the term means 'giant bird' or 'monster bird.' The word *skookum* once referred to legendary creatures such as the Sasquatch or Bigfoot."

"A flying Bigfoot?" Jon snickered.

Dr. Roberts suggested, "Maybe you found an obscure reference to the 'Thunderbird,' which figures prominently in Native American mythology—even here in the Pacific Northwest."

The volcanologist shrugged. "Perrrhaps. However, the inhabitants of other continents have reported seeing similar nocturnal lights. The natives of Papua, New Guinea have attributed theirs to a flying creature they call the *ropen*."

Something niggled in the back of Jon's mind. *Papua, New Guinea*. Where had he heard of that place before?

"But what *are* the Lake Lights exactly?" he asked.

Dr. MacKenzie patted his head affectionately. "Nobody rightly knows. Some people believe they're caused by burning methane—marsh gas, that is—bubbling up from the muck on the lake bottom. Others believe the lights are th' spirits of pioneers and Indians long dead. Then there's the 'ball lightning' theory."

"What do *you* believe they are?" Jon persisted.

"As a scientist and a Christian," the volcanologist answered, "I dinna believe in *wraiths*, and no methane cloud nor ball lightning can travel from one end of a lake to th' other end."

Dr. Roberts regarded his friend curiously. "So you've seen these lights yourself, have you? You've never mentioned them before."

Dr. MacKenzie nodded. "Indeed I have, and on many occasions, too. As you know, my wee house overlooks the lake. I didn't bring up the subject earlier because I didn't wish to be thought daft."

The professor chuckled. "You've been called worse!"

Dr. MacKenzie continued, "I've noticed those lights tend to travel in straight lines, which flies in the face of conventional theories. It's a fascinatin' phenomenon but one outside my field of expertise. Now, let's have a look at this cliff o' yours, shall we?"

Jon and his grandfather followed Dr. MacKenzie across the well-worn path to the cliff base opposite the observation deck. After inspecting the rocks there, the volcanologist took off his backpack and removed a black-barreled, steel syringe from a side pocket. He also brought out several long glass tubes and attached one of them to the heavy-duty syringe's tip.

"What is that thing?" Jon asked, pointing at the plunger. It reminded him of the hefty hypodermic syringes he had seen Equestrian Club veterinarians use to inoculate horses in the spring and fall.

"It's a gas-sampling device," said Dr. MacKenzie, holding up the syringe. "I'll use it to draw air into these glass tubules, which I will later take back to my laboratory for analysis."

The volcanologist poked the glass tube into a crevice between two mossy rocks. After drawing back the plunger, he removed the tube, sealed it, and repeated the process in two or three other spots.

"That's done," he said. "Now we'll set up the tiltmeters, which will transmit data via radio telemetry to my lab. This way I'll have advance warning if a serious geological event is aboot to occur."

Moving down the trail, the two men found a natural ledge below the path. After climbing down and leveling the space with the shovel, they anchored the first tiltmeter in place with some metal stakes they drove into the moist but rocky ground.

"Let's find that second tiltmeter a home, Jonathan," said Dr. MacKenzie. Then off he went, his stout legs pounding along the trail.

Not far from the first tiltmeter, a rugged, stony outcrop rose as much as eighteen feet above the trail on its uphill side. A few scrawny oak trees bravely clung to the thin soil on its flat top. After scrabbling up the slope beside the extensive outcropping, the two scientists secured the tiltmeter on a slab where it couldn't be seen from the path below. Then they slid back down the hill to rejoin Jon.

Thunder rumbled as inky clouds piled up over Iron Mountain. Tipping back his head, Dr. Roberts frowned at the sky. "We'd better head for home now if we don't want to be drenched," he said. "My daughter wouldn't like us showing up on her doorstep sopping wet."

Rain was dripping through the trees' new leaves when the three passed the observation deck. Using a stick, Dr. Roberts swept aside some ivy vines above the trail, exposing a patch of gray stone about five feet across that contrasted with the darker rocks around it.

"I thought as much," murmured the professor.

"What do you mean?" Jon asked him.

"I'll tell you about it later," said his grandfather. "Let's just say this marks the final chapter in the saga of the Prosser Iron Mine."

Chapter 5
THE PROSSER MINE

The evening sky was dusky with a drizzling grey mist when Dr. MacKenzie stowed his shovel and the two packs in the back of his jeep. After shaking hands with Jon and his grandfather, the volcanologist climbed into his vehicle and was cranking the engine when Mrs. Oliver emerged from the house.

"Why don't you two join us for supper?" she called out. "We're having chicken pot pie. It's always been Dad's favorite."

Dr. MacKenzie shut off the jeep's engine and climbed out. "I've a feeling it's aboot to become mine, too," he said. "I'd be delighted to accept your gracious offer, Mrs. Oliver. I haven't enjoyed a home-cooked meal in quite a while." He pronounced "while" as "whale."

Inside the front door, Jon and the two scientists removed their muddy boots. Dr. MacKenzie hung his tweed coat on the hall tree. Then the three companions joined Mrs. Oliver and Jennica at the table. After Dr. Roberts had blessed the food, everyone tucked in.

Jon loved his mother's chicken pot pie, with its tender chunks of chicken and succulent green peas swimming in a creamy sauce. Jennica hated peas—canned, fresh, or frozen. She always fished them out and dropped them under the table for the stray animals Jon often brought home. Since the neighborhood was missing so many pets, Jon hadn't yet found a dog or cat to clean up after his sister.

Dr. MacKenzie laid down his fork, closed his eyes and sighed. "Ken, you never told me your daughter was such a good cook. You'll have to invite me over for dinner more often."

Olivia blushed her thanks and changed the subject. "What did you boys discover on our mountain this afternoon?"

"It has apparently heated up," said Dr. MacKenzie. "However, we won't know why until I analyze the gas samples I took."

"Is Iron Mountain gonna blow its top?" Jon broke in. He pictured red-hot, molten rock flowing down Glen Eagles Road and engulfing everything in its path. Of course, all the local schools would be closed during the disaster, making for a nice, long spring vacation.

"Not in the conventional sense," the volcanologist replied. "If I had to come up wi' a theory, I would say Iron Mountain has suffered what you might call a 'magma burp.'"

"A magma burp!" Jennica tittered. "What's that?"

"Magma is molten rock," Dr. MacKenzie explained. "A pool of it must be lying deep beneath this mountain. When magma escapes through cracks in the earth's crust, it releases trapped gases as it rises. If the release happens rapidly enough—like a 'burp'—those hot gases can make their way to the earth's surface and cause local heating."

"Not to mention really bad smells," Jon added.

"Very true," said Dr. MacKenzie with a grin. "What I don't understand is how those hot gases became so highly concentrated in the homes along this ridge. Most of the fumes should have dissipated harmlessly into the air instead of building up inside these houses."

Smiling mysteriously, Grandfather Roberts said, "I might have the answer to that question. The children and I have just learned that this mountaintop is honeycombed with the old tunnels, caverns and drifts of the now-defunct Prosser Iron Mine."

"What's a 'drift'?" Jennica asked.

Her grandfather said, "That's a mining term for a horizontal tunnel that follows a vein of ore—in this case, iron ore."

"Could we explore the mine?" Jon eagerly asked.

"Over my dead body!" Mrs. Oliver snapped with a stern frown. "There will be no spelunking in this family till I say so."

"Spelunking?" asked Jennica, sipping her milk. Sometimes Jon thought his sister sported a perpetual milk mustache.

"She means exploring tunnels and caves," he explained.

"Your mother is right," said Dr. Roberts. "Those mine shafts are a death trap. Their supporting timbers probably rotted away long ago. That's why the City has sealed up the main entrance. Remember the ivy-covered patch of cement I showed you on the hillside?"

"Yeah." Jon didn't like where the conversation was going.

"That was the concrete plug the City of Lake Oswego poured into the mine entrance," the professor explained. "Left open, that entryway might have lured curiosity-seekers inside to their deaths. Those tragedies happen all too frequently, unfortunately."

"Was that . . . the *only* way into the mine?" Jon asked casually.

His grandfather answered, "As far as I know, all the other entrances have also been sealed up or have collapsed."

Jon sagged in his seat. His spelunking dreams were being dashed almost as quickly as they had taken shape. What good was a mysterious old mine if he couldn't explore its tunnels, nooks and crannies?

"I still don't understand what all this mine business has to do with us," said Mrs. Oliver. "Are you saying our house is in imminent danger of collapsing into one of those old tunnels?"

"Not at all," Grandfather Roberts hastily replied.

"Let me guess," said Dr. MacKenzie thoughtfully. "Ye are thinkin' that the hot gases have been traveling through these mine drifts and collecting under the houses on this bluff."

"That's exactly what I've been thinking," Dr. Roberts said. "Taking the path of least resistance, those noxious fumes have been concentrating in the mine's old sealed-off tunnels and seeping into the houses above them. At least sulfur dioxide isn't a flammable gas."

Looking worried, Jon's mother suggested, "Maybe we should hire someone to seal our basement to keep out those fumes."

"It couldn't hurt," her father agreed.

"If the iron ore was so plentiful here," Dr. MacKenzie broke in, "why did the owners shut down the mine? Did it play out?"

"That's a good question," Professor Roberts answered. "I've been wondering the same thing. According to Lake Oswego historical records, competition from cheaper pig iron overseas—specifically Scotland—killed the Prosser Mine in its heyday."

Dr. MacKenzie chuckled. "My grandfather was a Glasgow collier, a *coal* miner, so ye canna blame my family. But why was this mine more costly to operate than Scotland's mines?"

Dr. Roberts explained, "Smelting iron in those days required limestone and coal or charcoal. Since Oregon lacks any coal deposits, the smelter had to burn charcoal made at great expense from local Douglas-fir trees. Then there was the cost of shipping limestone from the San Juan islands, not to mention disputes over water rights."

"You're saying economics caused the mine's downfall," Dr. MacKenzie said with a sympathetic headshake.

"That's what I had concluded, too, before I came across a copy of an old diary someone posted online," said Dr. Roberts. "The diary belonged to a miner named Duncan J. McCaw."

"Och!" exclaimed the volcanologist. "There's a fine Scottish name if ivver there was one. Scotsmen are plentiful in these parts."

"A diary?" Jon repeated. *Girl stuff*. He had sneaked a peek at his sister's diary once or twice. It was mind-numbingly boring, filled with sketches of horses and gossipy references to her friends.

"What did the diary say, Grandpa?" Jennica piped up.

"Mr. McCaw hinted that shrinking profits weren't the only problem plaguing the mine. He claims the miners refused to work the Prosser any longer because of an incident that badly frightened them.

"'The Prosser Mine Disaster,' as he called it, left some of the men raving lunatics. They were committed to the Oregon State Insane Asylum, which was built in 1883—just before the mine closed."

"What kind of disaster was it—a cave-in?" Jon asked.

"Not exactly," said his grandfather. "According to McCaw, the miners were following a new vein of iron ore when they broke through into a cavern filled with man-like creatures wrapped in gray cloaks and having great, shining eyes. He called them 'brollachans.'"

"Brollachans!" Dr. MacKenzie burst out. "Are you sairtin that was the word he used? I haven't heard o' those creatures since I was a child, and that has been a very long time ago."

"Yes, I'm quite certain," Professor Roberts replied.

"What are brollachans?" Jon asked the volcanologist.

"My grandmother told me they are big beasties of indeterminate shape tha' live in caves, where they guard their treasure-hoards of gold and silver. Supposedly they like to carry off naughty boys."

Jon didn't like the sound of that. Being naughty seemed to come naturally for him, especially when his sister was involved.

Dr. MacKenzie laughed. "Naturally, those were old wives' tales. There was nothing to 'em, except as a way of keeping the likes o' me and my brother on the straight and narrow."

"McCaw also mentioned 'gobs,'" said Grandfather Roberts.

"Gobs, you say?" his friend remarked. "That's a Scottish Gaelic term for a 'beak' or a 'bill,' for which we Scotsmen are famous." The volcanologist rubbed his reddish, bulbous nose.

"Those miners probably just saw some bats," said Jon's mother. "People back then were more superstitious than they are these days. Now, can I interest anyone in some dessert?"

After generous helpings of Marionberry pie and vanilla ice cream, the two scientists took their leave. Jon retreated to his room, where he entered the word "ropen" in his laptop's search engine. The term brought up several websites featuring grainy photos and videos of long-beaked, flying animals.

"Humph," Jon grunted in disdain. All the images looked like birds or fruit bats to him. However, he did learn that Papua, New Guinea was situated only a hundred miles from Australia, a fact he could put to use in his geography class. He closed his laptop and crept downstairs into the basement.

"Phew!" he gasped. Still reeking of sulfur, the room greeted him with a bizarre scene. Striped with evenly spaced, vertical white bars, the sheet-rocked left wall had turned a sickly yellowish-brown. *That looks like water damage*, he thought. *Must be a leak somewhere.*

Scritch-scritch. The scratching sound was back! The skin prickled between Jon's shoulder blades. Taking the stairs two at a time, he fled the basement without looking back. He would have to tear open the wall and drop some rat poison inside—or call an exterminator.

Before he crawled into bed that night, Jon made sure his bedroom door was securely shut. He fell asleep listening to a pattering on the roof, wondering whether it was rain or skittering rodents.

Long-beaked birds flittered through his dreams.

Chapter 6
CRYPTIDS

Jon was sitting in church with his family the following Sunday when he remembered where he had heard about Papua, New Guinea. As soon as the service was over, he slid across the pew—bumping his sister's shins—and trotted up to the crowd of admiring parishioners surrounding the minister.

Squeezing between a couple of elderly ladies, he caught the preacher's eye and said, "Excuse me, Reverend Sanford, but could I . . . could I talk with you privately for a minute?"

"Of course, young man," said the minister. Wrapping an arm around Jon's shoulders, he took him aside and asked, "What did you wish to speak with me about?"

Glancing around to be sure his mother and sister weren't listening, Jon said, "Do you know what a *ropen* is?"

The reverend's eyes flew wide in surprise, and his arm dropped nervelessly from Jon's shoulders. "Where did you hear that word?" he asked in a lowered voice.

Sticky sweat trickled down the small of Jon's back. He had really stuck his neck out this time, but it was too late to backpedal. "My grandfather's friend told me the natives of Papua, Gew Nuinea—I mean, Papua, New Guinea—use that name for some sort of bird or bat or other flying animal there."

"I see," said the reverend thoughtfully. "He's right. The natives in parts of PNG do refer to some flying creatures by that name. What made you ask me in particular about *ropens*?"

Jon took a deep breath and exhaled a quick prayer. "Weren't you and your wife missionaries in New Guinea?"

Reverend Sanford laughed quietly. "You've got me there. Yes, we served as missionaries in that region of the world. But first things first. I don't believe we've met. Your name is—?"

"Jonathan. Jonathan Oliver." He stuck out his hand and the minister warmly shook it in a stout grip.

"It's a pleasure meeting you, Jonathan Oliver," he said. "We should set aside some time to speak further on this subject."

Jon felt a hand on his shoulder. "You must forgive my outspoken son," said Mrs. Oliver, eyeing Jon severely. "Sometimes his curiosity gets the best of him. Have you forgotten your manners, young man?"

"No harm done," Reverend Sanford assured Jon's mother. "He's been a perfect gentleman. It turns out that the two of us might have something in common—besides Jesus Himself, that is."

Mrs. Oliver stared quizzically at the minister, then at Jon. "And what might that be? Do you enjoy skateboarding, too?"

The reverend chuckled, and his eyes took on a distant look. "It seems we both share an interest in a particular branch of zoology," he said. "More specifically, *cryptozoology*."

Jon's mother relaxed. "In that case," she said, "why don't you and your wife come over for a bite to eat after the evening service? I've been meaning to invite you for supper to get acquainted."

"Why, thank you for thinking of us," said Reverend Sanford, smiling broadly. "I'd like nothing better. Amy and I were just saying we're long overdue in meeting some of our newer families."

That evening, dusky shadows were creeping up Iron Mountain's wooded flanks when Reverend and Mrs. Sanford took their seats with Jon and Jennica around the Oliver dining-room table. With her usual efficiency, Mrs. Oliver was preparing a light supper.

"You have a lovely home here, Olivia," said Amy, a petite brunette with soulful dark eyes. "And the view out this picture window is gorgeous! Bob and I bought a quaint little cottage in Lake Grove. We love the pace of life there, but we can't see the sky for all the fir trees in our yard. We do like having shade trees, of course."

"We're very blessed to have this place," Jon's mother modestly replied as she set a big pot of bubbling chili on the polished-wood table, followed by a steaming pan of cornbread. Jon's mouth watered at the scrumptious odors filling the room.

The minister rubbed his hands together. "My favorites!" he said. "I missed chili and cornbread in Papua, New Guinea, not to mention burgers with the fixings. Amy and I never could stomach raw sago palm grubs, which are considered a delicacy over there."

Jon quietly retched. *Grubs?* Raw, baked, fried or stewed, grubs were still grubs, and they would never pass his lips.

"Reverend," said Mrs. Oliver with a wry smile, "I'm happy to report that grubs are not on the menu tonight. I've baked an apple pie for dessert, though. Now, would you please bless the food?"

Bowing his head, the minister thanked God for the Oliver household and for the food—and asked Him to watch over Matt Oliver. A lump grew in Jon's throat at the mention of his father's name.

"Bob and I are looking forward to meeting your husband when he returns," said Mrs. Sanford when the reverend was done praying.

"I'm sure he'd love to meet you, too," said Olivia with a catch in her voice. "When we last spoke on the phone, I told him we had found a nice church to attend. He was concerned we might not find a good church to plug into after we moved here from Beaverton."

Bob Sanford beamed. "I'm glad you have enjoyed becoming a part of our little church family. You've been a blessing to us."

Conversation fell off as everyone dug into big bowls of chili and thick slabs of buttered cornbread. Then Jon heard a soft plopping sound near his feet. His sister was dropping pieces of stewed onion under the table. Jon doubted any stray pet would eat onions.

"What exactly is 'cryptozoology'?" Mrs. Oliver asked.

Seeing that Reverend Sanford's mouth was full of cornbread, Jon pinch hit for him. "Cropozyptology—er, *cryptozoology* is the search for undiscovered animals. I looked it up on my laptop after church."

Mrs. Oliver grunted. "You could start by looking under your bed. I'll bet you would find plenty of undiscovered animals there. I don't think you've cleaned beneath it since we moved into this place."

Jon blushed and stared down at his bowl and plate. He hated it when his mother criticized him in front of others.

Reverend Sanford swallowed his cornbread and cleared his throat of the dry crumbs. "Jon is right. Cryptozoologists search for and study hidden animals previously unknown to science."

Jon's mother frowned. "What sorts of 'hidden animals' are we talking about here? Giant rats and alligators in the sewers?"

The minister laughed infectiously. "Cryptozoologists make a serious career out of separating fact from fiction. All sorts of creatures are rumored to lurk and breed in New York's sewer system, for instance, but most of those stories are urban legends. Still, even the wildest myths often contain a kernel of truth."

Mrs. Oliver took a spoonful of chili and slowly chewed. "Forgive my frankness—I can be blunt sometimes—but I thought you and your wife were missionaries, not zoologists."

"That's true," said Reverend Sanford. "We served with IBT—International Bible Translators—in Papua, New Guinea for about ten years. It was a challenging but rich experience."

His wife added, "My husband's master's degree in linguistics came in handy, since more than eight hundred and fifty languages are spoken in PNG. We finished translating the New Testament into one of those languages just before we left the mission field."

"Amy has a degree in cultural anthropology, which also proved useful when working with the indigenous people," said the minister with a smile. "We made a great team back then."

"And we still do," said Amy warmly, patting his hand.

"Then why did you leave?" Jennica asked as she slathered butter on her cornbread. Her mother shot her a warning look.

By way of answer, Reverend Sanford bent down and pulled up his right trousers leg. He exposed a mass of disfiguring red scars that marred his shin and calf like ropy globs of congealed lava.

Jon's spoon fell from his fingers at the sight. "Wh-what happened to you?" he gasped. "Did you get burned?"

The minister straightened his pant leg. "No," he said. "A Papuan *taipan* bit me—repeatedly." He grimaced at the memory.

"What's a taipan?" Jennica asked him.

The reverend calmly replied, "It's one of the world's most venomous snakes. By all accounts, it is a miracle I even survived. A single drop of taipan venom is enough to kill a hundred grown men."

"We had to fly him to Port Moresby for treatment," Mrs. Sanford added. "For a while, the doctors there thought he would lose his leg, if not his life. After a couple of months in the hospital, he could walk again—but our missions board decided to sideline us because of the ongoing risk of infection in the bite wounds. We also had two young children at the time and wanted to spend more time with them."

"Wow. It must have been hard to leave Papua," said Jon, spitting cornbread crumbs across the table as he pronounced "Papua."

"It was," sighed Mrs. Sanford. "We had made many friends there, but the Lord evidently had other plans for us. He opened the door for us to minister in several churches here in the States."

"To answer your original question," said Reverend Sanford to Jon's mother, "zoology held no special interest for Amy or me before we were called to the mission field. Once we started working with the remote tribes of PNG, though, we began hearing tales of unusual creatures inhabiting the mountains and rainforests. The island is evidently home to a number of *cryptids*—unknown animal species."

Jon leaned forward intently. "Did you ever see one?"

"Did I ever see a cryptid?" Reverend Sanford shook his head. "I didn't—at least not up close. By nature, most cryptids are shy, elusive creatures. Some of them are active only at night. That makes it easy for scientists to dismiss stray sightings as the fantasies of backward, superstitious savages. However, Amy and I found the natives of PNG to be quite intelligent, honest and resourceful."

"I've always admired missionaries," Mrs. Oliver told her guests with a wistful look. "When my husband returns home, I'd like our family to help build a new church in the state of Veracruz, Mexico."

"Are there cryptids in Mexico?" Jon innocently asked.

Reverend Sanford chuckled. "I suppose there are cryptids everywhere, if you just look long and hard enough for them."

Jon wondered how long and hard he would have to look to find cryptids around Oswego. Probably the most he could hope for was a new species of slug or mosquito. If only the minister could see what Jon had seen, he might get some answers.

"Reverend Sanford," he began, "what did you mean when you said you had never seen a cryptid *up close* before?"

"Ah!" said the minister, wiping his mouth with a napkin. "I'm not sure you want to hear about those experiences, especially after supper. What I meant is that neither Amy nor I ever personally came face to face with any cryptid-like animals."

"Then what did you see?" Jon persisted.

The two former missionaries glanced at each other. "Several times," the reverend began, "we observed half-eaten animal carcasses wedged in the tops of trees. Most of the remains were those of goats or wild pigs. Once, I saw a sheep. As I say, this is hardly a proper topic for after-dinner conversation, especially for the young people."

Mrs. Oliver laughed. "Don't worry about my children. They like to watch gory wildlife documentaries. But couldn't a leopard or a python have killed those animals and left them hanging in a tree?"

The minister shook his head. "PNG doesn't harbor any big cats, at least none known to science. And the Papuan Olive Python likes to swallow its prey whole. The older natives of PNG blame these cached carcasses on a specific type of large, winged animal."

"Like a giant eagle?" Jennica suggested.

"Something like that," said the reverend, studying his empty bowl and plate. "Now, didn't your mother mention apple pie?"

With a guilty look, Mrs. Oliver jumped up and served the pie, doling out juicy wedges to her children and guests. Jon listlessly picked at his slice. Why was Reverend Sanford being so evasive, changing the subject whenever anyone cornered him on the question of cryptids? Was the minister trying to hide something?

"Thank you for the excellent meal," said the reverend. "However, we must be going. I promised Amy I would clean out the garage tomorrow, and I want to get a head start on it this evening. It's a mess."

"Thank you for coming over," said Mrs. Oliver, presenting the minister's coat to him. "Since we're new to Lake Oswego, we don't often have the chance to entertain guests."

Jon glanced out the dining-room window. Spring's stealthy darkness had already engulfed the Oliver house and its extensive back deck. Jon's heart sank to a new low. If only he could find an excuse to detain the Sanfords a little while longer!

Thuppa-thuppa-thuppa WHUMP. The window shook as muffled noises from outside jarred Jon out of his blue funk. Jumping up from his chair, he rushed into the kitchen, shoved open the sliding glass door and scanned the deck.

As soon as he opened the door, a gigantic, coal-black shadow rose from the deck and whirled into the night like a wind-driven leaf. Jon stood frozen in the doorway, hardly believing what he had just seen. Jennica and the grownups joined him in the kitchen.

"What was that sound?" his mother asked him. "Did you see any lightning flashes? It might have been thunder."

Jon shook his head. "I don't know what it was. Maybe I had better check out there to make sure everything is all right."

"I'll go with you," Reverend Sanford offered.

Nothing appeared amiss outside. Perhaps a fierce wind gust had blown someone's black-plastic tarpaulin across the deck. Jon looked up, and his breath caught in his throat. The flickering stars massed overhead shed a remote, milky light that awed and humbled him.

"See the Big Dipper there?" Reverend Sanford said, pointing up at the breathless heavens. "It's my favorite constellation, next to the Southern Cross in the skies over PNG. I love stargazing."

Jon tugged on the minister's coat sleeve. "C'mere a minute," he said. "I want to show you something on the lake."

Jon led his guest to the deck's back railing and pointed out the dark blotch that was Oswego Lake. Swarms of glowing objects were dancing and swirling above the water in a graceful aerial ballet.

"Our friend Dr. MacKenzie calls those 'Lake Lights,'" Jon said. "Supposedly they're caused by ball lightning or burning marsh gas."

The minister's jaw seemed to unhinge as he gripped the railing with white-knuckled fingers. "It's just not possible," he muttered hoarsely. "They're here, too. I thought we'd seen the last of them. They've followed us halfway around the world to Oregon."

Chapter 7
BROLLACHANS

J on asked the minister, "Who is here? What has followed you?" Reverend Sanford replied, "I don't know what they are. Those bobbing lights look like the ones we used to observe back in PNG hovering over rivers, lakes and the like. For a long while, I also assumed they were pockets of flaming marsh gas.

"One night, I had to rethink the marsh-gas theory. Some friends of ours had invited us to visit Lake Kutubu in the southern interior of PNG. Kutubu's water is crystal clear, meaning it contains no rotting vegetation to generate methane gas. We were camped out on the lakeshore the first evening when the lights began gathering over the lake after dark. Our friends jokingly called them 'giant fireflies.'

"Then one of those 'fireflies' swerved and headed directly toward us. It was so enormous that it blotted out the moon and stars. I heard a swishing sound as it passed overhead. That's when I knew it wasn't burning methane or even ball lightning, for that matter."

"Did you see what it was?" Jon eagerly asked.

"I'm afraid not. Its light dimmed and went out just before it flew over us. I saw only a dark shape hurtling through the night."

"Maybe it was a kind of giant sea-bird coated with phosphorescence from swimming in the water," Jon suggested. He had read about such phenomena and was pleased with himself for correctly pronouncing "phosphorescence" without tripping over his tongue.

"It's doubtful," the minister replied. "Phosphorescence is most commonly found in salt water, but Kutubu is a freshwater lake. On the other hand, many organisms chemically produce their own light as fireflies do. It's called *bioluminescence*."

"Huh," Jon grunted, digesting what the reverend had just said. "Why didn't you tell me before about Lake Kutubu?"

Reverend Sanford sighed. "I didn't mention my sighting earlier because I didn't know what it was I had actually seen."

"Do you think the Lake Lights are *ropens*, then?" Jon asked.

"Whatever the *ropens* are," the reverend replied, "they thrive in PNG's tropical conditions. That's why I'm surprised to find them here in Western Oregon's cooler climate—and why I hesitate to say they are the same phenomenon Amy and I saw that night."

"We need more proof, like a photo," Jon declared.

"That we do, my young friend. However, photographic evidence may be hard to come by, since I suspect these creatures are extremely secretive." The minister laughed. "And so you and I have traveled full circle to our mutual scientific interest—cryptozoology."

Excusing himself to rejoin his wife, Reverend Sanford left Jon in a mixed state of wonderment and puzzlement. Only then he noticed a fresh gouge marring the deck's railing. Reflecting the wan starlight, something white gleamed in the groove. With some effort, Jon pried the object out of the wood. It was a sharp, tapering claw. Longer and thicker than an eagle's talon, it resembled a curved, pointy finger.

Taking the specimen into his bedroom, Jon dropped it into a jar that held a few small seashells and promptly forgot about it.

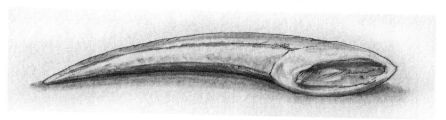

For days afterwards, the words *cryptozoology* and *ropens* rattled around in Jon's head like twin loose marbles. He had plenty of time to think, because the predictable spring rains refused to pack up and leave. Spring vacation came and went, but water was still sluicing along the steep, skateboard-friendly streets and swirling down the storm drains. The gutters plugged up with debris and overflowed.

One rainy Saturday morning, Dr. Roberts popped in with his old umbrella for a snack of cinnamon rolls. Jon and his sister were already at the kitchen table, armed with tall, cold glasses of milk.

The professor joined his grandchildren at the table as their mother laid out plates and the pan of cinnamon rolls. After blessing the food, she doled out the fragrant, doughy spirals to her family.

Jon had devoured his first bun and was working on another when his grandfather's cell phone chirped. The old paleontologist wiped off his sticky fingers, dug out his phone and answered it. Jon could hear Dr. MacKenzie's rapid-fire Scottish brogue on the other end.

Dr. Roberts interrupted him. "Hold on, Graham," he said. "Let me put you on speaker. I've got the rest of the family here with me."

Dr. MacKenzie's deep voice boomed out of the phone. "I tested those gas samples, and as I suspected, the sulfur dioxide levels were quite high. I've a hunch these releases ha' been going on for quite some time but were of such a low magnitude they escaped notice.

"But that's not the main reason I'm callin'. The first tiltmeter we placed shows no bulging on tha' part of the mountain. Readings from the second unit, though, are highly irregular. Either your mountain is erupting, or the tiltmeter is malfunctioning. Ye haven't felt any tremors or seen anything, er, *unusual* outside, have ye?"

"No, we haven't," Dr. Roberts replied, glancing out the window.

"In tha' case," the volcanologist continued, "would ye terribly mind checking on that second tiltmeter for me? I want to be sure it's still workin' properly. Maybe it got knocked over."

Dr. Roberts spoke into the phone. "I'd love to help you, Graham, but I'm afraid I've got some urgent errands to run this morning."

"I can check out your tiltmeter, Dr. MacKenzie!" Jon piped up.

"That's very kind of ye, Jonathan," the Scotsman replied. "I would come meself, but I'm bogged doon in my lab. Please let me know what ye find on tha' trail." He disconnected the phone.

"What if Iron Mountain erupts while you're down there?" Mrs. Oliver fretted. "You won't have any way to escape the lava!"

"Dr. MacKenzie wouldn't have let Jon take on this task if the mountain was about to explode," Grandfather Roberts reassured her.

"Well, all right," said Mrs. Oliver reluctantly. "Just don't dawdle along the way, young man. It's awfully wet outside, and you don't want to catch a cold or the flu or pneumonia."

"Don't worry, Mom; I'll be quick," Jon promised her.

Throwing on his boots and jacket, he headed out the door and trotted around the corner to the trailhead. Enticed by the sweet scents of rain-washed earth and foliage, he set out on the muddy path. Wispy steam-sprites swirled around him as if inviting him to dance. Stepping onto the observation deck, he gazed down at the hillside forest and tried to imagine what Iron Mountain must have looked like in the heyday of the Prosser Mine.

Jon stopped at the plug sealing the mine's entrance and climbed up to rap his knuckles on the concrete. Although someone had broken off a few thin pieces along the bottom edge, it felt all too solid. Only a jackhammer could break through into the tunnel beyond.

He passed the first tiltmeter on the right before the flat-topped outcropping came into view on the left. At its foot, the second tiltmeter lay in a patch of silver-dollar plants, apparently undamaged.

After brushing dirt off the instrument, Jon struggled with it up the hillside to the cliff's top, where he set up the tiltmeter beside an oak tree. Farther back on the outcropping, someone had apparently sloshed whitewash over a talus field of jumbled basalt slabs.

A spindly steam-plume was rising lazily from among the slabs. At first, Jon assumed the steam was boiling off damp, sun-warmed rocks. However, it was a typically drippy Oregon spring morning.

Curious as to the steam's source, Jon navigated through the rocky obstacle course until he came to a couple of basalt slabs propped precariously against each other. Behind them, a four-foot-wide gash gaped in the slope. Wisps of fetid steam were wafting out of it.

Jon's mother and grandfather had warned him against spelunking in the Prosser Mine. However, they hadn't forbidden him from checking out natural features—and this fissure was not man made. Besides, the hole probably didn't lead anywhere. He could poke his head inside and look around without anyone's being the wiser.

After ducking between the stone slabs, Jon peered into the opening. A thick, clammy twilight greeted him. His nose wrinkled at the faint, familiar stench of steamy sulfur dioxide. Using his cell phone as a flashlight, he climbed through the cleft into a narrow passage with rough, slate-gray basalt walls unmarred by any tool marks.

He felt his way some fifty yards along the winding tunnel. Then his fingers lost touch with the dank walls. Something brushed by his face, and he cried out, his voice echoing through a space whose limits were swallowed in suffocating darkness.

It was just a bat, he told himself.

Scritch-scritch. Scritch-scritch.

Jon froze. He had company. Dozens of pairs of glowing red eyes glared back at him through the blackness. He knew bats clung to cave ceilings while resting, but these eyes floated some seven feet off the ground. Behind them, Jon could see a pack of shapeless forms swaddled in dark hooded cloaks or veils. The figures hissed at him.

He recalled Grandfather Roberts' words: . . . *the miners were following a new vein of iron ore when they broke through into a vast cavern filled with man-like creatures wrapped in gray cloaks and having great, shining eyes. He called them brollachans.*

Brollachans. The word seared itself indelibly on his brain.

Terror clutched at Jon's throat with bony fingers. He was unarmed and greatly outnumbered by these red-eyed beast-men.

As his eyes adjusted to the dim cell-phone light, he saw he had entered the cavern near its left wall. Part of the wall was breached, leaving a pile of rubble on the floor. Perhaps this was the very spot where the miners of old had broken through—to their lasting horror.

All at once, the brollachans advanced upon him with a grotesque, lurching gait that reminded Jon of old men hobbling along on crutches. The creatures moved surprisingly quickly.

Jon fled back through the lightless passage, heedless of scrapes, bumps and bruises to his head and elbows. Hissing and scratching noises pursued him. He refused to look back until he had clawed his way through the entrance and into the blessed sunlit world.

He gulped in the forest's sweet, fresh air. Though the brollachans had not as yet followed him outside, he was taking no chances. Abandoning the outcropping, he slid down the hillside in a rattling avalanche of loose rocks and dirt. After landing in a heap on the trail, he picked himself up and ran the rest of the way home.

Chapter 8
VORCATS

"Help!" Jon bellowed as he burst through the front door. "Brollachans! Burligans! Branigans! Thousands of 'em. They nearly got me! They're living under our house! They're everywhere! Call the police! Call the fire—"

He ran headlong into Dr. Roberts, practically bowling him over. The professor was chatting in the hall with Jon's mother. Taking in Jon's wild eyes, torn, muddy clothing and scraped skin, they ushered him into the kitchen and sat him down. His mother made him a mug of hot chocolate, which he held with trembling hands.

"Why don't you tell us what happened?" she asked him.

"Don't make me go back there!" he babbled. "They'll kill me! They'll eat me! We've gotta move. It's not safe living here."

Hearing the commotion, Jon's sister rushed into the kitchen. "What's wrong? What's going on?" she demanded.

Bit by bit, the two grownups coaxed Jon's tale out of him. Describing his encounter with the creatures in the cavern, he shook uncontrollably. "Red eyes," he murmured. "They had terrible red eyes and walked like the living dead." Jon had once watched a zombie movie, and he had regretted it ever since.

"It's fortunate I came back for my umbrella, Liv," said Dr. Roberts. "Whatever the boy saw, it scared him witless. Maybe he just mistook a colony of bats for larger animals in the dark."

Jon shook his head. "No," he said. "Those things didn't fly at me; they *walked*, and they were taller than I was. I remember how Duncan McCaw described them. They were brollachans! I'm sure of it."

His mother growled, "And I'm sure I told you not to go spelunking without permission. You could have gotten yourself killed!"

As her words sank in, Jon started shaking again. He had taken some very foolish risks and had nearly paid for it with his life. If he had died in that cavern, nobody would ever have found his body.

"I'm sorry, Mom; I won't do that again," he said, and he meant it. He wanted nothing more to do with Iron Mountain or its trail, the Prosser Mine, and especially not with the brollachans.

Leaning over, his mother gave him a hug. "I'm just glad you survived your expedition," she said. "I don't know what I would do without you, now that your father is working overseas."

"What about the tilt-thingy?" Jennica asked her brother.

"Oh, that?" he absently replied. "The brollachans must have knocked it off its perch. I found it and put it back in place."

Dr. Roberts sat cupping his chin in his hands, deep in thought. Then his face lit up. "I'll be right back," he said. Pulling out his cell phone, he stepped through the sliding glass door and onto the deck.

Mrs. Oliver gazed meaningfully at Jon. "In the meantime, young man, I suggest you change out of those filthy clothes."

Jon quickly showered and pulled on a fresh sweatshirt and jeans. He emerged from the bathroom to find his grandfather pacing the living room and looking out the front windows. The professor was still gripping his cell phone.

All at once, Dr. MacKenzie's jeep roared up and screeched to a stop outside the house. Jon and his grandfather hurried out to greet the volcanologist, who beckoned for them to climb in.

Dazed, Jon clambered into one of the back seats. No sooner had he belted himself in than Dr. MacKenzie turned to fix him with a penetrating look of urgency.

"How *faur* is the place from here, laddie?"

Jon shrugged. "I guess it's a few hundred yards or so."

"We're driving, then," said Dr. MacKenzie. "VORCATS may be a wee machine, but bless me if she doesn't weigh near nine stone."

Jon didn't know what a "VORCATS" was, much less how to calculate its "nine stone" in pounds. He wished he had a Scottish-English dictionary. The canny volcanologist tended to lapse into his native Scottish dialect and accent when excited, making him sound as if he were gargling with rocks in his mouth.

Before Jon could protest that the trail was too narrow for any four-wheeled vehicle, Dr. MacKenzie started the engine and executed a squealing U-turn, his tires smoking. Ten seconds later, the jeep was bouncing along the treacherous Iron Mountain footpath.

Dr. MacKenzie slowed the jeep to avoid the overlook deck. Then he sped up again. "Keep yer arms an' head inside!" he shouted.

Jon needed no reminding. He shrank back as branches and berry vines slapped at him through the open cab. On the right, the trail's shoulder dropped off so sharply that Jon was certain the jeep would tip over and tumble down the mountainside.

Crack! A crumpled rectangle of metal and glass whizzed by.

"Drat!" grunted Dr. MacKenzie. "Lost another side mirror. That makes three already this month. I need collapsible mirrors."

Jon's teeth rattled with each jounce of the jeep. "C-can y-you slow d-d-down?" he asked the Scotsman, who was urging his jeep along as if a river of molten lava were pursuing him down the trail.

"I'm not sure how long this excursion will take," Dr. MacKenzie replied. "VORCATS doesn't like to be hurried, ye see."

Jon didn't like being hurried, either. Landmarks were whipping by so rapidly that he almost missed the hulking, flat-topped outcropping. "Here! Stop here!" he cried as the jeep careened past.

The vehicle swerved to a halt, sending a flurry of stones and dirt cascading off the path and into the forest below. Dr. MacKenzie and the professor hopped out, followed more slowly by Jon, who felt as if he'd been beaten all over with a baseball bat—or an iron pipe.

"Where is the entrance?" the volcanologist asked him.

Jon pointed up the slope, and the two men took him to the back of the jeep, where a tied-down tarpaulin concealed a bulky object. Dr. MacKenzie released the tarp and yanked it off with a flourish, revealing a miniature, six-wheeled tractor sprouting wires, dials, tubes, turrets and even a robotic manipulator arm.

"What is this thing—a digger?" Jon asked. He pointed at the manipulator arm, which resembled a scorpion's stinger poised to strike.

"Meet VORCATS—<u>V</u>olcan<u>o</u> <u>R</u>oboti<u>c</u> <u>A</u>ll-<u>T</u>errain <u>S</u>ensor," Dr. MacKenzie said, unstrapping the contraption. "I built this remote-sensing platform for use in extreme environments, such as inside the craters of active volcanoes. Those big beasties have an unfortunate habit of gassing or incinerating anything and anyone that comes too close to their business end. Much as volcanologists love studying volcanoes, we would prefer not to be entombed in one."

"But why did you bring 'CORVATS' up here?" Jon asked him.

"That's *VORCATS*," the Scotsman corrected him. "Your *granda* tells me ye've had a run-in with some 'brollachans' hereabouts. VOR-CATS will take a wee look at them while we watch safely outside."

Jon helped the scientists lift VORCATS out of the jeep and set it on the ground. From the back of the jeep, Dr. MacKenzie also removed a thick coil of electrical cable sheathed from end to end with a braided sleeve of some type of brown material.

He plugged one end of the cable into a port on VORCATS. Then he raised the jeep's hood and plugged the cord's other end into a small box attached to a complex array of wheels and belts fixed to the alternator. Last of all, he started the engine.

"VORCATS is ready to rumble," he said with a satisfied grin. "She has her own battery, but I'd rather spare it and rely on the power from my jeep's special alternator-inverter instead."

"What's covering the extension cord?" Jon asked him.

"That's a Nomex® sleeve," Dr. MacKenzie explained. "It's heat resistant to seven hundred degrees Fahrenheit and also prevents cuts and abrasions. Without it, my electrical cables would quickly melt or tear inside an active volcano's crater."

With Jon's help, the scientists lugged VORCATS up the hill and onto the rock outcropping, where Jon pointed out the nearly invisible tunnel entrance. Wisps of steam still puffed from the dark fissure.

"Aha!" crowed his grandfather. "We are fortunate Iron Mountain has been overheating lately. Without that telltale steam plume, I doubt you would have noticed this opening in the first place."

Jon and the men carried VORCATS through the field of basalt slabs and lowered it inside the tunnel entrance. "Keerful!" warned Dr. MacKenzie. "I dinna want her to take a tumble. Then all would be for naught. She'd cost fifty thousand dollars to replace."

After powering up the machine, the volcanologist pulled out a device resembling a standard video-game controller, only with a large video screen, a joystick and more buttons. He pressed one of the buttons, and VORCATS' small but powerful searchlight blazed to life, illuminating the passage's rough walls and floor.

Jon stepped back and picked up a jagged rock, just in case VORCATS stirred up a hornets' nest. Whatever was lurking in the cave probably would not take too kindly to a mechanical intruder in their lair, and nobody had thought to bring along so much as a knife on this impromptu expedition. It never hurt to be prepared.

However, no hopping-mad brollachans boiled out of the cleft. While Dr. MacKenzie manipulated the controller's joystick and Jon paid out the electrical cord, VORCATS lurched down the passage.

No one spoke as the volcanologist twitched the joystick, his eyes glued to the controller screen. Soon, the whine of VORCATS' motors died away, though the electrical cable continued steadily snaking into the tunnel, proof that the robotic sensor was still moving.

Dr. MacKenzie heaved a sigh and dabbed the sweat from his forehead. "Here," he said, handing the controller to Jon. "Have a look. I reckon she's about to enter the cavern ye spoke of. So far, I hanna seen anything unusual, but your eyes are better than mine."

Jon gingerly took the controller, reminding himself that this wasn't a video game where the worst that could happen was losing a few game points. There was no telling what might befall VORCATS once it had rolled inside the brollachans' cave.

Squinting down at the screen, Jon saw only a collage of light and shadow. Then the image resolved into a bright white cone fading into a deep darkness that had never seen such light before.

"May I?" he asked. Dr. MacKenzie nodded. Touching the joystick, Jon sent VORCATS trundling into the unknown. The searchlight lanced through more sticky blackness.

To Jon's relief and dismay, he saw no brollachans. Maybe they slept during the day and hunted at night—an unpleasant thought.

He was handing the controller back to its owner when something fluttered in the screen at the boundary between light and darkness. Then a shadow loomed, and the screen went black.

"What happened?" cried the volcanologist. Taking the controller, he stared down at it. "Ye've run her into a wall," he growled, but as he jiggled the joystick to and fro, the image on the screen remained unchanged. Muttering to himself, he pronounced, "Either summat's covering the camera lens, or the searchlight's stopped working. I canna navigate if I canna see. What a pickle!"

He pushed a couple of buttons and jiggled the joystick. "Och!" he said. "I still canna see a blessed thing. I'm stuck."

Professor Roberts asked, "Does that mean we'll have to go in there with flashlights and retrieve VORCATS ourselves?"

Jon shrank back. VORCATS or no, nothing in heaven or on earth could persuade him to enter that tunnel again.

"I dinna think so," the volcanologist replied. "That's one reason I plugged her in. The socket has a lock on it, so if worse comes to worst, we can drag her back wi' the cord. It's a last resort, because she's sure to sustain some damage during transit."

He flicked the joystick once more, and his face relaxed. "I moved the camera again. This time, the lens partly cleared. Since the searchlight is still workin', I can see well enough to bring her back. It's gaun to be nip and tuck, but I've been in worse fixes with VORCATS."

A tense half-hour passed before the sensor's whining motors broke the silence. Still trailing its electrical cord, VORCATS emerged from the fissure, its front end dripping with a white liquid.

"Ugh!" said Jon. "What is that stuff? It looks like bat poop."

His grandfather's brow furrowed. "Good question. It's not bat droppings. Bats produce little brown pellets that resemble mouse droppings, only larger. This stuff looks like fresh bird guano. It reminds me of the droppings we found underneath the fir tree. However, I don't know of any birds that like to roost in tunnels or caves."

"Swifts do, or so I've heard," said Dr. MacKenzie.

"Of course!" Dr. Roberts exclaimed. "Chimney swifts! They build their nests in caves, flues and smokestacks. They can even echolocate in the dark the way bats do. When Olivia was three, a family of swifts clogged up our chimney with their nests. We had a terrible time getting rid of them. They were also making an awful racket."

The two scientists stared at each other. Then they burst out laughing. "Jonathan's 'brollachans' are nothing more than common swifts!" chortled Dr. MacKenzie, beaming with relief.

"Swifts are small birds, and they don't have big red eyes," Jon pointed out. He knelt next to VORCATS and examined the whitish substance, which appeared to be laced with tiny, ivory-colored twigs.

Jon motioned to his grandfather. "Look at this," he said.

Still chuckling, Dr. Roberts crouched beside his grandson. Using a stick, Jon teased one of the small objects out of the dung and delicately laid it on a rock. Donning a pair of reading glasses, Dr. Roberts bent down to study the specimen.

"Lord have mercy!" he said. "I believe that is a bird bone."

"A *bird* bone?" Dr. MacKenzie repeated incredulously. "Let me see." He peered down at the thing. "Why, so it is. But in the Pacific Northwest, only raptors prey on other birds."

"Do you mean like falcons and hawks?" Jon asked.

"Yes," said Dr. Roberts absently. "But raptors don't ordinarily live in caves." Both men put on perplexed scowls.

"What about owls?" Jon suggested.

"That's a possibility," said his grandfather, rubbing his chin. "Some owls do nest in caves. Encountering a whole 'parliament' of those birds could have given rise to the miners' spooky tale of 'brollachans.' Owls regurgitate indigestible bones, fur and feathers in dry pellets, but they also produce typical bird droppings." He pointed at the whitewashed boulders and slabs.

"I dinna agree with your owl theory," Dr. MacKenzie argued. "It would take hundreds of adult owls to coat those rocks so heavily. The cavern should be knee deep in pellets, too. Yet, we hanna seen any pellets anywhere up here."

"I'm taking a sample of this stuff back to the university," Jon's grandfather declared. Pulling out a plastic bread bag, he scooped some of the guano into it and secured it by knotting the neck.

"Do you always carry around a bread bag with you?" Jon teased.

"You never know when a plastic sack will come in handy," replied the professor in a mock injured tone. "I have a biologist friend at the university who has a Ph.D. in ornithology—the study of birds, that is. I'll ask him to take a look at this sample."

"Ugh," said Jon again, this time with more feeling. He didn't envy the university biologist his bird-poop analysis. He also wasn't looking forward to helping pack the robotic sensor back down the hill.

After securing VORCATS in the jeep, Dr. MacKenzie drove his passengers farther down the trail until it joined a paved street. Then he circled around to the Oliver home, where he hosed off his contraption in the driveway. Jon helped him hoist VORCATS back into the jeep. Finally, with a cheery wave, the Scotsman sped away.

When Grandfather Roberts had also left for home, Jon knelt in the driveway to gather up some of the bones Dr. MacKenzie had washed off VORCATS. Most were small and fragile, but Jon was surprised to find fragments of much larger bones. Whatever the brollachans were, they could crush the bones of their prey to splinters.

Chapter 9
MISSING

Whats in the jar?" Jennica asked her brother. Jon was sitting at the kitchen table examining the bone fragments he had recovered from the driveway. After hearing what VORCATS had turned up in the cave, Jon's mother and sister seemed satisfied with the owl explanation, but Jon was not. The largest barn owls rarely reached two feet in height, whereas the creatures he had encountered were at least three times taller.

He withdrew to his bedroom, where he slapped a lid on the bone jar and placed it on a shelf beside other jars and shoeboxes filled with feathers, nuts, agates, geodes (thunder eggs), seashells, arrowheads, dried flowers, fossilized leaves and assorted other natural curiosities. Flopping down on his bed, he nursed his wounded spirit. Both his grandfather and Dr. MacKenzie had been all too eager to dismiss his brollachan tale in favor of their owl theory.

"Owls, shmowls," Jon muttered. He was tempted to collect some "photographic evidence," as Reverend Sanford had put it. Then people would believe him—if they didn't accuse him of faking the photo.

On the other hand, since VORCATS had detected nothing noteworthy with its own video camera, Jon wasn't sure he would fare any better. In fact, things might turn out a great deal worse for him if he returned to the brollachans' lair with the aim of filming or photographing them. Exhausted, he closed his eyes and slept.

The following Saturday, Grandfather Roberts dropped in again. This time, his hazel eyes were sparkling with excitement. Jon wondered whether the paleontologist had found a rare fossil.

"I received the report back from my ornithologist friend," Dr. Roberts announced as he munched on a buttered bagel.

"What did it say?" Jon and Jennica asked him.

"Whatever is in that cave, it isn't owls," said their grandfather. "My friend was certain of that. He ruled out chimney swifts, too. Having conducted a DNA study of those droppings, he concluded they don't belong to any known organism. In other words, Jon, you may have discovered a new species. Congratulations!"

Jon's heart swelled with pride. A new species! Perhaps he would name it, "Brollochanus oliveri." He'd be famous! As proof of his find, he needed only a clear-cut photograph of the red-eyed creature.

Dr. Roberts wasn't finished. "My friend also analyzed the bones in that guano sample. It turns out they are a mixed bag."

"What do you mean?" Jennica asked him.

Her grandfather stroked his chin. "Most of them are fish bones, but others belong to mice, rats, raccoons, possums, bats, birds—even dogs and cats. I don't know of anything that preys upon such a wide assortment of animals. Bears will eat fish and small mammals, but they can't catch birds or bats."

Jon's heart skipped a beat. "Lots of dogs and cats have gone missing in our neighborhood. Maybe now we know why."

The professor reared back. "You don't say. Normally I would blame coyotes, because they will catch and eat many of those same animals—including cats and dogs—but not bats. Besides, the animal scat VORCATS 'collected' was nothing like a coyote's. I just wish I knew what was living in that cave."

"Me, too," Jon said.

"My friend suggested we set up motion-sensor cameras outside the entrance," Dr. Roberts continued. "I'll see if I can borrow some from the university. In the meantime, I advise you both to watch out for any unusual animals in the neighborhood."

Jon and Jennica promised they would. Then Jon slipped off to his bedroom, where he quietly pumped his fist in the air. He was vindicated! The brollachans were not owls after all. He was feeling very pleased with himself when the doorbell rang.

Jon rushed to the door. He found a starched military man standing outside. The somber soldier was wearing a belted black jacket, shiny black shoes, pressed blue pants, white gloves and a white cap.

"Is your mother at home?" the visitor stiffly asked.

Jon nodded and wordlessly fled into the kitchen, where his mother was spreading chicken salad on slices of rye bread. "Mom," he said, "there's someone at the front door who wants to see you."

Mrs. Oliver put down her knife. "Who is it?"

Jon shrugged. "I dunno. He must be one of Dad's friends."

Giving him a perplexed look, Mrs. Oliver left the kitchen. Jon followed her to the door, which still stood half open.

When she caught sight of the stranger, Jon's mother let out a strangled gasp, and the blood drained from her face. She gripped the door jamb with white-knuckled fingers as a drowning man clings to a piece of driftwood. Her mouth opened and closed soundlessly.

"Are you Mrs. Matthew Oliver?" the visitor asked.

Jon's mother nodded mutely. Her lips were trembling.

"May I come in?" asked the man.

"Yes, of course," said Mrs. Oliver in a hollow voice. Standing aside, she let the soldier through and slowly turned to face him. He stood ramrod-straight in the corner like a second hall tree.

"Liv, who is it?" came Grandfather Roberts' voice from the kitchen. When he entered the hallway, he stopped short, and his face turned a sickly gray. "They sent a Marine," he murmured.

"Ma'am," the man began, with pity in his gray eyes. "My name is Lieutenant James Mitchell. I regret to inform you that your husband, Dr. Matthew Oliver, is missing in action. We don't ordinarily offer personal notification for the families of civilians, but Dr. Oliver has been such a valuable asset to our operations in Afghanistan that my superiors felt this visit was amply justified. If there is anything I can do for you, please don't hesitate to call me at this number."

The lieutenant handed Mrs. Oliver an embossed business card. She stared blankly at it. "Missing? What's he missing from, pray tell—his laboratory? He's a research physicist, not a combat soldier."

Removing his spotless cap, Lieutenant Mitchell explained, "Your husband was en route to a secure research facility when his vehicle was attacked by enemy combatants. The driver was killed, and another man was wounded. Military personnel conducted an extensive search for your husband, but they were unsuccessful in locating him. I can assure you the search will continue until he is found."

Covering her face, Jon's mother wept. Her wracking sobs tore at his heart like a dinosaur's cruel claws. Beside him, Jennica scrunched up her face and also burst into tears, wailing pitifully.

"Will we ever see Daddy again?" she whimpered.

Jon hugged his sister. "Don't worry," he said, trying to sound convincing. "I'm sure Dad will be all right. He'll turn up soon."

Jon didn't believe his own words. Somewhere on the other side of the world, evil men had kidnapped or killed his father. That much was plain. He had seen enough news stories about the Taliban to know those insurgents showed no mercy toward their enemies.

Yet, Matthew Oliver was nobody's enemy. He was just a very bright man trying to help others in a fallen world.

"Jon is right," Dr. Roberts chimed in, embracing his daughter. "Just because the military hasn't found him yet doesn't mean Matt is dead. We'll have to pray for his safety—and for his captors as well."

Still offering his condolences, Lieutenant Mitchell backed out the door and drove away, leaving the weight of his words to sink into grief-numbed minds. Jon then joined his family on a living-room couch as Grandfather Roberts prayed for them.

While listening to the professor, Jon let his mind wander back to the special moments he and his father had shared crafting fishing lures, building soapbox derby cars, and creating clever contraptions.

When Jon was ten, his father built a water rocket from soda bottles. It could soar nearly five hundred feet in the air. After that, Jon's popularity likewise soared among the local boys.

Mr. Oliver also constructed a miniature flare-launcher small enough to fit in a shirt pocket. Once, Jon "borrowed" one of the devices and shot off the flare, which landed on the roof and set it afire.

After the fire trucks had left, Jon was grounded for a month.

It didn't seem possible someone so clever and kind as Matthew Oliver could have been ambushed and declared "missing in action" in Afghanistan. Maybe there had been a mix-up. Lieutenant Mitchell would return to break the news that someone else had been kidnapped and that Dr. Oliver was safe and on his way home.

However, Lieutenant Mitchell did not visit the house again.

Over the next few weeks, the Oliver home saw a bewildering flurry of food, flowers, cards, and well-wishers. "You poor dears," the older women would croon over Jon and Jennica as they rubbed their hair the wrong way. No comb was a match for Old Ladies' Fingers, as Jon and his sister liked to call them.

After delivering their overcooked casseroles to go with their cards and shallow condolences, most of the well-meaning visitors excused themselves with, "I'm sorry for your loss."

Jon wanted to scream, "My dad isn't DEAD; he's MISSING!"

Only Mrs. Sanford visited often and stayed long enough to help out with the laundry and other household chores. She also offered a listening ear to anyone who needed to talk.

Lonely and frustrated, Jon holed up in his bedroom, poring over a few faded photos of his father he had found in an ancient scrapbook. School became a living nightmare as Jon's classmates and teachers avoided him or fumbled through awkward expressions of sympathy. No one knew what to say to him. Jon wished he could hide in a broom closet, preferably for the rest of the school year.

His sister didn't fare any better. For the first time in her life, she was getting into fights at school. Both the Oliver children neglected their schoolwork, and their grades suffered.

Often when Jon got up at night to grab a snack, he could hear his mother praying and weeping in the next room. During the day, she put on a brave face, but Jon knew a pool of tears lay just below the frozen surface of her forced cheerfulness.

The days and weeks crawled along like bugs on the wall calendar hanging beside the refrigerator, and still there was no news of Matt Oliver. Then late one Friday afternoon, the doorbell rang again. Jon's stomach spasmed as he went to see who it was. Like the raucous school bell, the doorbell usually brought bad news.

Jon found a stoop-shouldered, bespectacled man fidgeting on the front step. Impeccably attired in a gray wool suit, white shirt, red silk tie and gleaming black Oxfords, he gripped the handle of a polished leather briefcase that matched his shoes.

"Is Mrs. Oliver at home?" the stranger asked in a dry voice.

"No, she's still at school," Jon replied. He was about to close the door when his mother's old black Malibu pulled up. As she got out of the car, Jon waved to her and pointed at the caller.

"Why, Mr. Ellsworth!" she cried. "What brings you out our way?"

Dodging her question, Mr. Ellsworth said, "May I come in?"

Mrs. Oliver nodded to Jon, and he stepped aside, allowing the man to pass through. As she followed him inside, Mrs. Oliver whispered to Jon, "Mr. Ellsworth is our family's attorney."

In the living room, Jon launched himself onto his father's green "man-couch." Now that he was the nominal head of the family, it was his responsibility to guard the stained, swaybacked sofa from girls, wayward animals, and uninvited attorneys.

The lawyer primly seated himself on a different sofa and clicked open his briefcase, murmuring, "Please forgive the unannounced intrusion. I need only a few minutes of your time. I've already prepared all the paperwork for you in advance of my visit."

Mrs. Oliver pulled up a chair to face the attorney. "I trust nothing is amiss with Matt's affairs, is it?" she asked anxiously.

"Not at all," said Mr. Ellsworth kindly. "I am merely carrying out your husband's most recent wishes. Ah, here is what we need." The lawyer removed a single sheet of paper from his briefcase.

An electric shock stiffened Mrs. Oliver's frame. "That's not his will, is it? You're not supposed to read someone's will until they're legally declared dead, right? You know Matt is *missing*."

"Yes, I am aware of that fact, Mrs. Oliver," said the attorney with a trace of irritation. "This is merely a codicil to his will."

"A codi-*what*?" Jennica burst out as she entered the room and plopped down on the man-couch beside Jon. He scowled fiercely at her, but she ignored him. There was nothing he could do. He didn't dare make a scene, though he would have liked to.

"A codicil," explained Mr. Ellsworth patiently, "is an addendum or a supplement to a will—in this case, your father's will."

"What does it say?" Jon asked.

Adjusting his glasses, the lawyer read, "'I, Matthew Ellis Oliver, being of sound mind and body, do hereby authorize my legal representative, Wendell G. Ellsworth III, to distribute the enclosed items to my designated heirs per my written instructions in the event of my untimely death or disappearance.'"

Mrs. Oliver looked baffled. "*Or disappearance*? You're saying Matt made arrangements even if he went missing? How could he possibly predict what would happen to him in Afghanistan?"

Mr. Ellsworth replaced the codicil in his briefcase and took out three manila envelopes sealed with metal clasps. "That I do not know, Mrs. Oliver," he smoothly replied. "Your husband directed me to give you all one of these envelopes. He did not disclose their contents to me, however. I will begin with your son, Jonathan."

Jon's hands shook as he accepted his packet, which was addressed to "Master Jonathan Matthew Oliver." The envelope's weight shifted as a cylindrical shape inside slid or rolled.

After handing Jon's mother and sister their envelopes, Wendell G. Ellsworth III snapped his briefcase shut. "Mr. Oliver instructed me to depart immediately after fulfilling his request," the lawyer announced. "Thank you, and good day to you all. I will see myself out."

With that, the attorney silently glided out the front door.

Jon hurried to his room with his envelope. Tearing it open, he found a silky black sack inside—and a key. He upended the bag, and out dropped a six-inch, jet-black metal tube resembling a penlight. It was wrapped in a curl of folded paper held in place by a rubber band. After removing the rubber band and paper, Jon studied the tube.

Oddly, only a single pinhole pierced its end where a glass lens or reflector ordinarily belonged. Aside from a metal nubbin protruding from the other end, the penlight was smooth and featureless. Jon pressed the nubbin and twisted the tube, but nothing happened.

Laying aside the cylinder, he unfolded the slip of paper. It was a letter written in his father's elegant hand.

Dear Jon, the letter began.

If you are reading this, then I have been taken from you, either by death or by some unfortunate circumstance that has prevented me from returning home. Whatever the case, I am sorry for leaving you, your mother and sister, and I would give anything to be reunited with you all. I know this must be a very difficult time for you and Jennica and for Mom as well.

I need you to be strong in my absence, Jon. Please listen to your mother and help her, won't you? I am proud of the young man you have become, and I am sure you will continue to make me proud, whether I am with the Lord or still on this earth.

The objects I have placed in this envelope are for your exclusive use. Guard them well! The key belongs where you do not and leads to a gift with your name on it. Please forgive the encoded message below, but I cannot risk this knowledge falling into the wrong hands.

All in BASIN:

s1Pl1am—23-27
pai8nt7ac5 0a3ryg2
o18nh11j—6-11
tam5we16th—1-4
I-sin13rocha12tin—5-7

Here's a little practice to put you in the proper frame of mind:

"Meat grinds like a think."

Jon's world came to a sudden stop. His father often played word games with him as a way of helping him overcome his dyslexia. The technique had boosted Jon's confidence in his speech skills, though he still got mixed up when he was nervous. What was his father trying to tell him with these riddles?

Returning to the letter, Jon read further.

One more thing, Son: My business partner, Dr. Ingersoll, may stop by the house to pay you a visit. Do not tell him about the contents of this envelope. I have reason to suspect he may try to steal some of my most important private research, now that I am gone. Do not trust him! Instead, place your trust where it belongs: Proverbs 3:5-6.

With all my love and prayers—

Dad

A warm tear trickled down Jon's cheek. Where was his father now? Would he ever see or hear from him again? Perhaps if he could decipher the message, those questions would find some answers.

Chapter 10
MEAT GRINDS LIKE A THINK

Meat grinds like a think." Jon repeated the sentence aloud, transposing letters as he often did, this time intentionally. He produced nothing but gibberish. Then he tried turning off the sounds in his head and rearranging the syllables and letters again. *Geat mrinds like a think.* No, that's not it. *Great minds like a think. Great minds think alike.*

It was one of his father's favorite expressions.

Jon lay back on his bed, laughing softly to himself. He had passed the first test! He was about to tackle the rest of the riddle when his mother called to him through the door.

"Jon! Supper!"

Jon had been so engrossed in his father's message that he had lost track of the time. Cramming the note, key and penlight in his pocket, he loped down the hallway and turned the corner into the kitchen.

He found his puffy-eyed mother and sister seated at the table, helping themselves to steaming forkfuls of spaghetti and slices of fragrant garlic bread. When Jon popped in, the two stared at him with looks of curiosity seasoned with a generous pinch of suspicion.

"Well?" they said.

"Well what?" Jon responded warily. It was two against one.

His mother dabbed her eyes with a tissue. "We were wondering what your father wrote you. Would you mind sharing?"

Jon thought furiously. "Ah," he said. "You know—just the usual 'love and hugs' stuff. He wishes he were here, wishes he could see us again, sends us his love. Wants me to be strong and listen to you. That sort of thing." He faked a yawn.

"That's all?" asked his mother skeptically.

Eyes on the spaghetti bowl, Jon nodded. His father's penlight, key and note were burning holes in his pocket, but the riddle was meaningless until he had deciphered it. Since the other items were for his "exclusive use," he didn't dare show them to Jennica, or she would want him to share with her. A quarrel would surely ensue.

Mrs. Oliver said, "I know for a fact that something rolled around inside your envelope when Mr. Ellsworth handed it to you. What did your father put in there? I want the truth, now."

Swallowing, Jon replied, "He just gave me a cheap little flashlight I'd been wanting—something to remember him by." He hated lying to his mother or even telling her a half-truth.

Jennica sniffed, "Dad didn't give *me* a flashlight."

"That's because he knew you would lose it." Jon regretted his words even before he saw the tears welling in his sister's eyes. *Why do I always say the wrong thing?* he thought.

"I'm sorry, Jen," he said. "I didn't mean that. Really, I didn't."

To his surprise, she replied, "That's okay. I know you didn't."

"Let's bless the food before it gets cold," Mrs. Oliver suggested. After her prayer, Jon noisily slurped up all his spaghetti before his mother and sister were half done with theirs. Over their protests, he bolted out of the kitchen, rushed back to his room and knelt beside his bed to pray for the wisdom to decrypt the baffling phrases.

Afterwards, he dropped the key in a dresser drawer for safekeeping. Then he reviewed his father's encoded message. "All in BASIN" might refer to a programming language or encryption software. Jon searched the internet but found nothing along those lines.

Moving on, he examined the codes themselves:

s1Pl1am—23-27
pai8nt7ac5 0a3ryg2
o18nh11j—6-11
tam5we16th—1-4
I-sin13rocha12tin—5-7

The first line offered no clues, although the hyphenated-numeral format seemed familiar. However, the second line contained no hyphens. Instead, it appeared to represent two distinct words.

Guessing that the numbers were red herrings, Jon rewrote the two "words" on a separate piece of paper, omitting the numerals. This yielded "paintac" and "aryg."

The note had mentioned the message was "encoded." A true encryption required a special key to decode it. Without such a key, it was almost impossible to "break" the code. However, if the letters were merely transposed and weren't substitutions for something else, Jon reasoned it should be a simple matter to unscramble them.

This time, though, his dyslexia wasn't helping. Switching the first letter or two of the scrambled word pair yielded no solution. Having often played Scrabble™ with his parents and sister, Jon knew even a few letters could be rearranged in any number of random combinations. Unscrambling "paintac" and "aryg" could take him hours.

Frustrated, Jon pounded his fist on the bed. Why couldn't his father have plainly said what he meant instead of using this cryptic code? Was he mocking his dyslexic son from the grave?

Jon needed outside help. "Unscramble words," he typed in the query field of his internet search engine. To his surprise and delight, one of the listed results was for a free, online word-unscrambling utility. He clicked on the utility's link, typed "paintac" in its word field, said a quick prayer, and hit the "Enter" key.

In seconds, the web page presented him with a list of possibilities. The very first unscrambled word was "captain."

The hair prickled on the back of Jon's neck. He was right! The random numerals in the original riddle were just filler intended to throw snoops like his sister off the track.

Next, he typed "aryg" into the unscrambling utility. Out popped "gray" as the top selection. *Captain Gray.*

Jon stared at the words on his laptop screen. What did the original owner of his father's office chair have to do with this riddle?

Jon was determined to find out. He returned to the code's first line: *s1Pl1am—23-27*. Stripping out the "1"s resulted in *sPlam*. When he ran that letter combination through the online word unscrambler, *palms*, *plasm*, *lamps* and *Psalm* were the first results to come up. Since the scrambled word included a capital "P," Jon suspected the unscrambled word also was capitalized. That meant the riddle's most likely solution was *Psalm*.

Applying the same technique to the next two coded phrases after *Captain Gray*, Jon came up with *John* and *Matthew*—two more books of the Bible. However, the final phrase—*I-sin13rocha12tin* (which read "sinrochatin" without the numbers)—stumped the online unscrambler. The closest match the software could offer was "stanchion," which contained nine letters instead of eleven.

He needed an eleven-letter solution.

The first character—"I"—gave him the hint he needed. Roman numerals prefaced only a few books of the Bible: I and II Samuel, I and II Kings, I and II Chronicles, I and II Corinthians, I and II Thessalonians, I and II Timothy, I and II Peter—and I, II and III John.

Based on letter counts, Jon was able to eliminate all the books except Corinthians I and II—and rearranging the letters of "sinrochatin" confirmed his hunch. I Corinthians it was.

Unfortunately, I Corinthians contained sixteen chapters. Did his father really intend for him to read them all? If so, how would he know which verses held the key to Dr. Matthew Oliver's secrets?

Then Jon remembered the numbers he had stripped out of the original Corinthians riddle—13 and 12. Maybe those numerals weren't just filler after all. Most scripture references followed the same format, as in "I Corinthians 13:12."

He catapulted off his bed onto a cushiony pile of dirty laundry. Holding his breath, he waited for his mother's usual, "Why-can't-you-get-off-the-bed-like-a-normal-person?" lecture.

When no motherly reprimand pierced the door, he grabbed a Bible propped up on his bookshelf. Flipping the volume open to the New Testament and I Corinthians, he found verse twelve of chapter thirteen: *For now we see through a glass darkly, but then face to face; now I know in part, but then shall I know even as also I am known*.

Even if he had correctly interpreted the coded phrase, this verse offered no hints as to his father's intended meaning. Jon knew only that the "glass" in the first part of the verse referred to a mirror.

Returning to the original Corinthians code to verify his interpretation, he realized he'd overlooked the numerals "5-7" appearing at the end. He groaned. It seemed that for every piece of the puzzle he deciphered, another piece took its place.

Since a dash separated the additional numbers from the rest of the phrase, maybe they were word counts.

To test this theory, Jon rechecked the first sections of his father's code. Psalm 1:1 read: *Blessed is the man that walketh not in the counsel of the ungodly, nor standeth in the way of sinners, nor sitteth in the seat of the scornful*. Words 23-27 were "in the seat of the."

Jotting down the phrase, Jon ran through the rest of the riddle. John 18:11, words 6-11 read, "Put up thy sword into the." Matthew 5:16, words 1-4 produced, "Let your light so." And I Corinthians 13:12, words 5-7 were, "through a glass."

Taken together—with "Captain Gray" thrown in after Psalm 1— the decoded phrases made absolutely no sense whatsoever.

Jon had reached a dead end. Slamming the Bible shut in frustration, he was about to give up when he noticed the words, "King James Version" stamped in gold on the book's black leather cover.

King James Version—KJV. The title branded itself on his brain. The Holy Bible came in scores of translations and paraphrases. Each version rendered the scriptures with slightly different word choices. Jon liked the NIV—the New International Version. His father preferred the New American Standard Bible—the NASB.

"NASB." Jon pronounced the acronym aloud, rearranging the letters in his head. ASBN . . . BNAS . . . SANB . . . ANSB . . . ABNS . . . ASNB . . . SABN . . . BSAN . . . BSNA . . . BASN . . .

BASN. He stopped in a cold sweat. Borrowing the "i" from the word "Bible" in "New American Standard Bible" would complete the only code word yet to be unscrambled: *BASIN.*

Jon let the King James Bible fall from his trembling hands onto the bed. His father's love for the New American Standard Bible—and his offhand written remark ("All in BASIN")—were actually the keys to decrypting the entire scrambled puzzle.

Revisiting his bookshelf, he pounced on a dog-eared NAS Bible. He flipped back and forth through its pages, counting out the words for each of his father's encoded scriptures.

Once connected, the phrases now read, *Sit in the seat of Captain Gray. Put the sword into the sheath. Let your light shine in a mirror.*

Chapter 11
CAPTAIN GRAY'S SEAT

Jon stared at the piece of paper where he had hastily recorded the decrypted NASB scripture references. Even though they made better sense than the King James versions, each phrase still seemed completely unrelated to the others.

Sit in the seat of Captain Gray might refer to the bolted-down antique in Matthew Oliver's office, but what did a chair have to do with a sword or its sheath? To Jon's knowledge, his father didn't collect medieval weapons—or any other weapons, for that matter.

Exiting his bedroom, he hurried down the hall to the forbidden office and unlocked the door with the key hidden behind the family photo. The room looked just the same as he remembered it from his last visit—except for one detail. Approaching the Captain Gray chair from a different angle, he noticed a black electrical cable snaking down the back of one varnished leg and into the floor. Why would an antique wooden chair require an electrical source?

Cautiously, he settled into the chair and felt around the thick arm rests for an electrical switch or button. He found only the angled hole in the left arm that served as a pencil-holder. Jon wondered why his father needed pencils when he used computers for all of his work.

Besides, the holder's three-quarter-inch opening seemed rather large for a pencil. *Put the sword into the sheath.* If the hole was a "sheath," what kind of "sword" would fit into it?

Jon's gaze wandered around the office. On the desk lay Dr. Oliver's special ballpoint pen that he often used for making notes to himself. However, the pen looked too slim to fit the "sheath."

Discouraged, Jon rose from the chair. As he did, something fell out of his pocket and clattered to the floor. It was the heavy-duty black penlight his father had left him in the envelope.

Picking it up, he was struck by the object's diameter, which was very similar to the pencil-holder's. On a whim, he sat down again in the chair and with his left hand, shoved the nubbin end of the flashlight back into the angled opening as far as it would go.

Click. The metal tube seated itself at the bottom of the hole. Instantly, a hair-thin, bright green light-beam shot out of the tube's top end and struck the mirror hanging on the wall above the desk.

Jon's mouth fell open. *It's a laser!* Bouncing off the mirror, the light-ray traveled across the room to reflect off a multi-faceted disco-ball doubling as a light fixture. All around the office the laser beam lanced, glancing off mirrors built into books and bookends, trophies, ventilation grills and even a ceiling fan. In milliseconds, the laser beams had spun an intricate green web throughout the room.

Jon sat very still, hoping not to be caught in the web.

The laser light's path ended at a round sensor mounted on the wall behind him. Masquerading as a thermostat, the sensor glowed green, and with a humming vibration, a thin, dark ring appeared on the floor around the chair. The ring widened as a circular section of the flooring moved downward, taking Jon and the chair with it.

Before Jon could budge, the chair had dropped through the floor into another room. The laser beam shut off as banks of LED lights snapped on, revealing a high-ceilinged workshop crammed with gleaming machinery arrayed on work benches and tables. The chair stopped at floor level, and Jon hopped off. To his relief, the antique "elevator" stayed put, though he kept a hand on it for fear it would return to the office without him.

Feeling like an intruder, he surveyed the lab. Sure enough, his father had stashed his equipment in storage—right under his office floor. Judging from all the stainless-steel instruments set up in the work spaces, Dr. Oliver had conducted clandestine experiments in this laboratory—instead of wreaking havoc in his wife's kitchen.

On a nearby table lay a rumpled cloth bag. A yellow sticky note clung to it. "Jon" was scrawled on the note in Dr. Oliver's hand, almost as an afterthought. Jon was reminded of his father's hint about the envelope key: . . . *and leads to a gift with your name on it.*

Jon yanked open the sack's mouth. Peering inside, he found only a coiled-up construction belt with some aluminum canisters riveted around it, probably for holding small tools, screws, nuts and bolts.

His mother had once mentioned an old tool belt belonging to his Grandfather Oliver, who had been a building contractor in Beaverton. Jon's father must have left him the belt as a keepsake.

If so, why had the man taken such elaborate, cloak-and-dagger measures to conceal a utility belt? Maybe it was all a practical joke.

Beside the sack lay a gas mask Jon's father must have worn to guard against chemical fumes. Thinking it might come in handy in case Iron Mountain "burped" again, Jon stuffed it into the bag, which he recognized from somewhere. He couldn't place it until he recalled his mother's questioning him about her missing laundry sack.

Jon grinned. It was just like his father to appropriate household items for his science projects without asking his wife's permission. He remembered the time Mr. Oliver had used Mrs. Oliver's clothes-iron to seal the seams on a high-altitude box kite. That iron had never worked the same afterwards. The kite, however, had worked very well, generating enough lift to drag Jon across the ground.

"Jonathan Matthew! Where are you? It's time for dessert," Mrs. Oliver's voice faintly echoed down into the secret laboratory. Jon's heart nearly burst out of his chest. In his haste, he had forgotten to close the office door behind him. He couldn't let himself be caught in his father's office, let alone down in the laboratory.

Grabbing the sack, he plopped back into Captain Gray's chair and pawed at the arms in search of a button or lever that would send the chair back up to the office. Finding nothing of the sort, he plucked the laser pen out of its niche—and the chair began to rise.

"Jon!" his mother called again. The lab lights clicked off as the chair ascended. Jon anxiously squirmed in his seat. Apparently the chair had only one speed, and that speed was S-L-O-W.

As he emerged headfirst into his father's office, *ka-chunk*—the chair's mechanism neatly plugged the hole in the existing floor. And just in time, too. His mother's footsteps were clicking down the hallway past his bedroom. In moments, she would see the open door.

Jon dropped the laser pen into the bag and left it on the chair seat. Then he hurled himself through the office door and flung it shut behind him, just as Mrs. Oliver turned the corner.

"There you are," she said. "Didn't you hear me calling? I baked a nice berry cobbler for dessert. Now come along before it grows cold. You shouldn't be hanging around your father's office, anyway."

Jon froze. *The key belongs where you do not*, his father's note had said—and the one place Jon didn't belong was in this office.

"Yes, Mom," he croaked and followed her down the hallway.

After gobbling up his cobbler in record time, he went to his room and from the dresser drawer removed the key his father had left him. Then he took the office key out of his pocket and compared the two.

They were identical. Unaware that Jon had found the key behind the photo, Dr. Oliver had supplied this copy. Jon put it back in the drawer as a spare. Then he returned to the office to retrieve the laundry sack, lock the door and replace the old key in its hiding place.

It all made perfect sense now. The laser pen hadn't worked before because it lacked a power supply. The chair was wired to provide that power, and it was bolted to the floor to ensure the laser beam struck all the mirrors in sequence at precisely the proper angles. No wonder Dr. Oliver kept his office locked, lest people disturb those mirrors.

Jon recalled how his father had insisted on purchasing a house with a basement. He had also delayed his family's moving into their new home for six weeks while the kitchen cabinets were being replaced. Jon had never understood why. Cabinet installations were messy, but plenty of people stayed in their homes during the process.

There had to be another reason for the delay.

Now Jon realized his father had used that extra time to construct his covert laboratory by walling off the rear portion of the basement. That explained why the basement's back-wall sheetrock looked newer than the rest: It was only recently installed. It also explained Dr. Oliver's absence when Jon had peeked inside his office at three-thirty in the morning. The scientist had descended into his workshop and somehow sent the chair back up empty to deceive prying eyes.

Sitting on his bed, Jon opened the laundry bag and took out the laser pen, gas mask and tool belt. The mask he shoved under his bed amongst the dust bunnies. It was the last place his mother would think to check when searching for candy or comic book contraband. He put the laser pen in the dresser drawer with the key.

On inspecting the belt, Jon realized it wasn't designed to carry a builder's tools after all. The aluminum canisters were completely sealed, top, sides and bottom—and they didn't rattle when shaken.

The belt also lacked loops or holsters for holding hammers, pliers, screwdrivers and the like. Was it a lifejacket that used air-filled canisters for buoyancy? Jon tried on the band, securing it around his waist with a series of snaps provided for that purpose.

Then he noticed the electrical wires. Coded red, green and white, they ran to each of the sealed canisters from a boxy plastic case at the back of the band. What sort of belt was this, anyway?

Opening his laptop, Jon searched the internet for "belt." He found ladies' belts and men's belts; leather belts, fabric belts and designer belts; belts for vacuums and engine belts, and even the constellation known as "Orion's Belt." Then he lit upon photos of belts and vests with explosive-filled pouches that sprouted wires.

He was wearing a suicide belt.

Scarcely daring to breathe, Jon gingerly unsnapped it and laid it on the bed. Unlike the flimsy cotton bomb vests and belts he had seen on the internet, this heavy-duty, nylon-webbing belt had been built to last. The seamless lightweight canisters evenly spaced around its circumference were reinforced with thick aluminum bands. Why would someone go to the trouble of crafting such a sturdy piece of equipment when it was designed only to explode?

Afghanistan. That country had to be the key connection. Suicide bombers—and suicide belts—were commonplace there. In preparation for his hazardous work overseas, Jon's father must have designed this belt as a mock-up for research purposes. Perhaps it contained no actual explosives—and perhaps it did.

Running his fingers along the belt, Jon found a green button recessed in the front. Bomb belts required a detonator, but here the wearer would have to expose the belt in order to get at the button, sacrificing the element of surprise.

Moreover, it seemed a waste of time to install a button that would be pressed only once before being obliterated. Jon certainly didn't want to be the one to press it, especially not while wearing the belt.

Aside from cutting the belt's wires to defuse it—and possibly setting off any explosives instead—Jon couldn't think of a way to safely discover its function. Why his father would leave him such a potentially dangerous device remained a mystery.

A knock came at the door. Startled, Jon hastily rolled up the belt and shoved it into the drawer holding the key and laser pen. The door cracked open, and his mother's head poked through.

"Time for bed, Jon," she told him.

"Aw, Mom," Jon said. "Why can't I stay up a while longer? Tomorrow's Saturday, so I can sleep in as long as I want."

"Not tomorrow, you can't," Mrs. Oliver snorted. "I need your help with the housework. You can start by cleaning your room. It looks like a cyclone hit it. No, make that *two* cyclones. Then you can sweep and mop the kitchen floor and launder your dirty clothes."

Jon groaned as his mother blew him a kiss and closed the door. At this rate, he would never finish analyzing the belt. If only his father would come home and set matters right!

Jon was nearly asleep when a muffled thumping sound startled him. Assuming his mother was knocking on his door, he got up and opened it. No one was there. Jennica had tricked him again.

Muttering dire threats against his sister, Jon crawled back into bed and fell into a dreamless sleep.

Chapter 12
BLUE HERON IN A SUIT

Early the next morning, Jon's mother rousted him out of bed to tackle his chores. After breakfast, he was straightening his shelves when he found the jar of bones he'd recovered from the brollachans' scat. To photograph the creatures, Dr. Roberts had promised to borrow some motion-sensor cameras from the university, but since Jon's father had gone missing, the cameras were forgotten. Jon would have to take matters into his own hands.

He needed to get back inside the brollachans' cave. Unfortunately, Dr. MacKenzie was gallivanting around the globe exploring his pet volcanoes, so borrowing VORCATS was out of the question.

Jon would have to build his own VORCATS.

After scrubbing the kitchen floor and doing his laundry, he went out to the garage, which reeked of engine oil and rubber tires. Rummaging through the odds and ends his father had left behind, he found an old laptop, two webcams, his blue soapbox derby racer, a new car battery, and a boxful of electromagnets.

Given a few chore-free weekends, he was confident he could construct another VORCATS out of those spare parts. Then nothing would stop him from tracking down the elusive brollachans.

It wouldn't hurt if they had hoarded a little gold and silver, as Dr. MacKenzie had mentioned they were fond of doing.

But what should he call his invention? VORCATS II? No, he wanted to create a sensor robot that was uniquely his own. He would christen his creation "CORVATS," after his first dyslexic attempt at pronouncing "VORCATS." The new acronym would stand for <u>C</u>ave <u>O</u>bservation <u>R</u>emote <u>V</u>ehicular <u>A</u>ll-<u>T</u>errain <u>S</u>cooter.

"Jon! Mom says you gotta come inside. We have company."

Standing in the garage doorway, Jennica smiled sweetly at him. Jon gritted his teeth. It seemed every time he put his hand to an important project, his sister interfered. Who could be visiting them on a Saturday morning? No doubt more gushy well-wishers had popped in to say what a fine man Matt Oliver was, how they missed him, and would you like another tuna-and-rice casserole?

When he entered the living room, his mother was speaking with a lanky, bespectacled man dressed in an immaculate, three-piece suit. Turning to Jon, he said, "Ah, you must be Jonathan. Your father has told me much about you. It is a pleasure to make your acquaintance, young man. A pleasure indeed. You do resemble your father."

Jon shook the man's proffered hand, which felt like a limp, slimy eel. Behind his thick-lensed glasses, the visitor's pale, watery eyes floated like magnified twin moons. With his rakish haircut and rail-thin limbs, the fellow reminded Jon of a long-legged blue heron.

"This is Dr. Ronald Ingersoll," Jon's mother told him. "He's your father's business partner. He wanted to pay us a visit."

Jon stiffened with a vague suspicion. He had heard that name somewhere before, probably from his father. However, Matthew Oliver rarely spoke about his business associates or dealings.

Then Jon remembered. His father's letter had warned him against this very man. Dr. Ronald Ingersoll hardly seemed a threat, but Jon didn't trust him or his oily-palmed intentions.

"What kind of doctor are you?" asked Jennica.

"I'm a research physicist at GyroSensors," Ingersoll replied. When he spoke, his bird-like Adam's apple bobbed up and down.

"Er, how is GyroSensors coming along these days?" Mrs. Oliver brightly asked, evidently wishing to avoid ruffling the feathers of this annoying blue heron in a suit.

"That's the main reason I came to see you," said Dr. Ingersoll, cleaning his glasses with a cloth. "GyroSensors Laboratories is thriving nicely, although we do miss Matt—Dr. Oliver, that is."

"So do we," said Jon's mother softly.

Dr. Ingersoll hurriedly added, "Of course, I also wished to convey my heartfelt condolences for your loss. Your husband's disappearance is a terrible shame—and a waste of expertise. I warned Matt not to volunteer in this futile overseas war, but he wouldn't listen to reason. I was afraid something like this would happen to him."

Volcanic heat rose in Jon's neck and flooded his face. Who was this prissy scientist to pass judgment on his father's choices?

Oblivious to Jon's anger, Dr. Ingersoll lowered himself like a cat onto the Oliver man-couch. He wore a distasteful expression.

"Hey!" Jon protested. His mother silenced him with a look.

"That's just it, Dr. Ingersoll," she told the physicist. "We don't understand why Matt went to Afghanistan in the first place, either. He's a research scientist, not a military man."

Ingersoll looked genuinely—if owlishly—surprised. "You didn't know? Dr. Oliver told me he was working on an IED detection system to help protect the troops in Afghanistan. However, I have no idea whether he succeeded in producing such a device or not." He stared narrowly at Jon and his family, as if somehow suspecting they were concealing the IED detector from him in the next room.

"What's an IED?" Jennica asked.

The physicist peered down his pointed nose at her. "An IED is an 'Improvised Explosive Device.' IEDs range from roadside explosives made from modified mortar shells to suicide vests and sophisticated car bombs. My knowledge of that subject is limited. Weapons detection was—is—your father's specialty."

Suicide vests. Jon shivered. His first guess hadn't been far off the mark. Maybe the peculiar belt wasn't an IED but a cutting-edge IED detector. Either way, he wasn't about to reveal its existence.

Addressing Jon's mother, Ingersoll asked, "I don't suppose your husband left you any research notes or electronic mechanisms, did he?" The man's casual words floated lazily on a smoldering undercurrent of pure menace as he leaned forward intently.

Jon's mouth went dry, and an invisible boa constrictor squeezed the air out of his lungs. Dr. Ingersoll *was* trying to steal Matt Oliver's research. What might this scheming scientist do to get his hands on a game-changing invention like the one in Jon's dresser drawer?

"No, he didn't," Mrs. Oliver answered truthfully. As far as she knew, the only electronic device the family had inherited was Jon's "flashlight"—and he couldn't as yet tell her its true function.

"He just left us a few preliminary legal instructions," she added. "I suppose *if* he is officially declared dead, we might find more information in his will, which he may have modified. It's difficult living in this state of limbo, as you can imagine."

Dr. Ingersoll nodded without relaxing his tense posture. His eyes turned to steely gray marbles behind his thick glasses.

"Matt told you nothing of his experiments?" he asked.

Thump.

Jon's head snapped up as everyone's eyes turned toward his room. It was the same sound he had heard the night before. He couldn't imagine what it was, but he had to concoct an explanation before Dr. Ingersoll barged into his bedroom.

"Uh, the dog is trying to get out," he lamely explained.

His mother and sister stared at him in undisguised shock. Jon had a well-deserved reputation for honesty, a trait his parents had instilled in him. In truth, nobody in the family owned a dog—or any other pet. Jon knew his mother wouldn't let this lie pass.

"Then why don't you let him out?" said Dr. Ingersoll silkily.

"Oh, he bites people," Jennica jumped in. "We have to keep him in the bedroom whenever company comes over."

"I see," said the scientist, rising to his feet. He handed Mrs. Oliver a card. "If you do find something, please contact me."

"Yes, of course," she said, shaking his hand.

After Dr. Ingersoll had left, Jon's sister and mother turned on him. "What made that bumping noise?" they demanded. "You're not keeping any animals in your bedroom, are you?"

Jon shook his head. "No, I'm not. It's—it's just an experiment I'm working on. I didn't want Dr. Ingersoll to see it. I was afraid he would try to take it away from me."

It was a half-truth at best. Jon didn't want anyone having a look at the mysterious belt before he figured out what it was actually for. And he really was working on an experiment—CORVATS—which he also wished to keep under wraps for the time being.

"What kind of experiment?" his mother asked suspiciously.

"Don't worry; it's nothing dangerous or messy," Jon assured her. "I'm working with batteries and wires and stuff like that."

Mollified, his mother said, "Very well. Just clean up afterwards. And for Heaven's sake, don't electrocute yourself."

Avoiding his sister's curious gaze, Jon returned to his room. After closing the door, he searched the place from floor to ceiling without finding the source of the odd thumping sound.

Then he opened the drawer. The belt still lay inside—in a tangled heap. A pang of raw fear knifed through his chest. He knew beyond any doubt whatsoever he had left the belt tightly coiled. Someone— likely his sister—had meddled with the device behind his back.

When he removed the belt, the button in front was glowing a bright green. In his haste to put away the belt the day before, he must have accidentally pressed the button, completing an electrical circuit.

If this were an IED, it should have exploded. Was it a dud, or was it actually an IED detector, as Dr. Ingersoll had suggested? Either way, Jon didn't know what to do with the strange device.

The button-light began to blink, and a chime repeatedly sounded. The belt wasn't a dud; it was counting down to detonation!

Jon was doomed. He tossed the belt back into its drawer and dove under his bed, where he waited to be blown into oblivion, or at least through the wall and out into the street.

Nothing happened. Feeling faint from holding his breath, Jon crept out of hiding to inspect the still-chiming device. He noticed its blinking button displayed a lightning-bolt electrical symbol. His tension dissolved in a nervous laugh. After being left on for a while, the belt evidently needed recharging.

But how? On a hunch, Jon followed the colored electrical wires that ran from each of the canisters back to the heavy, square plastic case he had noticed before. He assumed it was a battery pack.

Prying off the cover, he found a tightly wound electrical cord packed into a cramped compartment above a compact battery. The cord ended in a conventional, three-pronged plug.

Jon unwound the cord and plugged it into the wall. The chiming stopped and the button's light turned to a steady green glow with the lightning-bolt symbol still displayed in the background. Flushed with success, Jon relaxed. He had only to wait for the unit to recharge. Then he would find out just what the device was capable of doing.

An hour later, the belt chimed again, and the button's electrical symbol no longer showed. To Jon's surprise, the belt felt lighter than a leaf in his hand. He pressed the button to shut off the power, and the belt regained its former heft. He hadn't been imagining things after all. His father's device evidently multiplied muscle strength. *The belt was designed to make a super-soldier out of anyone who wore it.*

Across the street, a silver Mercedes with tinted windows sat parked out of Jon's view. The driver's-side window slid partway down, and a gloved hand gripping a black, remote-like instrument reached through. The instrument's red indicator light began flashing, accompanied by a distinctive warbling tone.

The gangly scientist nodded his satisfaction. *Something* out of the ordinary was operating in the Oliver home, something he would like very much to see. The Olivers were definitely hiding an important discovery from him—but not for long.

Rolling up the window, Dr. Ronald Ingersoll drove away.

Chapter 13
OF DINOSAURS & DATING

That night, Jon slept fitfully. When his alarm went off the next morning, he leapt out of bed and threw on his clothes. Racing into the kitchen, he shoveled down the plate of eggs and toast his mother had prepared for him. As he ate, she stood gazing at him in wonderment, arms folded and foot idly tapping.

"What's gotten into you?" she remarked. "Sunday mornings, I usually have to crowbar you out of bed. Is something special happening today at church—or did you find a girlfriend in Sunday School?"

Jon blushed. He was painfully aware of his shortcomings in the girlfriend department. With the possible exception of Renée Doulière, a French exchange student at his school, Jon had little use for girls. Their cruel, cutting remarks made his life miserable. His peers saw him as a gawky geek who loved playing computer games and reading. He was always the last to be picked for sports teams.

"Mom!" he protested. "It's nothing like that. I just want to get to church so it can be *over*. I have plans today—big plans."

"So do I," said his mother. "My plans include a nap after lunch. Whatever your plans are, they had better not interfere with mine."

Jon assured her they wouldn't, though he couldn't be certain.

Despite Reverend Sanford's inspiring message on the subject of God's grace, mercy and forgiveness, Jon's eyes kept straying to the sanctuary clock. He was counting the seconds and minutes until he could return home and conduct some experiments while wearing the Belt of Power. Maybe he could even lift the Malibu effortlessly!

The clock appeared to have stopped.

As soon as the worship service ended, Jon raced out to the church parking lot and jumped into the family car. When his mother and sister caught up to him, he willed the vintage vehicle to fly home.

Mrs. Oliver had scarcely pulled into the driveway when Jon leapt out of the car, tore into the house and took refuge in his bedroom. After closing the door, he removed the belt from its drawer, fastened it around his waist and pressed the green power button.

The belt made a whirring sound, but Jon felt no different. He tried hoisting his floor lamp straight-armed with one hand, but it was too heavy. To his disappointment, it seemed the belt didn't grant its wearer superhuman strength after all.

He heard the front door open and close, followed by a murmured conversation. Then his mother called, "Jon? Will you please come out here? Your grandfather has stopped by for a visit."

Jon flinched reflexively. Something struck his head. Then stars pricked the blackness behind his eyes before winking out.

When he came to, he was looking down on his bed.

His mother was still calling for him. "Jon! I need to see you—now!" The door flew open, and Mrs. Oliver glanced around inside.

"Didn't you say he was in his room?" she barked to someone.

"I'm sorry, Mom. I thought he was," Jennica's voice replied. "Maybe he went out to the garage when I wasn't looking."

Jon's mother left and closed the door behind her, leaving him dreamily gazing down on his bed. Perhaps he had died. He had heard of people having near-death experiences in which they left their bodies and floated around the room, unobserved by the living.

If he was dead, why did his head hurt, and where was his body? He didn't see himself anywhere on the bed or the floor.

He was floating just below the ceiling, which bore a shallow, head-shaped dent. Then he remembered the belt. He was still wearing it, and its power button still glowed greenly.

"Jon? Jon! Where did that boy go?" his mother called.

Jon had to get down—and quickly. Pressing the green button, he shut off the belt's power. *Kerthump!* He fell flat onto his bed.

The door banged open. "There you are!" said Mrs. Oliver. "Where were you, anyway? I've been searching all over for you."

"I've just been taking a nap," said Jon weakly. He pulled a pillow over his waist to conceal the belt.

"Then what was that noise? Did you break something?"

Jon thought quickly. "Oh—I rolled off the bed on the wall side."

His mother nodded. "Maybe that's why I didn't see you earlier. Can you come out now? Your grandfather wants to have a talk with all of us. I honestly don't know why."

"Sure, Mom," Jon dazedly replied. "I'll be out in a minute."

After his mother had left, Jon unsnapped the belt and stowed it in his drawer again. Despite his muddled mind, he realized the device generated a gravity-cancelling field. When his mother had called him the first time, he had flexed his muscles enough to propel him off the floor and into the ceiling, where he hit his head and blacked out. He was thankful he hadn't been outside, or he might have floated off into the clouds with no way to safely return to good old terra firma.

That also explained the strange sounds in his room. When he had turned its power on, the belt had levitated and uncoiled, bumping around inside the drawer. Later, as the battery ran down, the belt had dropped back onto the drawer's bottom, making the knocking noise.

No wonder Ingersoll was so keen to acquire Dr. Oliver's research. A breakthrough in anti-gravity technology was worth a fortune.

Pulling himself together, Jon emerged from his room to find his family all waiting for him in the kitchen. He collapsed onto a chair.

"You look awfully pale, Jon. Are you all right?" his mother asked him as she removed a glass mixing bowl from a cupboard.

"Sure, I'm fine," Jon replied, though he felt anything but fine. His body was shaking from the shock he had just experienced, and he was breaking into a clammy sweat. He wanted to tell his family about the belt but decided against it, since he still needed to learn more about his father's remarkable invention and how it worked.

Grandfather Roberts cleared his throat, and his eyes clouded over like a western Oregon sky in March. "Everyone," he announced, "I'm sorry to say that I lost my job at the university last Friday."

Crash! Jon's mother dropped the mixing bowl, and it shattered on the floor into a million glass shards. Jon grabbed the dustpan and broom to sweep up the jagged pieces before they could cut someone.

Dr. Roberts wrapped a comforting arm around his daughter's shoulders. "Liv, I apologize for springing that news on you so abruptly. I know it's a lot to process on top of Matt's being MIA."

"I'm sorry, too, Dad," said Mrs. Oliver. "I don't understand. You were one of the most popular professors at the university. Everybody loved you. Why would they let you go like that?"

Dr. Roberts took a deep breath. "It's because of an article I published this month in a professional journal called the *Paleontology Review*. In my article, I suggested that we scientists ought to reexamine our assumptions about the earth's age, based upon new research data. In a word, I challenged the establishment's sacred cow."

Jon's mother buried her head in her hands. "Dad, how could you? I admire and respect you for standing on your convictions, but why did you have to stir up that old hornets' nest?"

"Somebody has to," he retorted. "Evolutionists deride us young-earth creationists for not publishing our research in secular journals, but they rarely accept our articles. When they do, they refuse to review our data with an open mind. Dr. Arnold, my department head at the university, told me Friday that my views are 'incompatible with the pursuit of scientific inquiry at this institution.'"

"Mom and I warned you something like this would happen if you didn't stop sticking your neck out," Mrs. Oliver sighed.

Agitated, Dr. Roberts paced around the kitchen. "For too long, evolutionists have ignored inconsistencies in their pet proposition. Science is supposed to operate according to certain basic principles, but those principles don't seem to apply in the realms of evolution and geology. There's abundant evidence that our world isn't billions of years old—that in fact it is much younger."

"I know, Dad," said Jon's mother wearily. "You're preaching to the choir. I don't mean to be rude, but I've got baking to do."

Mrs. Oliver left the kitchen, but her reproachful words hung in the air like tiny daggers that pricked at Jon's burning ears.

"What principles do you mean?" he asked his grandfather.

"Scientific inquiry requires collecting data by observing natural phenomena and conducting experiments," Dr. Roberts replied. "Based upon those data, we formulate hypotheses that must be proven or disproven by further experimentation and observation."

"What?" said Jennica, looking glassy eyed.

Dr. Roberts chuckled. "Sorry. I got carried away again. To prove something is true scientifically, you must demonstrate that it's true every time, everywhere. Different researchers conducting the same experiment should get the same results, if the hypothesis is accurate."

Warming to his subject, the paleontologist continued. "Determining the earth's true age is difficult because no human was here to observe its genesis. We have no way to document that event. Scientists can speculate as to how and when the earth formed, but they can't prove experimentally that the earth is of such-and-such an age."

"My teacher says the earth is four billion years old," said Jon.

His grandfather grimaced. "The usual number is around four-and-a-half billion years," he said. "Scientists typically arrive at that figure using a technique called 'radiometric dating.' They calculate the rate of radioactive decay of certain elements, such as uranium, which decays into lead. They also use potassium-40, which decays into argon-40 gas. If you measure the amount of lead or argon in a particular rock specimen and you know the decay rate, you can work backwards to calculate how old the sample is, at least in theory."

"So what's wrong with that?" Jennica asked.

"This method poses several problems," Dr. Roberts replied. "If you're using potassium-argon dating, for example, you must ask, 'How much argon was present in the rock to begin with?' Another question to ask is, 'Has the rate of decay from potassium to argon been constant throughout geologic time?' Neither question can be answered or proven empirically—by direct observation, that is."

Who cares about rocks? Jon thought. "How do you figure out the ages of other stuff, like things that used to be alive?" he asked.

His grandfather answered, "Scientists use a radioactive form of carbon called 'Carbon-14' to calculate the ages of dead plants and animals. Carbon-14 is present in all living things. Once an animal or plant dies, it doesn't absorb any more of this radiocarbon, which continues to break down. With a half-life of only 5,730 years, C-14 decays relatively rapidly. At that rate, virtually none of it remains after 50,000 years. Yet, many fossils that are supposedly millions of years old still contain measurable C-14. It is even found in natural diamonds, which are thought to have formed billions of years ago. Of course, diamonds are impervious to any form of contamination."

Jon nodded. "So if the earth isn't billions and billions of years old, does anybody know how old it really is?"

The paleontologist winked at him. "Members of the Young Earth Geological Society are working on that very question. Again, it is difficult to rely upon present observations as a foolproof window into the past. However, we are making great strides on several fronts. One is in measuring the amounts of helium present in granitic rocks as a clue to rates of radioactive decay. 'Radiohalos,' another key to our earth's past, are also found in granites. Our research may one day revolutionize dating techniques, if only the world will listen to us."

"Then what about evolution?" Jennica asked.

"That's a loaded question to ask a Bible-believing paleontologist like me!" said Grandfather Roberts with a grin. "First, I'm going to ask *you* both a question: When is a fossil not a fossil?"

Stumped, Jon and Jennica stared at each other. This was not the sort of riddle Jon could solve just by switching a few letters.

"We give up," he told Dr. Roberts. "When is a fossil not a fossil?"

"When it's not fully mineralized. A fossil is just tissue replaced by minerals. When that process is incomplete, traces of the original tissue remain. Recently, scientists have been finding soft tissues in lots of dinosaur fossils. They have also found that an iron-rich blood solution can preserve some tissues for two years, but many unfossilized dinosaur remains—such as mummified skin—lack any iron nearby. Besides, no Tyrannosaurus rex fossil ever soaked sixty-five million years in an artificially concentrated iron bath."

Jon jumped to his feet. "We could clone a T. rex?"

Dr. Roberts held up his hands. "Whoa! Hold on there, young fellow. I didn't say that. To clone a dinosaur, you would need enough viable DNA, though scientists are perfecting their tissue-recovery techniques in hopes of resurrecting the wooly mammoth and other extinct prehistoric species. Whether or not they succeed, those unfossilized dinosaur tissues could not have survived semi-intact for umpteen million years. They should have turned to dust ages ago."

"What's that got to do with evolution?" Jennica asked.

Dr. Roberts rubbed his hands together. "It's simple," he said. "If life on earth isn't millions of years old, then evolution is impossible.

"Remember what I told you about scientific observation? No one has ever observed a mouse evolving into a man—or an elephant. No one. An evolutionist would say that's because it takes millennia for evolutionary changes to occur. However, if we suppose the earth is as young as the Bible—and our tests—indicate, then mouse-to-man evolution would not have had enough time to take place."

"Don't fossils prove evolution?" Jon asked innocently. He already knew the answer, but he loved listening to his grandfather explain how fossils had formed during the Great Flood. Sometimes he wished he could have been a gecko on the wall inside Noah's Ark as the waters rose to inundate a world gone mad with violence.

"That's another good question," said Dr. Roberts. "Fossils offer abundant physical evidence that untold numbers of plants and animals were rapidly buried in a world-wide cataclysm, which most young-earth geologists believe was the flood of Noah's day. Though many species in the fossil record are now extinct, such as trilobites and ammonites, plenty of these petrified animals and plants are indistinguishable from their modern-day counterparts.

"For example, fossilized chestnut leaves look just like those of modern chestnuts. Fossilized redwood needles and cones are identical to those of the California redwoods and the Dawn redwood, though some species are extinct. Fossilized alligators and crocodiles also appear to have remained unchanged, along with horsetails, horseshoe crabs, the coelacanth fish and thousands of other species."

"Those are 'living fossils,' right, Grandpa?" Jon asked.

"That's correct," Dr. Roberts replied. "Recently, scientists have even discovered—and resurrected—bacteria dated 250 million years old containing viable DNA very similar to today's bacterial DNA.

"Aside from minor changes, why have so many organisms stayed the same over presumed millions of years, while evolutionists insist that other living things—amoebas and apes, for instance—have in that same time-frame metamorphosed into dinosaurs and human beings? It just doesn't make any sense. If evolution is true, it should be consistent in how it operates."

Jennica's forehead crinkled. "Does that mean some of those dinosaurs could still be alive here on earth, Grandfather?"

He nodded. "Possibly. If any real dinosaurs have survived, they are probably living in the remote jungles of Africa's Congo or in South America, where the tropical climate is more to their liking."

Mrs. Oliver bustled into the kitchen with a big sack of flour and set it on the counter. "I wouldn't mind living someplace warmer than Oregon," she said. "I doubt Matt would like it elsewhere, though. He has always loved the Northwest, despite all the rain here. He says it freshens the air and keeps everything lush and green. That's why I can't picture him tromping around the deserts of Afghanistan."

Wiping her eyes with a tissue, she sniffled softly. "Without his income, we'll be hard pressed to pay our bills."

Jon hated seeing his mother cry. He also didn't like listening to her argue with his grandfather over his creationist convictions. Jon, on the other hand, hoped he would grow up to become just like his father and grandfather—an inventor and a fossil-hunter.

That was assuming he would live to grow up. He rubbed the sore spot on his head where he had collided with the ceiling. The anti-gravity belt had already proven hazardous to operate.

Chapter 14
DR. STALKER

I'd like to discuss something else with you youngsters," Dr. Roberts went on. "Since I won't be employed at the university any longer, I want to use my free time to help your family the best I can. I know things have been difficult for you at school, so I am offering to teach you here in your home. That way, you can learn at your own pace without having to worry about the other kids. You wouldn't have to ride the bus twice a day, either."

Jon glanced over at his mother. She smiled back at him.

"It's fine with me," she said, measuring melted butter, milk, sugar and salt into a metal mixing bowl. "Your grandfather and I have talked this over, and we both agree that it would be a great idea."

"Yippee!" Jennica shouted, jumping out of her chair. "We're gonna be homeschooled! We're gonna be homeschooled!"

"She's been begging to be educated at home ever since two of her friends went that route," Mrs. Oliver told her father as she added eggs and flour to the bowl and slid it under her electric stand mixer.

Jon's head was spinning as fast as the mixer's beaters, and not just from hitting it on the ceiling, either. Maybe now he could learn more about dinosaur fossils and how to identify them.

He saw only one hitch in the plan. "But Grandpa, how will you have time to look for another job if you're teaching Jennica and me?"

A pensive look crossed the scientist's face. "I won't be applying for another higher education position," he said heavily. "No state university will touch me now. I've been blackballed because of my controversial views. But not to worry! To avoid a wrongful termination lawsuit, the university has agreed to let me continue conducting my usual free public seminars on campus.

"Moreover, I have been invited to join the *Journal of Creation Science* editorial board—a paying position. Frankly, I'm looking forward to working with a cadre of like-minded creationist colleagues."

Removing a sticky lump of dough from the mixing bowl, Olivia grunted, "When God closes a door, He usually opens a window."

"When can we start homeschooling?" Jennica eagerly asked.

"How about tomorrow?" Grandfather Roberts suggested.

"Yay!" Jennica squealed, hopping up and down with glee.

"What do you say, kids?" Dr. Roberts asked them with a lopsided smile. "Do we have a deal?" He offered them his weathered hand, and Jon and Jennica enthusiastically pumped it in turn.

The paleontologist beamed at the pair. "Where do you suggest we start? With Social Studies? Biology? English?"

"With CORVATS," said Jon. Everyone stared at him.

"It's pronounced 'VORCATS,' silly," Jennica corrected him.

"No, this one is called 'CORVATS,'" Jon shot back.

"CORVATS?" Dr. Roberts repeated. "What is that?"

"I'll show you," Jon cryptically replied. "Follow me!"

The whole family trooped out to the cluttered garage, where Jon pointed out the cast-off equipment he had been collecting. "Meet CORVATS, which stands for 'Cave Observation Remote Vehicular All-Terrain Scooter,'" he proudly announced.

"Huh!" said Jennica, flipping her hair back. "I think you should call it 'POUT'—'Pile Of Useless Trash.' It won't go anywhere till the garbage truck hauls it off to the city dump."

"Don't be unkind," Dr. Roberts admonished her.

Mrs. Oliver's eyes glistened. "You're becoming an inventor, just like your father," she said. "Just keep your oddball inventions out of my kitchen, you hear? I don't want my walls and ceiling painted with orange juice again—or with any other kind of juice, either. Promise?"

Jon laughed. "I promise," he said.

"But why would you want to build another VORCATS?" Grandfather Roberts asked him. "Why not simply wait until Dr. MacKenzie returns from his travels and borrow his unit? I'm sure he would be happy to bring it over again."

Jon squirmed. "I can't wait that long. Besides, I want to design CORVATS with tunnels in mind, not volcanoes. I would feel terrible if VORCATS got lost or stuck or broken exploring those nasty mine passages. And you never know what the brollachans might do to it."

Suddenly, twin headlight beams flashed through the garage window. Jon's back prickled, as if bugs were swarming up his spine. "Jen, could you please turn off the light?" he asked.

As soon as the garage went dark, Jon pulled over his father's lawnmower and stood on it to peer out the dingy window. Despite the drizzly dusk falling outside, he could see a silver Mercedes parked across the street. The vehicle's tinted windows obscured the interior.

A yellow flame briefly flared inside the car as someone lit a cigarette. Then the driver's-side window rolled down, and a pulsing red light emerged from within. Jon's stomach jolted.

"What's wrong?" his mother anxiously asked him.

"I'll tell you in a minute," Jon replied. He asked Jennica to switch the garage light on again. Then he took everyone back to the kitchen, where he described what he had just observed on the street.

Grandfather Roberts looked worried. "Do the police have any reason to watch your house?" he asked Jon's mother.

She shook her head. "I don't think so. Maybe it's some military people sent to keep tabs on us, to make sure we're all right."

Keep tabs. The phrase set off alarm bells in Jon's head. Somebody was spying on the Oliver home. Jon was determined to find out who and why. It's what his father would have done.

"Excuse me," he told his family, and he bolted out of the kitchen. Going to the hall closet, he took down a pair of powerful binoculars that belonged to his father and a black stocking cap. Then he returned to the kitchen and threw open the sliding door.

"Where are you going?" his mother asked him.

"Up the street," said Jon, pulling on the stocking cap. "I'll be right back. Please don't follow me, either. I mustn't be seen."

Stepping onto the rain-slick deck, he took the stairs that led off the deck's west side. As he plunged into a swath of native shrubs, the smells of moist earth and wet leaves wafted into his nostrils.

After weaving through the bushes and a patch of thorny blackberries, he came out on Glen Eagles just below the brow of the hill.

Thankful for the concealment of the gray Oregon mist, he crept up the steep, rain-dampened street until the Mercedes came into view. It was still parked on Glen Eagles across from his house.

He brought the binoculars up to his eyes and focused the lenses on the car's license plate, which read, "BRAINY." He shook his head. No wonder they were called "vanity plates."

Next, he turned his attention to the driver, who was still smoking and watching the house while pointing a TV remote-like gadget through the window. Icy fingers squeezed Jon's heart. If his suspicions were correct, the device was designed to detect the anti-gravity belt's telltale signals when it was activated.

Falling to his knees, Jon crawled back down the street until he reached his backyard again. Then he tore painfully through the blackberry vines to reach the deck and the kitchen sliding door.

"Good heavens!" his mother exclaimed as he burst inside. She was kneading out the lump of dough on the floured countertop. "What on earth happened to you? Why are your clothes all torn?"

"You're bleeding!" cried Jennica, touching his arm.

"BRAINY!" Jon blurted out breathlessly.

"What are you talking about?" Dr. Roberts asked him.

"That's the Mercedes' license plate," Jon replied. "B-R-A-I-N-Y."

"I could look up the car's owner online," said Mrs. Oliver. "Just give me a minute to finish kneading out this cinnamon-roll dough."

After kneading and setting aside the dough to rise, she hurried off and returned with her ancient laptop, which she placed on the kitchen table. "I just need a website with access to license plate information," she murmured, launching her browser. "Let's see. I'm finding lots of sponsored links. Ah, here's a promising free site."

She tapped on the keyboard and waited. Then her eyes widened and she turned ghostly pale. "Oh, no. It can't be."

"What? What?" cried Jennica and Jon.

Mrs. Oliver pushed herself back from the table. "That Mercedes belongs to a Ronald Ingersoll," she said hollowly.

Chapter 15
NOT EXACTLY A FLASHLIGHT

I should have known," Jon groaned. Seated at the table, he buried his head in his arms. He was now quite sure Dr. Ingersoll knew precisely what was hidden in that dresser drawer.

It was only a matter of time before Ingersoll tried to steal the belt. Now that Jon and his sister were being homeschooled, at least the house would be occupied during the day, making it less of a tempting target for the scientist-turned-industrial-spy.

Grandfather Roberts' head was swiveling back and forth between Jon and his mother. "Who is Dr. Ingersoll, and what should you have known?" he asked, looking distinctly perplexed.

Jon cleared his throat. "Dad left us each a personal letter in case something happened to him. In my note, he warned me not to trust his business partner, Dr. Ronald Ingersoll. He suspected Dr. Ingersoll might try to steal his research. I guess he was right."

"You should have told me about that man earlier!" Jon's mother scolded him. "I had no idea what he was up to. Anyway, Dad, Dr. Ingersoll paid us a surprise visit yesterday morning. He asked about Matt's work and whether he had left us any notes or gadgets. He also told us Matt was developing an IED detector in Afghanistan."

"What did you tell him?" asked Dr. Roberts.

She shrugged. "Very little, actually. I didn't even mention those letters Matt wrote to each of us or the flashlight he left Jon."

Dr. Roberts shot his grandson a sharp look. "A flashlight, you say? That's a very peculiar inheritance. But why is this fellow hanging around your house? Either he suspects you were lying, or he knows something about Matt's research projects that you don't. Maybe we need to call the police or get a restraining order against him."

"No, don't do that." The words were spoken so softly that Jon couldn't believe they came out of his own mouth.

"And why not?" his mother demanded, hands on hips.

Jon wilted inwardly. He could no longer shoulder this burden of secrecy alone. "I know what Dr. Ingersoll wants," he declared.

His family gazed at him in disbelief. "You do?" said his mother. "Why didn't you tell us before? What is he looking for?"

Jon wanted to demonstrate the belt, but he knew that activating it would alert Ingersoll. He had to block its emissions—but with what?

"Everyone, meet me outside Dad's office," he said curtly.

Jennica's eyes narrowed in suspicion. "What for?"

"Just go, and I'll explain later," Jon told her.

Feeling the others' puzzled stares boring into his back, Jon raced to his room, where he retrieved the anti-gravity belt and the laser pen from his dresser drawer. With a profound sense of relief and excitement, he fastened the belt around his waist, double-checked the locks on his window and closed the curtains.

Next, he went around the rest of the ground floor, locking doors and windows and shutting drapes and blinds. He didn't want Dr. Ingersoll snooping about during his private demonstration.

Heart pounding with anticipation, he hurried to rejoin his family outside the locked office. The three were conversing in hushed tones as he rounded the corner. At his approach, they fell silent and stared curiously at the anti-gravity belt.

"What is that thing? A girdle?" Jennica teased him.

"You'll see," Jon shot back. *If only she knew.*

Eyeing the belt dubiously, his mother asked him, "What are we doing here? You know we're not supposed to enter your father's office. Even I am not allowed in there. It's strictly off limits—*verboten*."

"Don't worry; I have something important to show you," said Jon. Going to the family photo hanging in the hallway, he removed the key from behind it and unlocked the door to the office.

His mother's eyes bugged. "How did you know that key was there? Your father never told *me* where he hid it. Why have you been keeping this a secret? What else haven't you told the rest of us?"

"Dad didn't tell me where the key was, either. I spied on him," Jon confessed. His face burned with embarrassment. Escorting his family inside the office, he closed and locked the door behind them.

Red-faced herself, Mrs. Oliver rounded on Jon. "What do you mean, you 'spied on him'? Why would you do such a thing?"

Dr. Roberts laid a hand on his daughter's arm. "Let the boy explain himself, Liv," he told her. "I'm sure he had his reasons."

"All right," she said, folding her arms. "Talk."

"It was an *accident*," said Jon lamely, and he described the early morning scene when he had caught his father letting himself into the office—only to find the room unoccupied. "At the time, I couldn't figure out what had happened to Dad," he concluded.

Dr. Roberts scanned the office. "I don't see anything in here worth keeping under wraps. What did you want to show us?"

"Something you won't believe." Jon directed his family to stand with their backs against the wall. "And don't move a muscle until I tell you," he cautioned them, removing the laser pen from his pocket.

Pointing to the pen with a flour-tipped finger, Olivia remarked, "Is that the flashlight your father left you?"

Jon avoided her inquisitive gaze. "Yes, but it—it's not exactly a flashlight," he mumbled. "Dad designed it for a special purpose. Let me demonstrate." After seating himself in Captain Gray's chair, he inserted the laser pen into its arm-slot. *Click.*

Laser beams bounced around the room, and Jon felt the chair drop beneath him. His family's astonished exclamations followed him down into the laboratory. As soon as the laser had shut off and the chair stopped descending, he called up into the office, "All clear!"

Three heads appeared at the round opening in the ceiling. "Are you all right?" asked Jon's mother anxiously. She looked decidedly befuddled, as did Dr. Roberts. Jon couldn't read Jennica's expression, because her long hair was obscuring her face. However, she was making hysterical "Eek! Eek! Eek!" sounds.

"Hold on!" Jon shouted up to the onlookers. He jumped out of Captain Gray's chair and scoured the laboratory for a switch to control the chair's movements without requiring the laser pen.

There—a quarter-size, red button jutted from one of the laminated fir columns supporting the ceiling. Jon punched the button, and the chair jerked upward slightly before stopping. He pressed it again, and the chair dropped back down. *I found it, Dad!* he thought.

Peering up at his family's faces, he called, "When the chair rises to your level, get on, and I'll bring you down here." Then he pressed and held the red button. With the whir of electric motors, the empty chair ascended out of the laboratory and into the office.

When the LED lights snapped off, plunging the "dungeon" into darkness, Jon realized the flaw in his plan. He hadn't brought along a real flashlight, although he suspected his father had set up some backup lights somewhere. Using his cell phone to faintly illuminate the laboratory, he fidgeted impatiently until muffled shouts from above signaled the chair-riders' readiness to descend.

Jon pressed the red button again. A sliver of light appeared above him like a thin crescent moon, widening as the chair dropped. Because the antique could accommodate only one person seated, Jon's mother and grandfather were standing on it, arms interlocked, while Jennica perched on their shoulders as if in a circus act. They had almost reached the floor when the lights blazed back on.

Thunk. The chair jolted to a stop, nearly catapulting the three off its seat. Jon helped them hop down from their wooden "elevator."

"Incredible. Absolutely incredible!" breathed Dr. Roberts. "I've never seen a light-activated key mechanism before. How very clever! Without that custom-built laser pen, the chair won't descend."

"But where *are* we?" asked Mrs. Oliver, still looking bewildered.

"We're in Dad's secret laboratory," said Jon proudly.

"I had no idea this was here," his mother ruefully remarked.

Glancing around, Dr. Roberts observed with a trace of envy, "This lab is stocked with some state-of-the-art electronic equipment. I knew Matt was—is—brilliant, but this place is a work of genius."

"I'm starving," Jennica announced. "When can we get out of here? It's way past supper time. I want some French toast."

"How can you think of food at a time like this?" Jon chided her.

Jennica stuck out her tongue at him, but he could tell that even she was impressed with the lab and its high-tech fixtures.

"How did you know about this room in the first place?" Jon's mother asked him. "Did you see your father come down here?"

Jon shook his head. "There's something else I haven't told you." He described decoding Dr. Oliver's Bible-based cipher, yielding the cryptic instructions, *Sit in the seat of Captain Gray. Put the sword into the sheath. Let your light shine in a mirror.*

Mrs. Oliver gestured around her. "But why did you show us this lab? None of us knows how to operate your father's machines."

"But I do," Jon replied. Going to a lab bench, he turned on its overhanging work light. Then he sent Captain Gray's chair back up to the office, shutting off the banks of LEDs.

"There," he said. "Now we can still see without the overhead lights. The real reason I brought you all down here is the shielding."

His mother glanced nervously about. "Shielding? You mean shielding against radiation? Is this a nuclear bomb shelter?"

Jon laughed. "I suppose it could be. Remember what I told you about Dr. Ingersoll watching our house? He wants to steal this belt I'm wearing. Dad invented it down in this laboratory. I found it sitting on one of these benches—with my name on it. I'll bet Dr. Stalker is still parked on our street, just waiting for me to turn on the belt. It must give off electro—electro—"

"Electromagnetic energy?" Dr. Roberts supplied.

"Yes, electromagnetic energy," Jon said. "I'm sure that's what Dr. Ingersoll is waiting to detect." Jon described the blinking device he had seen the physicist holding. "It's why I couldn't turn on the belt upstairs," he explained. "Down here, I'm hoping all the concrete, rock and earth surrounding this lab will absorb the belt's energy."

"You sound just like your father," said his mother proudly.

"Yeah," Jennica said. "I can't understand either one of them."

Dr. Roberts scratched his head. "Ingersoll is going to all that trouble just to track down and steal a wearable IED detector?"

"This isn't an IED detector," Jon said softly.

"Then what is it?" asked Jennica.

Jon pushed the anti-gravity belt's green power button.

Chapter 16
THE BELT REVEALED

Right after he pressed the belt's button, Jon pushed off from the floor. Extending his hands overhead, he braked himself against the ten-foot ceiling and came to rest about six feet off the ground, gazing smugly down at his family.

Grandfather Roberts gazed back, his eyes as large as turkey platters. Choking sounds burbled in his throat.

Slack-jawed and tongue-tied, Jon's sister and mother stood staring up at him with unfocused eyes. Jon wished he'd used his cell phone to digitally capture their comical expressions.

"It's an anti-gravity belt," he explained. "Pretty cool, huh?"

"Very . . . cool," murmured Dr. Roberts.

Jennica was the next to recover her wits. "What would happen if you pushed that green button again?" she asked her brother.

Jon laughed. "I would fall on top of Grandpa."

Grandfather Roberts scooted out of harm's way. With one finger, he reached up and nudged Jon's leg, sending him back up to the ceiling like a free-floating, helium-filled balloon.

"Extraordinary," murmured the old man. "I never would have believed it if I hadn't seen it with my own eyes. Anti-gravity!"

Mrs. Oliver's uplifted face had turned a mottled red and white. Jabbing her finger at Jon, she cried, "Jonathan Oliver, you come down from there right now, or I'll ground you for a week!"

Dr. Roberts clucked his tongue. "You can't blame the boy for wanting to play with his new toy. If I were his age, I would, too."

"It's not a toy!" Jon's mother countered. "What if he sailed out through an open window or door? He'd float right into space!"

Jon was listening with only half an ear. From his vantage point, he had noticed a patch of darkness on the far wall. He tried "swimming" through the air toward it but for all his efforts got nowhere.

"Jonathan Matthew Oliver," his mother said, biting off the names like celery sticks, "stop showing off and get down here—now!"

Heaving a theatrical sigh of resignation, Jon asked his grandfather to pull him down. Dr. Roberts obliged by tugging on Jon's shoes.

As soon as his feet touched the floor, Jon pressed the belt's power button. Immediately, he felt the weight return to his body.

"I would give anything to know how that amazing device works," murmured Grandfather Roberts, staring at the anti-gravity belt.

"I'll bet Dr. Stalker would, too," Jon said grimly.

His grandfather warned him, "If I were you, I would avoid activating that belt except for purposes of scientific research."

"Why is that?" Jon asked him. "What's the harm in turning it on, as long as I'm in the lab or the basement?"

"Because we don't know how this new invention may affect the human body," Dr. Roberts explained. "I'm not a physicist, but I'm willing to bet your belt produces some potentially hazardous forms of radiation. What you're wearing is probably just a prototype—an experimental model that may be the only one of its kind. Your father may not have had sufficient time to test its safety."

"Oh," said Jon, hastily removing the belt. He hadn't considered the possibility the device might be dangerous. He didn't want to end up glowing in the dark like his sister's cheap watch.

"Do you feel any different after wearing that thing?" Jon's mother asked him. She looked him up and down, as if he had sprouted an extra appendage in the past ten minutes.

"I just feel heavier," Jon quipped. He also felt a little lightheaded as gravity drained some of the blood from his brain.

"I want to try it on," Jennica petulantly told him. She tried to grab the belt, but Jon held it just out of her reach.

"You don't know how to use it," he loftily told his sister.

"Mom!" Jennica protested. "It's not fair! How come Jon gets to use Dad's invention, but I don't? I want a turn, too."

Mrs. Oliver deftly relieved Jon of the belt. "Neither of you is going to wear it without proper supervision," she said firmly.

"I'm keeping it in *my* room, since it's *mine*," Jon declared.

"No, it's not! Dad gave it to all of us," wailed Jennica.

"No, he didn't!" Jon argued. "He gave it to me."

Dr. Roberts held up his hand. "Please!" he said. "Let's not bicker over it. You'll both have plenty of opportunities to try out the belt, once I've had a chance to examine it. In the meantime, I suggest we keep it down here in the laboratory. We don't want Dr. Ingersoll to get a fix on this marvelous invention with his detector."

Jon cast about for a place to hide the belt. Then he remembered what he had seen while floating above the floor. Weaving among the workbenches, he came to a breach in the sheet-rocked wall. Hunks of gypsum lay scattered about the floor. A musty odor wafted out of the hole, which was flanked on either side by two-by-fours. As in the open basement, the drywall was stained a dull, mustardy yellow.

"I wonder what happened here," mused Dr. Roberts. He bent to peer into the dark opening. Sniffing at the dingy sheetrock, he pronounced, "Sulfur dioxide. That's what has caused this discoloration. I must say this is shoddy work, though. Someone slapped this piece of plasterboard directly over the studs without a sheet of treated plywood under it or better yet, a concrete wall behind it to keep out the dampness. That's why the drywall is stained."

Jon smiled to himself. The arrangement of those two-by-four studs explained the pattern of vertical white stripes he'd noticed on the open basement's stained east wall. Evidently the studs had protected the sheetrock from discoloration.

"Oh, my. Look at this!" Mrs. Oliver cried. She was standing beside a compact refrigerator lying on its back with its door hanging open. The unplugged appliance looked as if someone had attacked it with a chainsaw. Deep gouges and scratches marred its white finish, while shredded plastic sandwich bags lay strewn about its interior. Though empty, most of them bore smeared traces of peanut butter.

In the midst of this culinary ruin lay a half-gallon peanut butter jar on its side, also empty. A jagged hole had been punched or bored through its red lid, which was still screwed on.

Mrs. Oliver laughed uneasily. "It's just like your father to keep a jar of Karl's Kreamy in his lab fridge. He loves his peanut butter sandwiches. I can't imagine what made that hole in the lid, though."

"When ya gotta have your peanut butter, ya gotta have your peanut butter," Jon quipped. "Maybe Dad was in a hurry, or he couldn't get the lid off." *Or maybe something else got into that jar.*

"Here's an idea," said Dr. Roberts. Righting the mini-fridge, he shoved it against the hole in the wall. The appliance neatly covered the opening. "We don't want any moisture getting into this laboratory, or the equipment will be ruined," he explained.

"What do you think made that hole?" Jennica asked him.

"Why, I imagine sulfur dioxide fumes built up in a pocket behind the wall and exploded," said the paleontologist innocently.

Jon snickered. He already knew sulfur dioxide wasn't flammable. Besides, his grandfather's glib explanation didn't account for the scratched fridge and punctured jar lid, not to mention the torn sandwich baggies. Whatever had caused that breach, it wasn't fumes.

"And here's another idea," said Dr. Roberts. "Liv, may I have the belt, please?" His daughter obligingly dropped the anti-gravity belt into his open hand. Then he placed the device on a bare shelf inside the compact fridge and closed its door. "There," he said. "That should make it harder for Dr. Ingersoll to ferret out our little secret."

Mrs. Oliver suggested, "Now, why don't we all go upstairs so I can finish preparing my cinnamon rolls and pop them in the oven?"

Everyone was happy to oblige. Once he had sent his family back to the office on Captain Gray's chair, Jon pressed the red button once more to bring it down again. Then he slid into the chair himself and removed the laser pen from its slot to ride the chair out of the lab.

Upon leaving the office, he locked the door after him and hid the key behind the photo. To be safe, he pocketed the laser pen.

That evening, over a plate heaped with warm, gloriously sticky buns, Jon described how he had discovered the belt's powers. "Originally, I thought it was a suicide belt," he said. "If I had known what it could do in the first place, I would have told you all about it earlier."

He kept his voice low, as if Dr. Ingersoll might overhear him. His hands were still shaking with excitement.

Grandfather Roberts' voice also quavered. "Kids, your father's invention could completely change the world as we know it. Beginning with Sir Isaac Newton and others, scientists have been trying to crack the gravity code for centuries. Physicists will tell you it is virtually impossible to disrupt our planet's gravitational force. Dr. Matthew Oliver has succeeded where many others have failed."

Mrs. Oliver said, "Once Matt puts his mind to something, he doesn't give up. He's convinced that the Creator of the universe can reveal to us the principles that govern it—if only we will ask Him. I just wish Matt had confided in me. I never dreamed he was working on anti-gravity research. He didn't even drop any hints about it."

"You mustn't take it personally, Liv," said Dr. Roberts. "Matt probably stumbled upon this gravity-cancelling effect by accident. That's how such discoveries usually occur. Besides, I'm sure he realized his invention could be misused if it fell into the wrong hands. I suspect he was trying to protect you from unscrupulous men like Dr. Ingersoll who would stop at nothing to steal his life's work."

Jon swallowed painfully. He hadn't considered the lengths to which Dr. Ingersoll might go to obtain the anti-gravity belt. So far, the scientist had been content to monitor the device from his car. What if he became impatient and tried to take the belt by force?

"And that reminds me," said Dr. Roberts, rounding on Jennica. "You must promise not to breathe a word about this belt to any of your old friends from school. Do you understand?"

Caught in the act of stuffing an entire cinnamon roll into her mouth, Jennica nodded. "I pwomuff," she mumbled.

"We cannot risk letting news of this invention leak out," Dr. Roberts briskly went on. "Are we all agreed on that point?"

His listeners solemnly bobbed their heads. If the good people of Lake Oswego ever learned that one of their own had devised a belt to nullify gravity's force, swarms of curiosity-seekers would descend upon the Oliver home. Their lives would never be the same again.

For his part, Jon found consolation in the knowledge that he alone possessed the laser pen. Without it, neither his sister nor Dr. Ingersoll could lay hands on the anti-gravity belt where it lay safely hidden inside the mini-fridge.

Outside in the silver Mercedes, Dr. Ingersoll shook his gravitational wave interference detector and scowled. One moment, it was registering a weak signal; the next, the waveform had flatlined. Unless the Olivers had figured out a way to disconnect the Device from its power source or contain its emissions, it should still radiate its unique energy signature—even when turned off.

If he was correct about that signature, the Device was worth billions. Assuming he could get his hands on his partner's invention, he had already lined up a willing buyer. The Device would make him one of the wealthiest men in the world—several times over.

He shook the detector again, to no avail. His batteries must have run down. Opening the battery compartment, he pried out four AA batteries and replaced them with fresh ones.

However, when he powered it up again, his detector still was not responding. Perhaps the Olivers had broken the priceless Device. If so, he would have to rummage through their garbage for the discarded prize. If its emissions were being shielded, he might be forced to break in and steal it. Either way, Dr. Ronald Ingersoll decided it was high time he took matters into his own hands.

And his hands were capable of anything.

Chapter 17
CORVATS

The next morning, Jon was vividly dreaming he was serenely floating over Lake Oswego's rooftops wearing his anti-gravity belt when he was rudely jostled awake. Opening his sleep-bleary eyes, he found Grandfather Roberts standing over him.

"Up and at 'em, sleepyhead!" said the paleontologist.

Jon groaned and rolled over to focus on his clock, which read, "6:30." He pulled the pillow over his head. "It's not time to get up yet," he mumbled. "I don't have to be at school till 8:00."

"You're already at school," Dr. Roberts reminded him. "This is your first day of homeschooling. Your mother left earlier for an in-service workshop, so I've prepared a hot batch of French toast with maple syrup for you and Jennica. When you're done with breakfast, we can try working on CORVATS together in the garage."

"But what about the anti-gravity belt?"

"That's a project best left for another day," Grandfather Roberts replied. "Besides, I want your belt kept strictly under wraps until we decide how we're going to handle our nosy scientist friend."

Jon crawled out of his warm bed and threw on a shirt and pair of jeans. Tinkering with CORVATS sounded a lot more fun than math.

Shuffling out of his bedroom, he discovered his sister was already eating in the kitchen, her plate heaped with French toast. Only a couple of curled-up slices remained on the serving platter.

"Hey!" said Jon. "You left me the heels." He hated eating the thick, dry, end-pieces of bread in sandwiches or as French toast.

"You snooze, you lose," his sister archly replied. She stuck her nose back in an English textbook Dr. Roberts had no doubt supplied.

Jon was trying to come up with a snide reply when his grandfather said, "Don't worry, Jon. We have plenty more bread and milk and eggs. You can help me whip up another batch. Homeschooling isn't all Biology and Health, you know. Unless you get married at age eighteen, you'll need to master the basics of home cooking."

"Married?!" Jon squawked. "I'm never getting married."

"Oh, I'm not suggesting anything," Grandfather Roberts hurriedly assured him. "It's just that you'll be a young bachelor before you know it, and you'll have to learn to fend for yourself."

"I already know how to make Mac and cheese," Jon muttered.

"Can you live on it three meals a day?" Jennica said with a grin. She skipped out of the kitchen before Jon could think of a comeback.

"Girls!" he grunted as he helped his grandfather stir eggs, milk and cinnamon in a mixing bowl. The two took turns dipping slices of bread into the mixture and frying them on a hot griddle.

This is more like it, Jon said to himself, sitting down to a stack of steaming French toast. He wondered whether Renée Doulière's ancestors had been responsible for inventing such a delicious dish.

Renée. Jon's first forkful of French toast briefly froze halfway to his mouth. Being homeschooled meant he would no longer be seeing his favorite female exchange student in the hallways. Maybe he would have to take a fresh interest in his ex-school's athletic events. He knew Renée loved watching basketball games.

Having returned with her diary, Jennica was now doodling in it. When Jon looked over her shoulder, she blocked his view. *Suit yourself*, he thought as he savored a maple-syrupy bite of French toast.

"You'd better not be writing about your father's anti-gravity belt in that journal," Grandfather Roberts sternly warned Jennica.

Blushing, she held up the booklet to reveal the horse sketches she had been working on. Jon grudgingly had to admit they were quite good. He wished he could draw even half as well.

"Very nice, Jennica," said her grandfather, smiling. "Now it's time for you to get back to your English studies, please." With a sigh, Jennica obediently returned to reading her textbook.

After Jon had finished eating, he followed his mentor into the garage. The pile of paraphernalia still lay where Jon had left it.

"This will do nicely," said Dr. Roberts, nodding approvingly at Jon's soapbox derby racer. "I do believe it has room to accommodate all our equipment, both on the inside and on the outside."

"But what will make it run?" Jon asked him. In all his scavenging around the garage, he hadn't found any suitable motors.

Grandfather Roberts grinned at him. "No worries, mate!" he said. "I've brought along a direct-current motor I salvaged from a cordless power drill. That motor will easily run off your auto battery. I also brought a cheap DC/DC converter to reduce the voltage from the battery to the laptop. Now, let's get to work, shall we?"

While Dr. Roberts cannibalized a rusty bicycle for its chain-and-sprocket drive, Jon took off the derby racer's wheels. After replacing both the wooden axles with heavy steel rods, he helped his grandfather rig up the bicycle's chain drive to the front axle and the drill motor inside the racer's shell. Next, Jon fixed the wheels to the axles and installed the electromagnets to swivel the wheels by remote control.

The two tinkerers then lowered the car battery into the racer's cramped cockpit and wired it to the motor, the converter and the electromagnets. Finally, they connected the converter to the laptop, which they attached to a metal frame duct-taped above the battery.

Four flashlights scrounged from the laundry room—two at each end of the racer—served as CORVATS' headlights and taillights. A webcam at the front and another at the back functioned as "eyes."

"Isn't she a beauty?" said Dr. Roberts. Soldering iron in hand, he stepped back to admire the modified racer, which resembled an amphibious blue submarine on wheels, with the flashlights standing in for torpedo tubes and the open laptop imitating a conning tower.

"Yeah, I guess so," said Jon. He just wished the clunky-looking contraption weren't so heavily cobbled together with duct tape, like a derby racer that had been gift-wrapped by a chimpanzee. Jon pictured CORVATS sitting outside the hidden entrance to the brollachans' secret lair, all equipped for some serious tunnel exploration.

By then, it was late afternoon, and Jon was hungry. Having arrived home from her workshop, Mrs. Oliver had left the two men to their own devices, but now the tantalizing aroma of baking peanut butter cookies was wafting into the garage. Jon's mouth watered; those cookies had won blue ribbons at the Oregon State Fair.

Just then, he heard a *tap-tap-tapping* from outside. Jumping up, he climbed onto a paint bucket and peered out the garage window. A hunched-over man was passing by the house, cane tapping as he went. Jon saw no sign of Dr. Ingersoll or of his silver Mercedes.

"What are you looking at?" Grandfather Roberts asked him.

"I was just watching some old guy with a cane hobbling down the street," Jon replied, hopping down from the bucket. "I guess that's how he gets his exercise. His cane was making a rapping sound."

Dr. Roberts raised an eyebrow. "'Old guy'?"

Jon blushed. "Oh—sorry, Grandpa. I suppose I should have said, 'elderly gentleman' or 'senior citizen.' I meant no offense. I would never call *you* an 'old guy.' You just seem, well, *ageless.*"

"You'd better quit before you dig yourself in any deeper, young fellow," Dr. Roberts laughed. He applied his smoking soldering iron and some solder to another electrical connection. "There. The wiring is finished. It's time we put CORVATS through its paces."

Bringing out his cell phone, Dr. Roberts added, "I downloaded a remote control application onto this smart phone. The app allows me to access the web cameras, DC motor and electromagnets via the laptop. Here, have a look for yourself."

Jon took the cell phone from his grandfather. The first thing he noticed was the divided screen. The left side displayed a live video feed streaming from the CORVATS forward webcam, while the right side showed the view from the rear webcam. Not even VORCATS boasted an aft web camera, which would have come in handy.

Jon pressed the phone's "HOME" button, and both images shifted as CORVATS trundled forward. He pushed another button on the keypad, and CORVATS reversed direction. Other buttons canted the front wheels left or right. It wasn't much different from operating a video game, except that CORVATS was more sluggish in responding to his commands than the average video game.

"Wow! This is pretty cool, Grandpa," Jon said. Using the cell phone, he sent CORVATS scrabbling around the garage floor like an overgrown blue beetle. Then the racer plowed into a stack of ceramic flower pots, pulverizing the pottery with a terrific crash.

"Where did you learn to drive?" Dr. Roberts teased him.

Ignoring his grandfather's gibe, Jon said, "I'm getting the hang of this. Just watch me." After guiding CORVATS in a few more turns around the garage, he helped the ungainly racer up the short flight of stairs and directed it into the kitchen. Startled screams ensued.

"Jon!" his mother bellowed. "Get this—this horrible *monstrosity* out of my kitchen before I take a broom to it!"

Jon shouted back, "It's only CORVATS. It won't hurt you."

"I don't care what it is," came the answer. "Just get rid of it!"

Grumbling, Jon traipsed into the kitchen, where he found his mother and sister trapped between CORVATS and the refrigerator. His mother was threatening the racer with a wooden mixing spoon.

"My word!" Mrs. Oliver cried, brandishing the spoon in front of her like a medieval sword. "Is *this* what you call homeschooling?"

Using the smart phone, Jon backed CORVATS out of the kitchen and down into the garage again. Shaking his head, his grandfather grinned ruefully at him. "Your mother already warned you to keep CORVATS out of her kitchen," he said. "You should have known she doesn't take kindly to science experiments invading her domain."

"I wasn't invading," said Jon. "I was just . . . *practicing.*"

"Supper's ready, you two!" called Mrs. Oliver crossly.

Jon hurried back to the kitchen and slid into the chair next to his sister's. Grandfather Roberts followed at a more leisurely pace.

Seeing a stack of pizza squares in the center of the table, Jon was about to grab one when he took a second look. The "pizza" was slices of leftover French toast topped with melted cheese, olives, pepperoni and onions. Some of the pieces were suspiciously curled.

Jon recoiled. Heels. Dried-up, crusty old heels.

"What's the matter, Jon?" asked his mother. "I put on the toppings you like best. We can't afford store-bought pizza, so this will have to do. Besides, your sister tells me you like the heels."

Jennica smacked her lips. "These are really good," she said.

Jon shot her a venomous look. He had been set up. Determined not to give his sister the satisfaction of seeing him squirm, he waited until his mother had blessed the food and then dug in. For once, Jennica was right. Smothered with cheese, the "French-pizza" was quite tasty. Jon left a slice on the counter in a baggie for later.

For dessert, his mother brought out a plate of the peanut butter cookies she and Jennica had baked. One bite made Jon's mouth forget all about the pizza he had just eaten. He would have wolfed down the whole plateful by himself if his mother hadn't whisked it away.

"You'll make yourself sick eating so many cookies," she told him, putting the plate on the counter. "Besides, we need to save some for later. I'll cover them with plastic wrap so they'll stay fresh for you."

After everyone had pitched in to clean up the kitchen, Mrs. Oliver saw her father out the door. Then she hauled out the garbage pail from under the sink. "Jon, the trash is full—and it stinks," she said.

Jon sighed. As the man of the house by default, he had inherited the unpleasant task of taking out the garbage. Holding his breath, he coaxed the bulging plastic liner out of the garbage pail, dragged the bag out to the garage, flicked on an outside light and exited through a side door leading to the trash enclosure—his least favorite place.

Inside the enclosure, he heaved the bag into the garbage cart. The nauseating stench of rotting food assailed his nostrils. However, not only the cart stank. The entire enclosure reeked of ripe garbage.

A vile stew of spent coffee grounds, pizza crusts, chicken bones, moldy cheese, spoiled fruit, and banana peels was fermenting on the cement pad. Amidst the rubbish sat one of Jon's hand-held games that had tragically fallen into his bathwater and shorted out.

Acid bile burned in Jon's throat as he gagged at the revolting odor. Had a foraging animal gotten into the garbage cart? If so, why were the chicken bones left intact—and why wasn't the cart tipped over? Something about this smelly scene just didn't add up.

Maybe Jennica the Horse Fanatic had accidentally tossed out one of her precious equine figurines and had pawed through the garbage trying to find it. Still, she wouldn't have passed over the hand-held game, broken or not. If anything belonged to Jon, she coveted it.

He spent the next fifteen minutes scraping up and discarding the garbage before returning to the house, where he found his mother and sister watching television in the living room. They looked up as he passed by on his way to the bathroom to clean up.

"Phew!" exclaimed Mrs. Oliver. "What is that stench? I asked you to take out the garbage, Jon, not roll in it like a stray dog."

"Yeah, Jon," Jennica teased him. "Take a bath, will you?"

"I intend to," Jon retorted. He described how he had cleaned up the garbage-strewn enclosure. "I wish I knew who made that mess," he grumbled, glaring at his sister. She stared back at him blankly.

Mrs. Oliver yawned. "We're going to bed early, Jon, so you'll have the house to yourself. Please don't stink it up too badly."

After sudsing himself under a hot shower to scour away the garbage odor, Jon dressed, went to the kitchen and made himself a peanut butter sandwich, which he washed down with a glass of milk.

That night, he dreamt the brollachans were chasing him through a maze of mine tunnels. When he reached a dead end, they surrounded him. The creatures resembled stooped old men like the one he had just seen tip-tapping with his cane along Glen Eagles Road.

A block north of Jon's house, Dr. Ronald Ingersoll sat fuming in his faithful Mercedes, which was parked in a quiet cul-de-sac, safe from prying eyes. All his windows were rolled down, but not for the purpose of spying on the Olivers. He was trying to rid his car of the garbage stench that had clung to his clothing.

He had spent most of the day perched in a fir tree, which afforded him the perfect vantage point from which to monitor the Oliver home for telltale emissions. Because the Mercedes sat in front of an unoccupied house with a "For Sale" sign by the sidewalk, people would assume the car belonged to a realtor or a prospective buyer.

Camouflaged in a green jumpsuit, Ingersoll had scaled the tree in the early-morning darkness to avoid notice. Ordinarily, he had no use for trees or tree-climbing, but he decided to make an exception in this case. Parking across the street from the Oliver house was becoming too risky, and he didn't want to spook his intended targets.

It had been a wasted day. His gravitational wave-cancellation detector hadn't blinked or chirped in twelve hours. Afterwards, stiff and sore and besmeared with pitch, the physicist clambered down and made for the Oliver house. He hoped his official-looking jumpsuit would throw off suspicion as he cut through people's yards and entered the enclosure where the Olivers kept their garbage.

An hour later, he had dumped out and sifted through the contents of every last bag, finding no electronics except a broken handheld game. Digging through the Olivers' garbage was humiliating and distasteful enough. Reversing the process added insult to injury. He finally gave up after having scooped most of the moist, rotting refuse back into the bags and dumping them into the cart.

Only a dedicated physicist such as he would climb so high—and stoop so low—just to acquire this revolutionary technology. Despite the day's smelly setback, the Device would soon be his.

Chapter 18
BAITING THE TRAP

J on, you PIG!" Jennica's strident voice cut like a siren through her brother's bedroom door. The door flew open, and Jennica marched in, her new braids swinging like tentacles.

Jon's eyes popped open. *What have I done this time?* he wondered. By unspoken agreement, Jennica wasn't supposed to barge into his room without knocking first, and vice versa.

"Wh-what?" he croaked in his morning voice.

"You *pig!*" Jennica repeated. "You ate all the peanut butter cookies! Why didn't you leave just one for me? I helped Mom bake them in the first place, remember? Now I won't have any snack today."

"I didn't—" Jon weakly protested, but Jennica was just getting started. She shook her small fist at him.

"We had only one jar of peanut butter left, and you had to eat all of that, too!" she screeched. "I wanted a PBJ for breakfast, but now Mom is at work and we're out of peanut butter! I should make you walk to the store and buy some more for me."

Jon rubbed the sleep from his eyes. He hadn't touched the plate of cookies since leaving the dinner table. As for the peanut butter, he couldn't imagine consuming a whole jar of it at one sitting.

When he had made his sandwich the night before, he'd used barely two tablespoons of peanut butter. Maybe his mother had emptied the jar to whip up another batch of cookie dough.

"You might try some hummus instead," he weakly suggested, but his sister had already flounced out of the room in a high huff.

Homeschooling had its drawbacks, he reflected. Dragging himself out of bed, he padded into the empty kitchen. The wall clock read ten-fifty. How had he managed to sleep so much of the day away? And why hadn't Grandfather Roberts rousted him out of bed?

Quite bare, the offending cookie plate sat on the counter beside its shredded plastic wrap. The empty peanut butter jar was lying on its side on the table with a note in his mother's hurried handwriting taped to it. The note read: *Jonathan: Did you eat all the peanut butter cookies and peanut butter? Next time, please leave some for the rest of us. I will try to pick up another jar or two after work. Love you, Mom.*

Jon tore off the note and crumpled it up. If he was guilty of anything, it was forgetting to screw the peanut butter jar lid back on. He examined the clear plastic container. It had been scoured clean, right down to the bottom. Had the mysterious dumpster-diver broken into the house to help himself to a snack? If so, he hadn't made any sandwiches; the loaf of bread and jam jar were untouched.

Maybe Jennica is trying to get me into trouble, Jon thought. But he had a hunch that wasn't the case. Jennica wasn't the scheming sort, though she knew how to push his buttons. Besides, this empty jar looked a lot like the one they'd found in his father's secret laboratory.

Jon still needed some breakfast, and his mouth was set on his leftover French-toast pizza slice. Searching the cluttered counter, he found a torn plastic bag. Like the peanut butter jar, it was empty.

He held the baggie up to the light. Only a few crumbs were left.

With a sigh, Jon discarded the ruined bag. Then he shook some nuggety cereal into a bowl, poured milk over it and began morosely munching on the nuggets. As usual, he was being blamed for something he hadn't done. Most recently, his sister had accused him of pinching her at the dinner table. Before that, she was convinced he had pilfered her secret stash of sugar-free caramels.

All at once, the doorbell rang. Jumping up, Jon accidentally knocked over his bowl of cereal. He hastily mopped up the mess with a dishrag. Things were going from bad to worse.

The doorbell rang again.

Grandfather Roberts was waiting on the front step, his arms heaped with scientific-looking texts and scholarly journals. "I apologize for arriving late," he said. "Aren't you going to invite me in?"

"Oh, sorry," Jon said, ushering him inside the house. "Let me help you with those. Where have you been, anyway?"

Dr. Roberts unloaded some of the textbooks on Jon and peered down at him. "I've been preparing."

"Preparing for what?" Jon asked him. He hoped all the books and journals weren't intended for an in-depth homeschool unit.

Grandfather Roberts winked at him. "I've been preparing today's biology lesson for you and your sister."

"Wait—what?" Jon protested as he dumped the materials on the kitchen table. "I thought CORVATS was our science lesson."

Dr. Roberts picked up a biology text. "CORVATS is your *physics* project, though if we do find some brollachans, we might be dabbling in biology, too. Between the anti-gravity belt and CORVATS, we've been a little heavy on the physics side of science lately."

What's wrong with that? Jon thought. *Who needs biology?*

"For today's lesson, I'll be teaching on the subject of natural selection and evolutionary thought," Dr. Roberts informed him.

Jennica's blond head popped around the corner of the kitchen door. From the alarmed expression on his sister's face, Jon gathered she had been eavesdropping on the conversation.

"*What* are you going to teach us today?" she asked.

"Natural selection," repeated Grandfather Roberts.

Jennica pouted. "I'd rather play with the gravity belt."

Dr. Roberts invited Jon and his sister to sit at the table. "Charles Darwin is credited with developing the principle of natural selection, which was central to his theory of evolution," the paleontologist said.

"In actuality, he borrowed his ideas from a Creation scientist named Edward Blyth, who was the first person to put forward the concept of natural selection in a paper he wrote in 1835. The difference between the two men is that Blyth saw natural selection as a God-designed means of preserving existing plant and animal species, whereas Darwin proposed natural selection as the mechanism driving the transformation of one species into another."

"But what *is* natural selection?" Jennica asked him.

Dr. Roberts smiled. "Have you ever seen a wild rabbit?"

Jon and his sister nodded. "Of course!" they chorused.

"What color was it?"

Jon had to think for a minute. Recently, he had spotted a rabbit darting across the Iron Mountain trail. "Brown," he said.

"Right you are," said his grandfather. "If such a rabbit were living in the Arctic, how do you suppose he would survive?"

"Not very well," Jennica said. "He'd prob'ly freeze to death. Besides, his brown fur would stick out against the white snow."

"Right again," said Grandfather Roberts, nodding. "Brown-furred rabbits thrive in the Northwest because they blend in well with our woodsy backgrounds. In the far north, though, their dark fur would stand out against the lighter snow and ice, making them easy prey for wolves, foxes, lynx, snowy owls and other predators."

"Poor bunnies," Jennica murmured.

"Fortunately," continued Dr. Roberts, "rabbits and hares have a wide range of fur colors already built into their collective genome— their genetic makeup. Since more white-furred hares have survived than pure-brown ones during the Arctic winter, the brown strain has died out, and the Arctic hare now lacks the genes for pure-brown fur.

"In the winter, you'll now find only white-furred Arctic hares. As Edward Blyth suggested, built-in genetic diversity helps organisms to survive environmental changes instead of becoming extinct."

"You're saying evolution is true?" Jon asked doubtfully.

"Not at all," his grandfather replied. "Brown or white, a rabbit is still a rabbit. It hasn't evolved into a rhinoceros, which would require entirely new genetic information. When natural selection operates, it almost always results in a loss, transfer, rearrangement or breakdown of *existing* genetic information, not the introduction of new genes."

Jon began to fidget. "But natural selection doesn't explain how life on earth began in the first place, does it?" he pointed out.

"No, it doesn't," Dr. Roberts agreed. "Though evolutionists have many origin-of-life theories, they cannot demonstrate how even the simplest cell could have arisen from random chemical reactions."

The front door opened, and Jon heard his mother's quick footsteps. She sailed into the kitchen carrying two large grocery bags.

"Can I get a little help here?" she said. "We worked only a half day because the school is closing for summer vacation."

Jon and Jennica helped their mother unpack the first sack. "Oh, goodie!" Jennica squealed, lifting out an oversized jar of peanut butter. "You got my favorite kind—Karl's Kreamy! I'm gonna have peanut butter-and-jelly sandwiches for breakfast, lunch and dinner."

"Oh, no, you won't," said Mrs. Oliver, taking the jar from her. "You may have a PBJ for lunch and one as a snack before bedtime, but that's it. I won't have you becoming a hard-core peanut butter addict like your brother." Her eyes twinkled as she spoke.

"I'm not a peanut butter addict!" Jon sputtered.

"Then what happened to all of our peanut butter?" Jennica sweetly asked him. "Did a gremlin eat it?" She sniggered loudly.

"You must admit you do like your peanut butter," Jon's mother told him. Unable to prove his innocence, he had no reply.

Judging from Dr. Roberts' amused look, not even he was sticking up for his grandson this time. Jon would have to fend for himself.

"Don't fret about it," Mrs. Oliver said, emptying the other bag. "I bought four jars—enough for all the peanut butter cookies and PBJs you could ever want, and then some."

Jon and his sister brightened at the prospect of more peanut butter cookies and sandwiches. Their faces fell like collapsing angel-food cakes when their mother reached up to set three of the jars on the topmost cupboard shelf. Then she firmly closed the cupboard doors.

"Now *someone* won't be tempted to raid my peanut butter supply late at night," she said with a sly glance at Jon. He looked away. Nothing he could do or say would convince his family he was not to blame. He simply *had* to catch the real culprit.

"What about *that* jar?" asked Jennica, pointing to the fourth container of peanut butter that Mrs. Oliver had left on the counter.

"This?" she replied with feigned innocence. "Why, I'm going to make another batch of peanut butter cookies with this one—that is, if I can find someone to help me. Otherwise, it's going up in the cupboard with the other jars. Do I have any volunteers?"

Jennica's hand shot up. "I'll help you!" she exclaimed.

"What about you, Jon?" asked his mother.

"No, thanks," he muttered sourly. He didn't want to be accused of filching cookies or peanut butter while helping out.

"In that case," said Dr. Roberts, "we can continue with our physics project. It's time to deploy CORVATS in search of brollachans."

Jon's heart leapt. "Really? Do you think it's ready?"

"I do," replied the paleontologist. "While we are remotely exploring the brollachans' lair, I suggest we also make CORVATS do double duty—in a manner of speaking."

Mrs. Oliver stopped scooping peanut butter out of the Karl's Kreamy jar and asked, "What *kind* of double duty? You're not thinking of turning that giant mechanized cockroach loose in my kitchen again, are you? That thing belongs outside, not in my house."

Her father laughed. "We're taking CORVATS outside, all right. We want to lure Dr. Ingersoll away from this house, correct? Otherwise, it's only a matter of time until he breaks in and discovers Matt's secret laboratory. We can't have him stealing the belt."

Jon couldn't argue with his grandfather's logic. Dr. Stalker was nothing less than a pit bull when it came to the anti-gravity belt. He would do anything to get his paws on it.

"By now," Dr. Roberts went on, "our friend with the Mercedes is undoubtedly fit to be tied. He knows we are keeping Matt's invention somewhere in the house, but now that its emissions are shielded down in the laboratory, he can't get a reading on it."

"Maybe he'll assume we took it out of the house for safekeeping," Mrs. Oliver suggested.

Dr. Roberts shook his head. "Not a chance. If we brought the device outside, I have a hunch he would know it immediately."

"Then it's a stalemate," said Jon's mother flatly.

"Yes, but it's a stalemate we can break," her father countered. "What if—and I'm brainstorming here—what if Jon were to briefly activate the belt outside the laboratory, to let Ingersoll detect it?"

"On purpose?" Jon exclaimed. "In two seconds, Ingersoll would be standing on our front porch with his hand out."

"Correct," said his grandfather. "Let's suppose, though, that you turn off the belt and return it to the refrigerator in the lab. And let's also suppose that shortly afterwards, you and I march through the garage door carrying CORVATS."

"You want to hand over CORVATS to Dr. Stalker?" said Jennica, licking a heaping spoonful of peanut butter.

"No, no. Not at all," Dr. Roberts said impatiently. "We want to trick him, remember? You have to think as a villain thinks."

"That shouldn't be too hard for Jen," muttered Jon.

Dr. Roberts ignored him. "Maybe it would help if I told you that I'm planning to strap a metal tube into CORVATS' cockpit."

"What kind of metal tube?" Jon asked.

"I'll show you," said his grandfather. Disappearing into the garage, Dr. Roberts returned with a red cylinder about three inches in diameter and ten inches in length, solid on both ends. A white plastic cap protruded from the top end.

"What's that?" Jennica asked him.

"This is a propane torch cylinder," Dr. Roberts informed her.

"Not *another* experiment!" groaned Mrs. Oliver.

"Oh, we won't be using the gas inside this bottle," the scientist hastened to explain. "It's the cylinder itself that we want. By now, Dr. Ingersoll must suspect that we are masking the device's electromagnetic energy signature. He doesn't know how, of course. I'm proposing that we disguise this tank and parade it right under his nose."

"You want Dr. Stalker to see it?" Jon asked him dubiously.

"I do indeed," said Dr. Roberts. "And what will he assume?"

Jon's mind reeled at the sheer audacity of his grandfather's brilliant plan. "He'll think we . . . we transferred the belt from one shielded spot to another. He'll assume the device is inside that propane tank, or else that the tank *is* the anti-gravity gadget."

"Right again," Grandfather Roberts replied. "He'll also assume we're using CORVATS to conceal the device somewhere, and he won't be able to help himself. He'll follow your blue racer through fire and water to retrieve that bottle."

"But what if he tries to steal CORVATS?" Jennica asked.

The scientist shrugged. "Let him try. CORVATS will be dead weight, and one person alone can't carry it. I suspect Jon and I will have enough trouble wrestling it down the trail as it is."

"Whoa!" Jon broke in. "What are you talking about, Grandpa? I thought we were taking CORVATS out for a spin. Why would we need to carry it? It's got wheels and a motor to move on its own."

Dr. Roberts replied, "Remember, it's a long way to that tunnel entrance, and if CORVATS had to get there under its own power, its battery would run down. We don't have the luxury of plugging our invention into an external power source, as Dr. MacKenzie did with VORCATS and his jeep.

"Besides, CORVATS isn't designed for speed. It's meant to muscle over obstructions in its path, much like a Mars rover. It could take all day for CORVATS to reach its destination."

"Huh," said Jon, disappointed. "I'll bet CORVATS could still beat VORCATS in a batteries-only race over level ground."

"You might be right about that," his grandfather agreed.

Brandishing a spatula thickly coated with peanut butter, Jon's mother said, "But if 'CORBATS' is so slow, what's to keep Dr. Ingersoll from catching up to it and taking the tank?"

Dr. Roberts winked at her. "We'll give CORVATS a head start. At any rate, we can well afford to lose a cheap propane cylinder. Ingersoll might figure out it's a ruse, but he won't be absolutely sure without cutting into the tank—and risking an explosion. The whole point of this exercise is to flush out our foe and make him tip his hand. Once he realizes that we're wise to his scheme, he might leave us alone and go in search of lower-hanging fruit, so to speak."

I'd like to detonate that propane bottle by remote control as soon as Dr. Stalker picks it up, thought Jon. However, he knew his mother and grandfather would never approve. Jesus taught His followers to love their enemies, not blow them to pieces.

"Don't forget about the brollachans," he told his grandfather.

"Oh, I haven't," he replied. "Whether our poky old CORVATS can track them down is quite another matter."

Dr. Ingersoll sat ruminating in his idling car on a turnout high above Oswego Lake. The rays of an early afternoon sun were slanting across the water, but the physicist hardly noticed. His Mercedes still reeked of decaying rubbish, reminding him of yesterday's disgusting foray into the wonderful world of garbage.

What was he overlooking? If the Olivers had broken the Device, why hadn't they tossed it in the trash? And if it wasn't broken, how had they cancelled its electromagnetic emissions?

He wouldn't find any answers sitting beside the lake. He needed to stake out the Oliver home again. This time, he would adopt a more aggressive strategy—and he was a master strategist.

The only hitch in his plan was the Olivers themselves. The girl and boy were staying at home during the day with their grandfather. The brats had probably flunked out of their local public school and required remedial tutoring, but that meant Dr. Ingersoll no longer had free access to their house during the daytime.

Instead, he would have to break in at night—very soon.

Chapter 19
OPERATION INGERSOLL

An hour later, the propane tank was ready. Dr. Roberts had split a balding tennis ball in half, gluing each of the halves onto opposite ends of the cylinder to help disguise its true nature. Jon then spray-painted the entire bottle a glossy silver until it shone like an oversized Christmas-tree ornament.

Dr. Roberts touched the tank. "The paint feels dry," he said.

"Do you really think this will fool Dr. Ingersoll?" Jon asked.

His grandfather grunted. "Maybe for a little while. It looks more like a hydraulic cylinder or an artifact from outer space."

"Do you mean part of a UFO?" Jon teased him.

They both laughed at that. Then Dr. Roberts' face hardened in a resolute expression. "It's time to launch Operation Ingersoll," he said. "Jon, will you check to see whether or not our nosy physicist friend is parked out on the street again?"

Climbing onto the lawnmower, Jon peered through the grimy garage window. Except for an idling UPS truck, Glen Eagles Road was deserted. Then a silver Mercedes cruised to a stop across from the house. Heart thumping, Jon jumped down from the mower.

"He's here!" he breathlessly announced.

"You know what to do now," Dr. Roberts told him. "CORVATS and I will wait here until you return. Thirty seconds should do it."

Jon charged into the house and down the hallway to his father's office. Once inside, he rode Captain Gray's chair down into the laboratory, retrieved the anti-gravity belt from the fridge and raced back to the chair. After rising into the office, he punched the belt's green power button, counted out thirty seconds and then turned off the belt. Finally, he returned it to its original hiding place.

Hoping Dr. Ingersoll's detector had registered the half-minute activation, Jon hurried back through the house, stopping only long enough to tell his mother, "Grandpa and I are taking CORVATS out for a test run to look for brollachans—and trick Dr. Ingersoll."

"That's fine, dear," she replied. "Just don't be late for supper."

In the garage, Dr. Roberts was cradling the silvery propane tank in his arms. He told Jon, "Go ahead and open the garage door now."

Jon flicked the wall switch that engaged the motor, and the door rose, creaking back along its metal railings. Then Dr. Roberts instructed him to push CORVATS out onto the driveway. The paleontologist followed with the propane tank. A warm, late-spring sun shone down upon them, glinting off the painted cylinder.

Dr. Roberts handed Jon the bottle and a bungee cord, saying, "We want to be sure Ingersoll gets a good look at our 'bait.'"

Following his grandfather's directions, Jon secured the tank inside the racer's cockpit with the elastic cord. He avoided gawking at the silver Mercedes. Ironically, the tank's color matched the car's.

Although he appreciated Grandfather Roberts' capable help in constructing CORVATS, Jon couldn't help feeling his original plan had been hijacked. He had hoped CORVATS' jury-rigged webcams would capture some clear images of the crafty brollachans in the flesh. Somehow, that plan had morphed into "Operation Ingersoll."

Once Jon had strapped in the propane tank where it was clearly visible, he and his grandfather slowly rolled CORVATS down the driveway and onto the steep slope of Glen Eagles Road. Both were sweating by the time they reached the Iron Mountain trailhead.

"Maybe we should have waited for Dr. MacKenzie to return with VORCATS after all," Jon panted. He wasn't looking forward to the task ahead. "Do you think Dr. Stalker noticed us?"

"I'm sure he did," Dr. Roberts grimly replied. "We can only hope he will follow us. We'll have to carry CORVATS from here."

Grumbling, Jon picked up the front end, while his grandfather lifted the back. "Ugh!" Jon grunted. "This thing is heavier than the old TV in our basement. Why can't we just let it run on its own?"

"No can do," said Dr. Roberts through clenched teeth. "As I told you before, we've got to spare the battery. If CORVATS runs out of juice while underground, we'll never be able to retrieve it."

"If its battery dies," Jon replied, "I say we leave it there. I don't want to lug this thing back home. It weighs a ton and a half."

"It's not any lighter on my end," grumbled Dr. Roberts.

Remembering Dr. MacKenzie's rugged jeep, Jon asked, "Why can't we use your pickup to haul CORVATS instead?"

The paleontologist explained, "If he takes the bait, Dr. Ingersoll will be on foot, and we don't want to lose him. Now, please be careful not to break off the web cameras or damage the laptop."

Staggering down the trail, the pair stopped to rest at the observation deck. "We can't stay here for long," Dr. Roberts said. "This is a popular trail, and a hiker could come by here at any moment. It might be awkward explaining what we're doing with CORVATS."

"What about Dr. Ingersoll?" Jon asked, stalling for more time to catch his breath. He glanced back up the path but saw no one. Was the scientist tracking them, or had he seen through their ruse?

"For our plan to succeed, we mustn't let on that we're watching for him," said his grandfather seriously. "If you spot the man, you should pretend not to notice him. Otherwise, all our efforts will be wasted. We want to lure Ingersoll into following CORVATS. Timing is everything. Speaking of timing, we had better move along now."

With a groan, Jon hoisted his end of CORVATS, while his grandfather picked up the other. Down the trail they shuffled under their burden like pallbearers with a coffin. Overhanging trees dappled the racer with leafy shadows, while a playful breeze toyed with Jon's hair.

After a sweaty eternity, the two reached the base of the rock outcropping. The hairs prickled on Jon's arms as he recalled his terrifying encounter with the brollachans in the hidden passage above.

"Now what?" he asked, athough he already knew what was coming. They had to drag CORVATS up the hill to the outcropping's top. When he had first conceived of CORVATS as a way of finding the brollachans, he hadn't given any forethought to the problem of transporting the remote-controlled racer up to the tunnel.

Evidently his grandfather hadn't, either. "Hmm," he said. "I had forgotten how steep this slope is. Since we can't carry CORVATS up there, we'll have to drag it. You push from the bottom, and I'll pull from the top, all right? It shouldn't take long."

"Just don't let go," Jon said as he positioned himself at the rear end of CORVATS. "I don't want this thing to run me over."

Scrambling to find footholds in the loose soil, Jon and his grand-father manhandled CORVATS up the treacherous slope and onto the outcrop. Stinging, salty sweat was dripping into Jon's eyes as he and Dr. Roberts carried CORVATS through the field of basalt slabs. Then they both collapsed on the outcropping, panting heavily.

"Whew!" gasped Dr. Roberts. "I'm getting too old for this sort of thing. Next time, let's give CORVATS enough speed and horsepower to climb hills on its own. And that reminds me: I brought along something to help us in climbing down again."

Reaching under the leading edge of CORVATS' cockpit, Dr. Roberts pulled out a coil of rope from the racer's hollow nose. Ex-pertly, he looped one end of the rope around a scrawny oak and tied it off. Then he tossed the rest of the coil down the hillside.

"There," he said. "No paleontologist worth his fossils leaves home without a rope. Besides, we want to make it easier for Dr. Ingersoll to find his way up here. To avoid spooking him, after we've properly positioned CORVATS, we must find a good hiding place. Speaking of hiding places, you picked an odd spot to stash your peanut butter cookies. I noticed them when I was getting out the rope."

Dr. Roberts pointed to CORVATS' cockpit, where several wilted peanut butter cookies were wedged between the battery and the racer's wooden shell. Jon slapped a hand over his mouth to bottle up his laughter. He didn't want to make any loud noises that might attract the attention of passing hikers.

"I didn't put those cookies there," he said. "They probably fell off the counter when I sent CORVATS into the kitchen."

"Then shall we leave them as a peace offering to the brollachans?" said Dr. Roberts with a grin.

Jon shrugged. "Why not?" he said. Stale peanut butter cookies tasted terrible, anyway—at least in Jon's opinion.

The two stationed the racer with its front end pointing toward the crevice in the rocks. Then they switched on all four flashlights. Finally, Dr. Roberts handed Jon the specially modified cell phone.

Hoping his racer would fare better than VORCATS had, Jon punched the phone's "HOME" button. With a whine, CORVATS lumbered into the crack like a remote-controlled mining machine.

"That's far enough for now," Dr. Roberts cautioned him. "We want Ingersoll to see CORVATS before it travels any further."

Jon took his finger off the button, leaving CORVATS hanging half in and half out of the fissure. "I still don't understand why we're doing this," he groused. "Why couldn't we have left that tank in the driveway for Ingersoll instead of dragging it all the way out here? The extra weight is just slowing down CORVATS. And maybe its shiny paint will scare off the brollachans before I can get a video of them."

Dr. Roberts' eyes ranged around the landscape before settling on Jon. "Think of it this way. First, we want to make Ingersoll work for that bottle. If we hand it to him on a silver platter, he'll suspect it's a fake. Second, CORVATS might give us a glimpse of the brollachans, and it might not. Human eyes and ears are much more sensitive than any camera. And if we're looking for volunteers, are you prepared to go back into that tunnel to scout around for brollachans?"

"Uh, no thanks," Jon quickly replied.

"Well then," said his grandfather, "that's where Ingersoll comes in. If he takes the bait, he'll be our guinea pig—our 'brollachan detector'—in that passage. If he sees and hears nothing, we've lost only a cheap propane bottle. But if he does encounter the creatures, we will see how he fares—assuming he survives at all."

Jon had to admit Dr. Roberts' argument made sense, though he wouldn't say as much. Following the old man, he used the rope to lower himself off the outcrop and down the steep hillside to the trail.

Dusting off his hands, Jon asked his grandfather, "How about I hide in this tree?" He pointed at a bigleaf maple standing on the path's downhill side. Its low-hanging branches beckoned to him.

Dr. Roberts nodded. "If you climb high enough, the cell-phone signal should have a clear line of sight to CORVATS and into the tunnel. Just be careful. I don't want you falling out of the tree. Your mother would never let me hear the end of it."

"What about you?" Jon asked him. "Where will you hide?"

"I'll just settle down behind your maple tree," Grandfather Roberts answered. "I'm betting Dr. Ingersoll will be too busy sniffing out our 'lure' to notice anything on the south side of the trail."

Jon stuffed the cell phone in his pocket, shinnied up the maple's trunk and pulled himself onto the lowest limb. After a short rest, he continued climbing higher until he could sit comfortably in the tree's crown. From there, he could see the back half of CORVATS jutting from the crevice like some alien creature entering its burrow.

"I'm ready!" he whispered down to his grandfather.

"Any sign of Ingersoll?" Dr. Roberts called back.

From his perch in the tree, Jon could view a long stretch of the trail in both directions without being seen. "Not yet," he replied. The words were hardly out of his mouth when he spotted a slender figure furtively darting from tree to tree alongside the trail. There was no mistaking Dr. Stalker's bony limbs and bird-like movements.

"He's coming!" Jon squeaked. "What should I do?"

"Just wait," Dr. Roberts quietly urged him.

He waited. Dr. Ingersoll continued slinking down the trail until he reached the rope's free end, which was dangling invitingly over some hillside rocks near the path. Without hesitation, the physicist grabbed the rope with both hands and began climbing.

Presently, Jon heard a faint exclamation from near the top of the outcrop. He aimed the modified cell phone at the half-hidden derby racer and pressed the "HOME" button, deploying the decoy.

CORVATS' electric motor responded with a faint but satisfying whine. Then the hillside swallowed the makeshift remote-controlled vehicle—wheels, flashlights, webcams, propane tank and all.

The trap was set.

Dr. Ingersoll snapped awake, startled by a buzzing noise. Parked on the street, he had been dozing in the warm afternoon sun. He stared blearily at the detector hanging around his neck. He'd rigged it to sound an alarm if the signal resurfaced, which apparently it had.

The buzzing abruptly stopped, and Ingersoll gasped. The signal was gone again. Impossible! That clinched it. The Olivers must have found a way to mask the unit's emissions. Either that, or his detector had completely gone on the fritz.

He was so busy shaking and prodding the device that at first he didn't hear the Olivers' garage door clanking open. Out rolled a grotesque conglomeration of plastic, wood and metal, all haphazardly duct-taped together, creating a crazy patchwork effect.

If Matthew Oliver were still alive, he never would have allowed such a mechanical monstrosity to be birthed in his garage. Clucking his tongue in disdain, Dr. Ingersoll christened the jury-rigged gadget, "DOW," for "Duct-tape On Wheels." He watched as the Oliver boy secured a silvery cylinder inside the wheeled contraption using an elastic cord his grandfather had handed him.

The physicist could hardly believe his eyes. Kendall Roberts and his dimwitted grandson had evidently brought the Device out into the light of day, oblivious to the spy observing them. In the midst of Ingersoll's elation, acid churned in his stomach. The metal cylinder must be shielding the Device's emissions from detection, but where were these two taking it—and why?

Being the brilliant scientist that he was, Dr. Ingersoll quickly hit upon the answer: Matt's kin had enclosed the Device in a metal tube and were transporting it somewhere for the selfsame reason—they feared it. Kendall Roberts was a paleontologist, not a physicist, meaning that not even he could deduce the Device's true purpose. And what humans feared, they tended to destroy. The silvery cylinder might even contain explosives! Ingersoll shivered at the thought.

He waited until the pair had trundled DOW over the brow of Glen Eagles before discreetly following them. If they were about to blow up the Device, Dr. Ronald Ingersoll would make sure he got there first before they could follow through with their plan.

It was absurdly easy to stalk his quarry, since they had to lug their primitive invention down the Iron Mountain trail. Apparently DOW lacked the necessary power to travel far on its own. Ingersoll lost track of the couple only once, when they unaccountably veered off the path with DOW and disappeared from sight.

They had conveniently left behind their calling card—a rope trailing down the hill—making it easier for him to scale the slope. He had, after all, been a star fencer in college and was quick on his feet.

The rope led him to the top of a rock outcropping studded with stunted oak trees and littered with bleached basalt slabs. A few yards away, DOW sat motionless inside a slab "tent" with its back end protruding from a hillside fissure. The silvery prize shone like buried treasure in the shadows. Ingersoll let out a cry of triumph.

Buried treasure, indeed! Evidently Roberts and his nerdy grandson were planning to conceal the Device inside this rocky cleft. But if that were the case, why go to all the trouble of building DOW and lugging it down the trail simply to hide the cylinder? Why not just place it inside the crevice by hand? And why leave the rope behind?

DOW wasn't moving. Was it stuck in the crack? Had it run out of power? Ingersoll had once watched an action film in which the police used a robotic vehicle to locate and defuse a bomb. The only logical reason for sending this wheeled scrap-heap underground was to blow it up along with the cylinder, just as he had feared.

If he wanted the Device, he had only one chance—and this was it.

The physicist was picking his way through the field of basalt slabs when he heard a humming sound. To his horror, DOW was rolling through the fissure. Now it had vanished inside.

Without hesitation, Ingersoll plunged into the dark opening to follow the duct-taped nightmare on wheels.

Chapter 20
INGERSOLL TAKES THE BAIT

Jon fidgeted in the maple tree. Five minutes had passed since he had sent CORVATS into the tunnel, and still he had detected no sign of Dr. Ingersoll in the rear-view webcam. Yet, he had distinctly seen the scientist dive into the tunnel's mouth just after CORVATS had entered the passage. Where was he?

"Grandfather Roberts!" he loudly whispered, but there was no response. Jon's heart clenched. He was all alone now, unable to rely upon anyone else for advice. Staring at the cell phone, he saw rock walls slowly sliding by on the left half of the screen, which displayed the view from the forward webcam. On the right side, daylight was dwindling as the entrance receded behind the lumbering vehicle. Where was Dr. Ingersoll?

Jon stopped CORVATS before it could venture any farther down the tunnel. He didn't want to lose Dr. Stalker. On the other hand, he wanted very badly to catch a glimpse of a brollachan while still safely sitting in his sunlit maple tree in the fresh air of the outside world.

He thumbed the "HOME" button again, and CORVATS lurched forward, jiggling the webcams. A few minutes later, the rear camera captured the fuzzy image of a hunched-over man scuttling crablike down the tunnel. Jon shuddered. Dr. Ingersoll was rapidly gaining ground on CORVATS. He would catch up to the vehicle in seconds.

Using the mobile phone, Jon deftly maneuvered the remote-controlled racer down the tunnel. In the right screen, the shadowy figure was still advancing upon CORVATS, stiffly holding his right arm straight out in front of him like a mummy in an old Hollywood horror movie. With his left hand, he was massaging his head.

Suddenly, CORVATS broke out into the brollachans' cavern, its headlights drilling holes into the dense darkness. On the screen's right side, Dr. Ingersoll was scurrying close behind the racer. Jon shrank back as the scientist's form loomed. His mummy-arm came down. When he raised it again, he was gripping the propane tank.

Ingersoll's leering face appeared on the screen. "You won't dare blow it up now!" he soundlessly mouthed into the rear webcam. Without warning, his smug expression contorted into a look of pure horror. The dual images on the screen wobbled. Then the forward screen went black, punctuated with wildly gyrating flashlight beams.

One beam waved around the cavern, while the other stabbed back at the tunnel's mouth. Then both light rays bobbed back into the passage, as seen in the rear-view webcam. Dr. Ingersoll had evidently torn the forward-facing flashlights out of their mounts to light his way back to civilization, leaving Jon with a half-blind CORVATS.

He groaned. Though the rear-facing flashlights were still intact, he would have to navigate backwards through the tunnel. Dr. Ingersoll had fallen for the propane tank ruse, but he had also turned the tables on Jon and his grandfather. Now they had nothing to show for their painstaking efforts except a crippled CORVATS—and Jon still had not captured the evasive brollachans on video.

He rubbed his eyes and stretched. The world rushed back into focus. Drenched with sweat, he was still perched in the maple, though a part of him remained in the underground cavern.

He was wondering what had become of Dr. Ingersoll when frantic screams broke out. The hollering scientist shot out of the hillside fissure like a cannonball. Still clutching the tank, he stumbled and rolled down the hill, fetching up against a boulder at the bottom. Undaunted, he bolted up the trail, hair askew and thin limbs windmilling, all the while casting terrified glances behind him.

Just before the bleating physicist rounded a bend in the path, Jon saw the back of his shirt had been sliced to bloody ribbons.

He climbed down the maple to find his grandfather sitting with his back to the tree. The old paleontologist was groggily blinking and looking around with a befuddled expression.

"What was all the shouting?" he asked. "Did I miss the show?"

"I'm afraid so," Jon told him.

Dr. Roberts shakily stood and brushed himself off. "Doggone it. I should have known better than to take an afternoon cat nap. I always oversleep. How did CORVATS fare?"

"Not very well," Jon replied. "Ingersoll took the bait, but he also took both front flashlights to light his way back. The last I saw of him, he was hightailing it up the trail with the propane bottle. Once he got what he wanted, he seemed awfully anxious to leave the tunnel. Something bad must have happened to him in that cave."

Jon described the bloody slashes in the physicist's sweat-stained shirt. "Maybe the brollachans got to him after all," he concluded.

"Maybe they did," said Dr. Roberts. "I wish I'd attached a tracking device to that cylinder so we could keep tabs on the fellow. Dr. Ingersoll won't be very happy when he discovers he's been duped."

Using the rope, the two pulled themselves up the ivied slope and onto the cliff's top again, where Jon came upon the stolen flashlights. Dr. Ingersoll must have discarded them there in his haste to make off with his fake prize. One of the flashlights was smashed beyond repair, but the other still worked, despite its badly dented casing.

Using the mobile phone, Jon was about to back CORVATS into the exit passage when he noticed a cluster of egg-shaped lights on the screen's left side. They were huddling around the robotic racer.

Peering over Jon's shoulder, Dr. Roberts asked him, "Since you've already found both forward flashlights, what are those ghostly images on the screen? They look like camera lens reflections."

"I dunno," Jon replied. "They're kinda like Christmas-tree lights, except that they don't blink. They remind me of the Lake Lights I saw before, but they don't move as fast as the Lake Lights did."

"Whatever they are, they're bright enough to light up that cave like Times Square on New Year's Eve," Dr. Roberts remarked.

Jon studied the screen again. His grandfather was right. Between the unearthly lights and the two remaining flashlights, the exit tunnel was clearly visible in the right half-screen. Even the stones lying on the cavern floor stood out in glaring detail.

Seating himself cross-legged on the rocky ledge, Jon pointed the cell phone directly at the shadowy opening in the hillside and poked the "HOME" button. He realized his mistake when CORVATS scooted farther into the cavern, scattering the mysterious lights.

"Darned dyslexia," he muttered to himself, tapping the phone's "REVERSE" button. Obediently, CORVATS began backing toward the exit. Regathering, the otherworldly "ghosts" hovered around the blue vehicle until glimmers of natural light began filtering into the tunnel, helping Jon guide CORVATS the rest of the way.

The sinister lights did not follow further.

As soon as CORVATS poked its tail end through the cleft, Jon and his grandfather hauled the vehicle the rest of the way out. Aside from missing its headlights, the cobbled-together creation appeared to have suffered little damage.

Looking his racer over, Jon noticed something else was missing. "It didn't get a bird-poop shower," he remarked. But why had VORCATS been sprayed, while CORVATS had not?

His grandfather didn't comment. He was gazing into the cockpit. "It seems Ingersoll made off with more than the propane tank. I don't know how he managed it. That gap is hardly a half-inch wide."

"What are you talking about?" Jon asked him.

The paleontologist pointed down beside the battery. "Our sticky-fingered friend also pilfered your peanut butter cookies."

Jon stared down into the narrow space between the battery and the racer's shell. Not even a cookie crumb remained.

"I hope he choked on 'em," Jon growled. Disabling CORVATS and stealing the propane tank had been bad enough, but Dr. Stalker had crossed the line when he filched Mrs. Oliver's fallen peanut butter cookies. One way or another, Jon would have his revenge.

As if reading his mind, Dr. Roberts said, "Love your enemies—remember? We may not like what Dr. Ingersoll has done, but that's all the more reason to pray for him, not hate him."

"Yeah, I know," Jon replied with a twinge of guilt.

"The main thing is you brought CORVATS back safe and mostly sound," Dr. Roberts exclaimed, clapping Jon on the shoulder. "Now let's carry our creation back to the garage for a checkup."

Jon groaned. In rescuing CORVATS, he hadn't considered the fact that he and his fellow conspirator would have to lug the heavy racer back to the house—and it was uphill all the way.

By the time they reached home, Jon's legs had turned to rubber. After helping his grandfather stow CORVATS in the garage, he staggered into the kitchen, where his mother and sister were sitting at the table eating sandwiches. Mrs. Oliver wore a disapproving look.

"You're late," she said reproachfully. "It's not like you to miss a meal, Jon. What took you and your grandfather so long?"

"We fooled Dr. Ingersoll!" Jon burst out.

"Wait a minute," said his mother. "I thought you were going out to test 'CRIBBET,' or 'CRAVAT,' or whatever you call it."

Jon rolled his eyes in exasperation. "It's called 'CORVATS,' Mom," he corrected her. "And yeah, we were testing it. We also used the propane tank to draw out Dr. Ingersoll."

"CORVATS passed its first trial with flying colors," Dr. Roberts put in as he ambled into the kitchen. "It doesn't seem much worse for the experience, either. May I have one of those?"

He pointed to the tall stack of peanut butter-and-jelly sandwiches sitting on the table. At his daughter's nod, he picked one up and started munching on it. Jon stared at him in disbelief.

Grandfather Roberts stopped chewing. "What's the matter?"

"Er, nothing," Jon replied, reddening. "It's just that I didn't think old—I mean, elderly—that is, grownups your age . . ."

Dr. Roberts chuckled. "I get it," he said. "You don't think 'old people' like peanut butter-and-jelly sandwiches. Is that it?"

Embarrassed, Jon nodded. Yet again, he had wounded someone with his words. His father once accused him of having "foot-in-mouth disease." Jon had an endless supply of feet.

"I was practically raised on PBJs," his grandfather went on. "I still enjoy them on occasion, especially with a tall glass of milk."

"We're out of milk," said Jennica glumly.

"What's this about Dr. Ingersoll?" Mrs. Oliver demanded.

When Jon described the scientist's dogged pursuit of CORVATS and his theft of the painted propane tank, everyone enjoyed a good laugh at Ingersoll's expense. However, Jon couldn't shake the image of the fleeing physicist's tattered, bloody shirt. Unless he had scraped himself on the rocks, some sort of creature had attacked him. Jon was betting it was the brollachans.

"That'll teach him to spy on us!" Mrs. Oliver declared. "We won't be seeing him and his pointy nose around here again."

"I wouldn't bank on it," said her father. "He's a very determined fellow. I only wish I could be there to see the look on his face when he realizes the cylinder he stole is a counterfeit. All it contains is liquid propane. It's rather like evolutionary philosophy—a clever hoax. And that reminds me—oh, no!" A panicked expression came over Dr. Roberts' features as he stared at the kitchen calendar.

"What's wrong?" Jon asked him.

Dr. Roberts flew out of the kitchen, exclaiming over his shoulder, "I'm supposed to be presenting my monthly lecture at the university in half an hour!" Grabbing his coat from the hall tree, he disappeared through the front door and roared down the street in his pickup.

"Wow!" said Jennica. "I didn't know Grandad could run so fast."

"And I didn't realize he was so scatterbrained," Jon said.

His mother laughed. "Your grandfather has always been a bit absent minded. One time many years ago, he took our family out to eat at a local restaurant. After the meal, he got up from the table to pay but never came back. He had driven off without us.

"Now, it's time for bed. Jon, if you want a late-night snack, I'm leaving out this fresh container of peanut butter. I don't care whether you eat it straight out of the jar, make a sandwich with it or smear it all over your body. Please just leave some for the rest of us, all right?"

Jon sullenly nodded. He would have been happy to swear off peanut butter the rest of his life if that's what it took to dispel the dark cloud of suspicion hanging over his head. *Peanut butter addict, indeed!* Excusing himself, he slunk off to his bedroom, giving the tempting jar of Karl's Kreamy a wide berth.

Still gripping his hard-won prize, Dr. Ingersoll leaned against his trusty Mercedes, gasping for breath. His head throbbed from having bashed it on a rock inside the tunnel, slowing his progress. Then he must have run afoul of an upside-down forest of spiky stalactites, which had torn his back and shirt. That was the only logical explanation for his wounds, and Ronald Ingersoll lived for logic.

He had finally secured the Device, and soon he would ferret out its secrets. Reverently he laid the cylinder in the trunk and closed the lid. Before long, he would be well out of range of any transmitter that might trigger a detonation, if he wasn't already. With that, he sped down Glen Eagles Place on his way to GyroSensors.

Nestled in the woods off Kruse Way, GyroSensors Laboratories consisted of nine blocky gray buildings. The main research facility was discreetly situated at the back of the complex, fringed by tall firs.

Dr. Ingersoll let himself into the building and padded down the hallway with his precious silvery cylinder. Since it was after five, the place was virtually deserted. He would have the facilities to himself.

Ducking inside an unoccupied laboratory, he laid the seamless tube on a table for examination. After a few moments of poking and prodding, he discovered the lumps at the ends of the cylinder were two halves of an ordinary tennis ball. He chuckled softly to himself. Roberts and his grandson had devised a crude yet ingenious solution for cushioning the sensitive components inside the canister.

With all the delicacy of a heart surgeon, he removed the two rubbery halves and set them aside for further analysis. Underneath one of them, a white-capped nub protruded from the cylinder's end. Faint alarm-bells went off in his head, but he ignored them. The nub was probably for attaching an antenna or other piece of equipment.

On the other hand, if he pressed the protuberance, it might open the canister—or trigger an explosion intended to prevent the Device from falling into the wrong hands. In this case, *his* hands. He smiled grimly at the irony. He was capable of defeating any booby trap.

He shook the cylinder, creating a sloshing sound. Liquid mercury. Of course. The mercury would dampen vibration and absorb any electromagnetic emissions. Still, he should proceed cautiously.

He secured the canister with clamps to a sturdy stand and aimed a powerful tabletop laser at the smooth end. When he activated the laser, smoke spurted from the cylinder's shiny surface as silver paint burned off. The metal underneath glowed a cherry red.

Dr. Ronald Ingersoll donned a pair of safety glasses and took cover behind a floor-to-ceiling Plexiglas shield, just in case. One way or another, he would find out what was inside that metal container.

Chapter 21
ACCUSATIONS

How was your seminar last night?" Jon asked his grandfather. The family was sitting around the breakfast table polishing off a platter of scrambled eggs with salsa, whole-wheat toast and orange wedges. In the living room, a local Portland station was broadcasting a news program on the television.

"The seminar went well, despite my being a tad late and out of breath," Dr. Roberts replied. "After my presentation, I enjoyed some lively discussions with members of the audience. The topic of natural selection as it relates to evolution always draws a mix of hecklers, genuine truth-seekers, and lots of curious folks, too. I'd be happy if even a few of my listeners reexamined their assumptions about the origins of life on earth."

"I'm sure your lecture was as brilliant as always," Jon's mother warmly declared. "And I do hope your Creation Science conference goes well today, too. You're the keynote speaker, right?"

"Yes. The conference theme is, 'Evolution or Devolution?' I'll—"

He stopped mid-sentence and cocked his head in a listening pose. "Hold on," he said. Then he jumped up and charged into the living room. Curious, Jon and the rest of the family followed.

"In breaking news," the television announcer was saying, "we have just learned that an explosion damaged a building at GyroSensors Laboratories last night. No deaths or serious injuries were reported. The cause of the explosion is still under investigation."

"Wow!" Jon said. "I'll bet that's the lab where Dad works! It's a good thing he wasn't there when—oh." Dr. Roberts had shot him a meaningful sidelong glance while raising an untamed eyebrow. Jon thought his grandfather could communicate better with his eyebrows than he could with speech.

A sick feeling churned in the pit of Jon's stomach. What he had wished for might actually have come to pass. Dr. Ingersoll could have been killed when the propane bottle exploded, except that nobody had died—at least according to the most recent news bulletin.

"When what?" his mother asked, her eyes darting between the two conspirators. "Do you know something I don't?"

Dr. Roberts cleared his throat. "Maybe, and maybe not, Liv," he said. "It's possible Ingersoll tried to cut open that propane tank in his lab. I honestly didn't think he would take things this far. The man has a Ph.D., yet he's so blinded by greed that he apparently failed to recognize the cylinder for what it was—a common propane bottle."

"What do you think happened to him?" Jennica asked.

"For now, that will remain a mystery," Dr. Roberts replied. "After I leave, though, I suggest you all keep watching for news updates."

Mrs. Oliver crooked a finger at Jon. "And here's another mystery I want solved," she said firmly. Jon followed her into the kitchen, where she thrust a clear plastic container into his hands. It was an empty, lidless Karl's Kreamy jar.

"What don't you understand about 'Leave some for the rest of us'?" she growled, her face rigid with restrained wrath. "And since when did you forget how to unscrew a jar lid, anyway? You've left a dreadful mess in my kitchen, and I expect you to clean it up before I return home this evening." Tears welled in the corners of her eyes.

Jon hadn't seen his mother so angry since the day he had scrawled, "Jennica was adopted" in lipstick on the bathroom mirror. That stunt had cost him a month's video-game privileges.

"What are you talking about?" Jon asked in a daze. His eyes focused on the floor and counter, where pieces of the jar's red lid lay scattered about, as though someone had run it through a shredder.

His mother sighed. "I'm talking about that empty peanut butter jar you're holding and the chewed-up lid. Don't pretend you don't know what happened to them, either." She snatched her purse from off the table. "I have to go to work. I'll be back in time for dinner."

Jon's head was spinning. "Why are you going to work? I thought your school already let out for summer vacation."

"I got a job working the front desk at the Lakeshore Lodge. We need some extra income until your father's invention starts to pay off. Since Dad's conference lasts three days, you and Jennica will have a nice break—till summer school starts. Please try to get along, keep an eye out for Dr. Ingersoll, and stay out of the peanut butter!"

"But Mom," Jon protested. "I didn't do it!"

"Then who did? The dog that we don't have? Why won't you just come out and admit what you've done? Honestly, Jon, I'm beginning to think I really don't know you anymore."

"That makes two of us," Jon muttered.

His mother gave him a parting hug. "I forgive you, and I will be praying that you can learn to be more truthful. In the meantime, if you could prepare dinner for us tonight, that would be helpful."

Mrs. Oliver stalked out of the kitchen, leaving Jon to scoop up the lid-scraps and dump them into an empty grocery bag. Then he retreated to his room with the bag in hand. Closing the door behind him, he shook out the red shards onto his bed. In five minutes, he had reassembled the shattered lid like a plastic jigsaw puzzle.

"Huh!" he said to himself. The pieces had fit together perfectly except for a gaping hole where something had pierced the lid in the center. Most of the fragments bore dimpled marks.

Jon flopped down on his bed. Maybe he had raided the kitchen while sleepwalking. If so, why had he jabbed a knife or a screwdriver through the lid to pry it off instead of simply unscrewing it? And how had he managed to scour out the jar so thoroughly? Even a spatula would have left telltale peanut butter streaks behind.

Moreover, consuming an entire jar of Karl's Kreamy should have glued his jaws shut for a week—and left a peanut butter aftertaste in his mouth. Equally puzzling, the loaf of bread looked undisturbed. If he had made peanut butter sandwiches, he would have used up most of the loaf—and left a dirty knife on the counter in the bargain.

Instead, all the knives, forks and spoons were still lying neatly compartmentalized in their proper drawer. Either he had washed the knife or he had scooped out the peanut butter with his fingers. Neither possibility was likely. He was a messy eater, but not that messy.

"Lord," he said self-consciously, staring at the ceiling. "I don't understand why everyone thinks I ate all that peanut butter. You know what it's like to be blamed for stuff You didn't do. How can I prove I didn't empty out that whole jar of Karl's Kreamy?"

First, you must forgive your mother and sister for falsely accusing you, came the reply. *Then you can try catching the real thief. But don't forget to help your mother by making supper.*

Forgiving his mother and sister was easy, considering how often they had forgiven him. But how was he supposed to apprehend the elusive peanut butter bandit? The answer was obvious. *CORVATS.*

He spent the rest of that morning tinkering with his revamped racer in the garage, whistling cheerfully all the while. First, he unplugged the laptop from the DC/DC converter box and plugged the computer directly into a wall outlet with a black extension cord.

Next, he positioned CORVATS with its rear webcam pointed at the door leading into the kitchen. He wanted the camera to record whatever entered the garage. Then he cleared a line-of-sight path to the door, reducing the background clutter viewed from the webcam.

That afternoon, he busied himself rinsing off the dirty dishes and stowing them in the dishwasher. He also threw a frozen pizza in the oven before sweeping and mopping the vinyl kitchen floor. Jennica slouched in the doorway, helpfully pointing out spots he had missed until he threatened her with the mop and she huffed off to her room.

When Mrs. Oliver dragged in like a wet cat, Jon met her at the front door. "Hi, Mom!" he said. "How was work? I've cleaned up the kitchen and prepared supper for you."

Dropping her purse, she stared at him skeptically with bloodshot eyes. "Thank you, but what do you want?" she said. "You rarely do any housework unless you're hoping for something in return."

Busted, Jon thought. He twisted his fingers into a nervous knot. "Well," he said. "I'd like to borrow a jar of peanut butter."

His mother scowled at him. "'Borrow'? Do you mean 'borrow' in the same way you 'borrowed' that jar of Karl's Kreamy last night? Let me give this some thought." Mrs. Oliver tipped her head to one side and stroked her chin, as if she were deep in contemplation. "No can do," she said. "Fool me once, shame on you; fool me twice, shame on me. Fool me three times, buy me some more peanut butter."

Jon groaned. He hated it when his mother resorted to sarcasm. "Mom," he pleaded with her. "Just listen. I really do have a plan—"

He broke off as gray tendrils wafted down the hallway. Glancing behind him, he saw smoke pouring out of the kitchen. He had forgotten to check on the pizza in the oven, and it was burning.

"What is that horrible smell?" Mrs. Oliver cried.

"Sorry, Mom!" Jon yelled and ran into the kitchen. Throwing open the oven door, he yanked the pizza out in a black cloud. All the smoke alarms in the house began blaring in jarring disharmony.

Fortunately, the pizza was still edible. It turned out some melted cheese had dripped onto the bottom of the oven and caught fire. After the smoke alarms and Mrs. Oliver had stopped shrieking, Jon speedily set the table and sliced the pizza.

While sharing the rescued pizza with his mother and sister, Jon posed his request again. Mrs. Oliver was too tired to listen and just picked at her slice. Muttering that she needed to "check into a mental asylum," she left the table and locked herself in her bedroom.

Exchanging guilty glances, Jennica and Jon polished off their pizza slices, cleared the table, and went their separate directions. For Jennica, that meant her bedroom and her drawing tablet. Jon remained in the kitchen to finish cleaning up the supper dishes.

In failing to win over his mother, he was left without any peanut butter to use as bait. He couldn't risk taking even a spoonful, since Mrs. Oliver had threatened to install locks on the kitchen cabinets to foil the Karl's Kreamy thief. Jon needed to find different bait.

But what would tempt the peanut butter bandit?

He had just scraped the pizza crusts off the plates into the garbage when the solution dawned on him: Rats, mice and other vermin would eat pizza crusts as surely as they would snack on peanut butter. Retrieving a couple of the crusts from the garbage, he took them out to the garage and placed them on the floor behind CORVATS' back end within the webcam's field of view.

Next, Jon powered up the laptop. Manipulating its touchpad, he downloaded and configured a basic video-recording application, which he used to create, name and save a new video file. Then he adjusted the web-camera until the pizza crusts appeared squarely in the screen's center and clicked on the software's "Record" button.

After rechecking CORVATS' systems, he vacated the garage, leaving the light on and the kitchen door open. He wanted to lay out the welcome mat for whatever was devouring his peanut butter.

That night, he couldn't sleep. Mulling over the mystery of the jar-licking thieves, he finally dozed off and dreamt of peanut butter cookies chasing him around the kitchen and into the basement.

In his darkened study, Dr. Ronald Ingersoll sat sullenly nursing his regrets—and his wounded ego. His ears were still ringing from the laboratory explosion. What a fool he'd been! How could he have let that bumpkin Oliver boy take him in with a common propane bottle? The blow to his pride had been worse than the inconvenience of the damage to the laboratory and his failure to obtain the Device.

Adding insult to injury, he also had to fend off a team of arson investigators and their nosy questions. They had all but point-blank accused him of deliberately demolishing the laboratory in order to collect an insurance settlement. Though their allegations were groundless, he couldn't tell them the whole truth—that he, Dr. Ronald Ingersoll, had been duped by an ignorant, snot-nosed brat and his dull-witted family.

More importantly, the *Korporatsiya*—his prospective buyer—would not be amused at these repeated delays. He would have to redeem himself by finishing what he had started, even if he had already shown his hand. But this time, he was playing for keeps.

Unlocking a desk drawer, he took out a Walther P99 semi-automatic pistol and checked to make sure it had a full magazine and that the safety was on. He didn't want to shoot himself in the foot accidentally while burglarizing the Oliver home.

If the Olivers gave him any trouble, he had only to point the compact weapon, pull the trigger, and Newtonian physics would do the rest. He sniggered to himself. It was about time the laws of physics started working in his favor instead of against him. Uncontrolled, an explosion could destroy an entire laboratory. Controlled, it could launch a bullet and snuff out a life.

If at that moment he had cared to glance out his picture window overlooking Oswego Lake, he would have seen scores of glowing orbs wheeling and gliding above the water like so many Chinese sky lanterns. However, Dr. Ronald Ingersoll was too absorbed in plotting his revenge to pay any attention to the Lake Lights.

Chapter 22
RATCAM

The next morning, Jon leapt out of bed and rushed out to the garage. CORVATS still sat where he had left it, but the pizza crusts were gone, right down to the crumbs.

"Jon!" his mother exclaimed. With rumpled hair, she was standing in the doorway wearing her favorite bathrobe. "Why are you up so early? Dad's conference isn't over yet, so there's no school today."

"Yeah, Mom, I know," he patiently replied. "I am just checking on my, ah, *experiment.*" Then he described how he had been using CORVATS to capture video of the mysterious peanut butter bandit.

His mother shook her head disapprovingly. "Don't you have anything better to do with your time than videotape rats and mice?"

"Mom, I want to prove to you that I didn't empty all those peanut butter jars and eat those missing cookies. That's why I'm doing this."

His mother's gaze softened. "I'm beginning to believe you," she said. "But if you didn't eat that peanut butter, then who did?"

"I am hoping CORVATS can tell me," Jon answered.

His mother cocooned herself more snugly in her bathrobe. "I don't care what you do with that souped-up derby car, just as long as you don't try to race it in my kitchen," she said sternly.

As she shuffled back down the hallway in her slippers, Mrs. Oliver muttered, "Now what did I do with the church directory? I need some pastoral counseling before I burst a blood vessel."

Returning to CORVATS, Jon opened the laptop's video software, stopped the recording, saved the file, and scrolled back to the beginning. Tapping the space bar, he played the saved video file.

The video showed nothing but pizza crusts lying on a concrete floor. Crusts . . . floor . . . crusts . . . floor. He might as well have been watching the moss grow on the trees behind the house.

After an hour of "crust watch," Jon fast-forwarded the video. Even at four times the normal playback speed, the crusts stayed put, as if they were pizza fossils or bizarre mineral formations that had oozed out of the cement and hardened like lava.

Jon must have dozed off, because when he next focused on the screen, the crusts were gone. He stopped the video and played it backward at three times normal speed until the crusts reappeared. Stopping the video again, he played it backward and forward until he caught a brown, furry animal scurrying across the screen.

A rat! At normal speed, the rodent slunk up to the two crusts and began gnawing on them. It had just finished devouring both when a shadow fell across the scene, and the rat vanished in a formless blur.

Jon rubbed his aching eyes. Where had the rat gone? He reviewed the section of video, slowing the action to a near stop. The rat disappeared as if by magic. Far from catching the Karl's Kreamy thief, all he had to show for his efforts was a rodent and a fleeting shadow.

Then he spotted a subtle movement buried in the darkness at the screen's upper edge. Freezing the video, he zoomed in on the anomaly. Though fuzzy, the image resembled a light-colored, curving tail or twig. *Probably the rat's tail*, he thought glumly.

"Jon! Breakfast!" his mother called.

Jon paused the video playback and dashed into the warm kitchen, where he found his mother with spatula in hand, standing like an orchestra conductor over a pan of steaming scrambled eggs.

"Well?" she said with raised eyebrows.

"It was just a rat, I guess," Jon mumbled. Taking the spatula from his mother, he eased a slab of eggs onto a plate.

"You guess?" said Mrs. Oliver. "Did you see a rat on your video eating those pizza crusts or didn't you? Which is it?"

"You saw a rat?" squealed Jennica, charging into the kitchen.

"On camera I did," Jon replied. "After it ate the crusts, something else grabbed it. Whatever it was, the video image was pretty blurry."

"Wow," said Jennica, helping herself to a plateful of scrambled eggs. "Maybe you should call your invention, 'RATCAM.'"

For once, Jon had to agree with her. "RATCAM," he repeated. "<u>R</u>odent <u>A</u>ctivated <u>T</u>racking <u>C</u>amera." He and Jennica laughed with their mouths full of eggs. Even their mother smiled at Jon's quip.

"That's enough talk about rodents in my kitchen," she told them. "By the way, your grandfather called. He will be joining us for dinner after his conference. Maybe you can show him your, er, rat video, Jon. I'm sure he would be interested, being a scientist and all."

After breakfast, CORVATS lured Jon back to the garage the way catnip attracts cats. Returning to the video clip of the crooked object, he enlarged the frozen frame. The blurry image still resembled the tip of a rat's supple tail. He applied a filtering algorithm to clean up the digital picture, and it snapped into sharper focus.

A glossy ivory-white, the curved feature was definitely the wrong color and texture for a tail. Its shape stirred a vague memory that—like the image itself—resisted coming into focus. The longer Jon stared at the thing, the more foreign it appeared.

If the thief wasn't a rodent, perhaps a possum had wandered up from the basement. After taking a screen shot of the object, Jon shut down the laptop and went outside to shoot hoops in the driveway.

Swish. He had just sunk his first basket when his skin tingled the way it often did when his sister was spying on him. Leaning on his stick, the shabby old man who spent his days shuffling up and down the street was gazing intently at him from the sidewalk.

"Don't mind me," he quavered. "I enjoy watching young fellers like you play basketball. If I might make a suggestion, try keeping your elbow closer to your body when you're shooting."

Jon grimaced. What did this old geezer know about basketball? He probably hadn't played the game in a half-century. Still, Jon didn't want to be rude. "Thanks," he said. "I'll have to try that."

With a polite nod, the stranger was moving on when Jon called after him, "Wait a second! I don't know your name."

"My name?" said the old man. "Why, you can call me 'Ted.'"

Ted shambled off, leaving Jon with a bad case of the goosebumps. Something wasn't quite right about the doddering old fellow, but Jon couldn't nail down his suspicions. His personal radar was working overtime now that Dr. Ingersoll had entered the picture.

A cold droplet splashed onto his forehead, derailing his train of thought. Dark clouds were roiling ominously above Iron Mountain. "Great," he groaned. At that time of the year, you could often count on a drenching cloudburst to spoil a lively hoop-shooting session.

In boyish frustration, he slammed the basketball against the backboard before heading for the porch. He had barely nipped inside the front door when the slate-colored sky opened up and rain sluiced down in silver sheets, drumming on the roof.

"Jon!" his mother called from the kitchen. "Could you please unplug the downspout back here? The gutter is overflowing."

Grumbling to himself, Jon reluctantly trudged into the kitchen. He hated cleaning out the gutters and downspouts, but now that his father was missing in action, he had inherited that chore along with a thousand others—or so it seemed. He found his mother standing at the half-open, sliding glass door watching water cascade out of the gutter and onto the deck in waterfall torrents.

"You see?" she said, turning toward him. "That much water will wash out the ground under our foundation. Nobody has cleaned out the gutters since your father left, and the downspouts are plugged."

With a theatrical sigh of resignation, Jon headed out to the garage. Taking down a folding aluminum stepladder, he manhandled it into the kitchen and hauled it through the sliding door—without breaking the glass. Once outside, he sidled along under the eaves to avoid the gutter's overflowing water. He still got soaked.

Coming to the downspout, he set up the ladder and climbed high enough to reach the plastic pipe's plugged intake. While steadying himself with one foot on the deck's railing, he dug out a debris dam of leaves and fir needles until he heard the satisfying gurgle of water rushing through the downspout. The gutter stopped overflowing.

Before backing down the ladder, Jon checked behind him to make sure his path was clear. As he did, he noticed a gash in the railing. The sight of that scar in the wood triggered a vivid memory that nearly knocked him off his perch.

Jumping backwards off the ladder, he rushed into the kitchen, leaving puddles of water—and loud motherly protests—in his wake. He then barged into his bedroom and began upending his glass specimen jars, dumping their contents onto his bed. It wasn't long before he found the one containing a handful of seashells—and a claw. It was the very claw he had pried out of the railing.

Gripping the artifact, Jon hurried out to the garage, where he powered up the ancient laptop. The outdated, poky computer seemed to take forever to boot up. In the meantime, his mother and sister had appeared at the door, concerned looks on their faces.

"Jon! What's wrong?" Mrs. Oliver asked him. "You know you left the stepladder outside in the rain. Thank you for cleaning out the downspout, by the way. But what are you doing out here?"

"Yeah, what are you doing out here?" Jennica echoed, a particularly annoying habit she had recently picked up.

"Come on over here, and I'll show you," Jon replied. Clicking on the screen shot of the mysterious object he had captured on video, he explained, "'RATCAM' recorded this image early this morning."

His mother squinted at the screen. "I thought you said you'd been recording rats. This doesn't look like a rat to me."

"That's because it isn't a rat," Jon replied.

"Then what is it?" asked Mrs. Oliver.

Jon held up the railing-claw. "I think it's one of these."

"Where did you get that?" Jennica asked. Her hand shot out to take the claw from him, but he held it out of her reach.

"I found it outside on the deck the night Reverend Sanford and his wife visited," he answered truthfully. "It was stuck in the railing."

"It looks like a bird claw," his mother observed.

"But how did a bird get into our garage?" Jon mused. He positioned the object alongside the laptop image for comparison. Although only the talon's sharp, tapering portion showed in the screen shot, it was nearly identical to the curved claw he held in his fingers.

He let out a low whistle. "It's a match, all right."

"What kind of bird has such big claws?" Jennica asked.

Just then, Jon heard a much-loved rattling sound. On tiptoe, he peered out the garage window and saw a beat-up red pickup chugging up the street. "Grandpa Roberts is here," he announced.

"He's a little early," Mrs. Oliver remarked.

"Maybe he knows where that claw came from," Jennica said.

However, after examining Jon's evidence, Dr. Roberts was also mystified. "This claw might belong to a large raptor, such as a hawk or an eagle," he said. "On the other hand, it might also have come from a mammal such as a fox or a coyote. One of the drawbacks to specializing in paleontology is that I'm more familiar with extinct animals than I am with modern ones. I must admit I've never seen anything like this before. If it belongs to the same animal we glimpsed in your video, how did its owner get into your garage?"

"I was wondering the same thing," Jon said. "Maybe it came in through the basement."

His grandfather stared at him. "How could anything sneak in from the basement? You've got no outside door down there."

Jon shrugged. "I have been meaning to tell you I've heard strange noises in the basement wall. I thought it was rats."

Dr. Roberts arched his bushy eyebrows. "Is that so?"

"Yeah," Jon said, suddenly feeling self-conscious. "If you follow me, I can show you where those sounds came from."

"Maybe we need to put out some poison," his mother suggested as she and the others trailed along behind him. "Rats carry terrible diseases, you know. Why, back in the Middle Ages, millions of people died of the bubonic plague from flea-infested rats."

Jon rolled his eyes. With his mother, a few rats meant an epidemic of the Black Death was about to wipe out all the residents of Lake Oswego, if not the entire population of the state of Oregon.

As he padded down the basement stairs, a dank smell tickled his nostrils. He saw the source even before turning on the lights.

To all appearances, a bomb had gone off behind a section of the yellowed sheetrock, hurling gypsum fragments and snowy powder everywhere. The resulting five-foot hole reminded Jon of the breach in his father's laboratory wall.

Aghast, his mother exclaimed, "Jon! What have you done?"

Even the normally unflappable Dr. Roberts was taken aback. "You cut a *hole* in the *wall*?" he rumbled. "Whatever for? There are easier and less destructive ways to kill rats, you know."

"Oh, boy. You are gonna be in big trouble now!" Jennica gleefully joined in. She winked at Jon to show him she wasn't serious. He could never be quite sure with his playful sister.

"I didn't make that hole!" Jon snapped. He plowed through piles of shredded plasterboard to reach the opening, which was too large for any rats to have created. Something much bigger had done this, something that wanted very badly to break into the basement.

Dr. Roberts was right behind him. Kneeling on the floor, the old man sifted through the wall's remains. "Take a gander at this, Jon," he said. He held up a handful of gypsum mingled with some coarse, blackish fibers. "Looks like raccoon hair to me. Don't you agree?"

Jon threw back his head and laughed. *Raccoons!* With their sharp claws they could tear through almost any building material except plywood or metal. Ripping open a peanut butter jar or demolishing a sheet of plasterboard would be a cinch for those band-tailed bandits.

Perhaps the brollachans Jon had disturbed in the cavern were actually raccoons standing on their hind legs, as the animals often did. Coons even had enough loose skin around their legs to mimic furry cloaks, and erect ears that could be mistaken for hoods.

Still, a seven-foot raccoon? And the guano Dr. Roberts had collected from VORCATS didn't belong to any known animal species.

"Let's have a look-see," the scientist said, pointing at the hole.

Jon unearthed a flashlight from a storage box and shone it into the opening. Wet, rotting timbers and damp rock glistened in the dim light. Jon's skin crawled with excitement. In excavating the basement, the builders had broken into one of the Prosser Mine's old drifts. Raccoons must have taken up residence there.

Grandfather Roberts echoed his thoughts. With a shaky laugh, he said, "Well, that neatly solves our brollachan mystery. You have a raccoon infestation. We'll have to close up this hole."

"I apologize for accusing you of eating all that Karl's Kreamy and my peanut butter cookies, too," Mrs. Oliver tearfully told Jon.

He hugged his mother. "That's okay, Mom," he said. "Who knew that raccoons liked peanut butter so much?"

"Uh, I'm sorry, too," Jennica mumbled.

Jon patted her head. Then he and Dr. Roberts shoved a wooden bureau in front of the raccoon hole, neatly covering it.

That night, Jon researched "raccoon claws" on the internet. The claw-photos he found were much too stubby in comparison with the talon he had found stuck in the railing.

Parked forty yards down Glen Eagles Road, Dr. Ingersoll fiddled with his battery-powered detector. If all went as planned, he would be using the instrument *inside* the Oliver house instead of *outside*.

Still smarting from his recent failure, he patted his inside jacket pocket and felt the solid, reassuring shape of his pistol. Soon, nobody could stop him, least of all Matthew "Jesus Freak" Oliver.

Dr. Ingersoll crossed himself and laughed scornfully. Despite his former business partner's sanctimonious talk of eternal life, dead men couldn't benefit from their inventions. Being very much alive, on the other hand, he himself was in an ideal position to rake in obscene profits from his sale of the device he was about to recover.

It was time to take back what rightfully belonged to him, by force if necessary. And he hoped force would be necessary.

Chapter 23
TERROR IN THE BASEMENT

Jennica's eyes flew open. Ever since seeing her brother levitate while wearing the anti-gravity belt, she had thought of nothing else. Vivid flying dreams invaded her sleep. More often than not, she awakened to find herself wrestling with her blankets on the floor and wishing her dreams weren't just dreams.

Weary of waiting for Jon to let her wear the belt, she decided to try it on anyway. Why should her brother have all the fun?

At around two o'clock Friday morning, she slid out of bed and threw on her clothes. Grabbing a flashlight from her bedside table, she tiptoed down the hall and opened her brother's bedroom door. In quietly searching his trousers pockets, she found the laser pen. Then she continued down the hallway to her father's office.

Following her brother's example, she removed the office key from behind the family photo, unlocked the office door and inserted the laser pen into Captain Gray's chair to lower it into her father's laboratory. Once in the lab, she wove among the metal tables to reach the damaged mini-fridge that held the magic belt.

When she removed the belt from the compact refrigerator, Jennica found it surprisingly heavy for something that could render its wearer as buoyant as the soap bubbles she loved to blow.

Using the built-in snaps, she fastened the belt around her slender waist and was about to press the green power button when she paused. With all its equipment, the laboratory was too cramped. She wanted enough space to float freely. If she went outside, though, she risked drifting away into the night, unable to return safely to earth.

She would test the belt in the basement, then. After savoring the experience of weightlessness there for a few minutes, she would return her father's invention to the mini-fridge. Nobody would be the wiser. Not even God Himself could object to her borrowing the belt for such a short time. It wasn't as if she was stealing it.

After riding Captain Gray's chair back up, she exited the office, locked the door and made a beeline for the basement. Darkness flowed down the stairway like a river of chocolate milk. Jennica flicked on the flashlight and crept down the steps, careful not to make the treads creak. It was fortunate she was such a lightweight.

Planting herself beside Jon's video-game table, she pressed the belt's green button. To her dismay, she felt no change. She had expected a tingling sensation or dizziness. Jon had once mentioned the belt's battery needed recharging. Maybe that was the problem.

Or maybe she wasn't supposed to feel any different. Tensing her leg muscles, she sprang into the air—and crashed headlong into the ten-foot ceiling, just as her brother had done in his bedroom.

Stunned, she dropped her flashlight. It clattered onto the concrete floor far below, shattering the light bulb. Now only the belt's dimly glowing power button still shone in the thick darkness.

Jennica pushed off from the ceiling, only to stop partway down. She couldn't safely reach the floor without a solid object to give her leverage, and she didn't dare cut the belt's power for fear of falling and breaking a leg or an arm. If only she had taken the precaution of turning on the lights before starting her forbidden experiment!

Flailing frantically about, she felt only empty space. She was doomed to hang between heaven and earth until the belt's battery ran down—and she plummeted to the unforgiving cement floor.

Searching for her cell phone, Jennica jammed her hands into her pockets. Her fingers found only the office key. Still, that key gave her a brainstorm. Fishing it out of her pocket, she tossed it away from her to gauge her distance from the floor. Instead of the *clink* of metal on concrete, though, she heard a soft, rustling sound, the sort of sound that sheets make when removed from a dryer.

Next came a sharp, click-clacking noise. *I'm not alone down here*, she realized. *Those pesky raccoons must be on the prowl again*. Did raccoons eat people? She didn't think so. At least she was out of their reach for the time being.

Click-clack. Click-clack. Jennica thought, *They're stalking me. They know I'm here. What if they can jump or climb?*

Without knowing how far off the floor she was, she couldn't risk shutting down the belt. The battery might run down by morning, but if not, her mother or brother would discover her helplessly floating in the basement. She would never live down the humiliation.

Either way, she was in a serious fix. However, her predicament was about to take a turn for the worse. An unpleasantly sharp smell stung her nostrils. The air was growing fouler by the minute, making her cough and gag. Her eyes started to water.

What was it Grandfather Roberts had called that poisonous gas? Sulfur dioxide. Yes, that was it. The gas was rapidly filling the basement, and if she didn't leave the room soon, she would die.

"Help!" she cried. "Somebody help me! I'm trapped in here!"

However, nobody came, because nobody could hear her pleas for help. Her mother and brother were fast asleep in their beds. She breathed with ragged, panting gasps as the sulfur dioxide burned her throat and lungs.

Jennica was praying and crying by turns when the clicking sounds came closer. She felt a sudden rush of air, as if someone had just turned on a ceiling fan—but the basement didn't have one.

Whish. Something smooth and leathery brushed Jennica's arm, and a glowing form shot by her like a small meteor. She shrieked into the darkness. *It's coming for me. I'm going to die. Jesus, please save me!* Mercifully, unconsciousness wrapped her in shrouds of oblivion before terror could snatch away her mind.

Clad all in black, Dr. Ingersoll was crawling through the Olivers' unlocked kitchen window when the powerful stench of sulfur dioxide seared his sinuses. Coughing and sneezing, he dropped back onto the deck. He had prepared himself for every conceivable contingency—except an outbreak of noxious gas. Entering the house without protective breathing equipment would be flat-out foolhardy.

He gritted his teeth in frustration. Either the Olivers had anticipated him and had released the poisonous gas on purpose to foil his break-in, or this was a rare natural occurrence. Whatever the gas's source, he was now forced to abort the operation and bide his time until another opportunity presented itself.

Of course, the malodorous fumes might just do his job for him by asphyxiating the Olivers in their beds. He would check up on the family in the morning to see whether they were still alive. If they had perished, he could waltz into the house and make off with the Device without the risk of being apprehended.

Cheered by this possibility, Dr. Ingersoll hurried off to his waiting Mercedes and drove home, whistling as he went.

Chapter 24
PTERA

A monstrous raccoon was slowly smothering Jon with its hairy, stinking bulk, pinning his arms to his sides with its sharp, wickedly curved claws. Gasping for air, he fought in vain to free himself from the hissing creature.

He forced open his heavy-lidded eyes. He was alone in the bedroom, which was quiet except for the faint hum of his electric clock. It read 3:10. In his violent tossing and twisting, he had trussed himself up in his bedclothes. However, his suffocation was all too real. *Sulfur dioxide.* Iron Mountain had chosen that particular Friday morning in June to burp again. *Why today of all days?* Jon wondered.

Coughing and wheezing, he threw off his blankets and fell to the floor. He had enough presence of mind to grope under the bed and grab the gas mask he had taken from his father's laboratory. As soon as he fitted the mask over his face, the air freshened and his mind cleared. He had to help his mother and sister before it was too late!

He rushed out of his room and into the hallway, flicking on lights as he ran. First, he flung open the front door to bring in some fresh air. Then he burst into his mother's bedroom. Mrs. Oliver lay pale and still upon her bed, scarcely breathing.

Tearing the mask off his face, he pressed it over his mother's nose and held his breath. Slowly, the color returned to her cheeks. After a few seconds, her eyelids fluttered open and she attempted to speak.

"What happened?" she asked weakly in a mask-muffled voice.

"Sulfur dioxide," Jon wheezed, losing precious air as he spoke. He helped his mother up, threw a bathrobe over her shoulders and took her out onto the front porch to catch her breath. After making sure she would recover, he reclaimed his mask and ducked back into the house to find his sister. However, her rumpled bed was empty.

Jon raced out of her room and down the hallway to check the bathroom, living room, dining room and kitchen, but Jennica wasn't in any of those places. Where could she have gone?

Then he heard a piercing shriek like the rending of sheet metal coming from below. Hurrying back down the hall to the basement door, he bounded down the stairs and switched on the lights.

The basement was quiet, but the echo of a scream—his sister's scream—still hung in the air. Wearing the anti-gravity belt, she was floating about eight feet off the floor like a magician's assistant in a clever illusion. Her limbs lolled limply, and her hair drifted around her head in a weightless halo as if she were in outer space.

Below her and beside the video-game table stood a brownish-black statue Jon hadn't noticed before. His mother must have bought it. She was forever bringing home yard-sale "treasures." One year, it was a bevy of pink plastic flamingos. The next, she found a giant in-flatable snowman that stood as tall as the house when blown up.

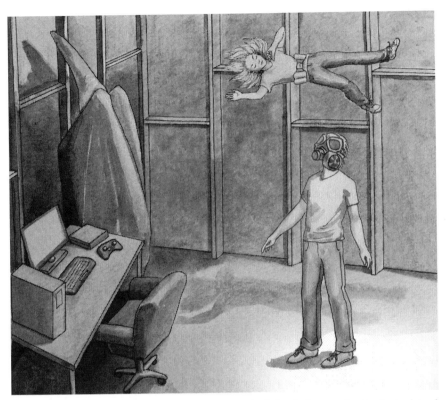

Shimmering sulfur dioxide fumes belched from the hole behind the bureau. Jon gagged as the fumes leaked around his mask. He had to get Jennica out of the basement before the gas suffocated her.

However, he couldn't quite reach his sister, even when he stood on the video-game table. Casting about, he found a rusty boathook his father used on a small sailboat he kept down at Oswego Lake.

Raising the pole, Jon hooked the anti-gravity belt. After dragging Jennica's slack, weightless form down to his level, he slung her over his shoulder, flew up the stairs and whisked her out the front door.

He found his mother sitting on the lawn, coughing and in a daze from her ordeal. She didn't seem to notice either Jon or Jennica.

Jon lowered Jennica's feather-light body onto the grass and shut off the belt's power. Then he pressed on his sister's chest to expel the noxious fumes she had inhaled. She shuddered and drew in a long, rasping breath. Opening her eyes, she sat up and began to wail as she rocked back and forth. "Where is it?" she cried, wildly looking about.

Jon removed his gas mask. "Where is what?" He lowered his voice. "Do you mean the, uh, *belt*? You're still wearing it."

"No, no. I'm talking about the *thing* that attacked me!"

Alarms went off in Jon's head. "Something attacked you?"

"Yes! A creepy creature got into the basement with me! I don't think it was a raccoon, either. Raccoons can't fly."

Jennica tore off the borrowed belt and cast it aside. Then she handed Jon the laser pen. "I'm sorry I took this," she tearfully told him. "I dropped the key downstairs. I'll look for it later."

Jon didn't have the heart to scold his sister. "That's okay, Squirt. I'm just glad I found you when I did. And I have a spare key."

Donning the gas mask again, Jon swung by his bedroom to pick up the extra key on his way to the office, where he replaced the anti-gravity belt in his father's covert laboratory. By the time he returned, his mother had recovered her senses and was looking more alert.

"Thank you, Son," she told him. "If it weren't for your quick thinking, your sister and I might have suffocated in our sleep."

Jon shrugged as he pulled off the mask. "You can thank Dad for leaving this gas mask in his laboratory where I could find it. He probably needed it whenever sulfur dioxide built up inside the lab."

By now, porch lights around the neighborhood were coming on, and people were pouring out of their homes. A police car and fire truck slowly cruised by, their lights flashing.

Fortunately, the gas-release episode was short lived. After huddling on the front lawn until dawn, Jon and his family returned inside and aired out the place. Still wearing her bathrobe, Mrs. Oliver then went back outside to pick up the newspaper from the porch.

Since sleep was impossible, she brought out packages of graham crackers, chocolate squares and marshmallows, and everyone melted gooey s'mores over a fire in the fireplace. Jon slathered peanut butter on his graham crackers before piling on the chocolate and marshmallows. Before long, he had smeared equal parts of marshmallow, peanut butter and chocolate around his mouth.

By the time he and Jennica had scoured the stickiness off their hands (but not off their faces), the sun was blazing above the eastern horizon, lighting up the kitchen. Eyelids drooping, Jennica slumped over the table, pillowing her head on her arms.

"I'm going back to bed," she announced, yawning hugely.

"Me, too," said Jon. His whole body felt as if it would sink into the floor if he didn't make up for his lost sleep.

He followed his sister down the hallway until she stopped outside her bedroom door. She turned to face him, her lip quivering.

"I'm sorry for using the belt," she said. "Thanks for not telling Mom about it. Now I'm gonna close my door an' brace it with a chair. I don't want that thing coming after me again."

"What *was* it?" Jon tried to ask her. He found himself talking to her door, which shuddered as she shoved the chair against it.

Jon stared blankly at the door. He knew better than to force it open. Then he trudged down the hallway toward his own bedroom. As he passed the basement door, he heard a rustling sound.

Jennica had been telling the truth. Something *was* lurking downstairs—and Jon intended to find out what it was. *It's probably just those raccoons*, he told himself, hardly believing his own words.

The blood roared in his ears as he headed into the living room, where he seized the still-warm poker propped against the fireplace. He didn't want to confront the intruder unarmed. If only his father were home! Matthew Oliver always knew what to do in a pinch.

Back to the basement door he went. Mingled with a fishy odor, the reek of sulfur dioxide wafted up from below. Crouching on the stairs with muscles tensed, he peered into the darkness. Nothing seemed amiss, though a flapping noise came faintly to his ears, as of a bird flying blindly in the blackness. *Raccoons can't fly*, as Jennica had pointed out. Hoping it was just a bat, he stole down the stairs.

As his eyes adjusted to the dim light, he noticed a ghostly pillar standing in front of his video-game table. Flipping the stairway switch, he flooded the basement with light. The yard-sale sculpture he had noticed earlier now stood where the luminous pillar had been.

No wonder his mother had brought the thing home. She loved glow-in-the-dark garden statuary—gnomes, fairies, butterflies, and the like. Most of her stock was still in storage after the move.

He froze. The statue didn't look right. It was too tall and misshapen to grace any self-respecting garden. Also, he had last seen it standing *beside* the table, not in front of it. Had someone moved it?

Cautiously, he approached the sculpture, holding the poker stiffly before him like a sword. At first glance, the statue resembled one of those fake tree stumps that people converted into waterfall features.

On closer inspection, what he had taken for bark ridges were actually smooth folds very similar to umbrella pleats. One of the pleats twitched, and Jon jumped back. As he did, the figure expanded like a futuristic robot. Clawed, batlike wings splayed out on either side, nearly spanning the seventeen-foot-wide room; a narrow, crested head with a long, toothless beak unfolded from narrow shoulders; and a saucer-size pair of luminous, red eyes glared back at him.

The creature opened its jaws and hissed.

The poker dropped from Jon's slack hand, and all the air left his lungs. He willed his body to flee the basement, but his muscles refused to cooperate. What sort of nightmarish prehistoric animal was this, and if it had gotten in through the hole in the wall, how had it managed to squeeze past the massive bureau?

The truth struck him with the force of a physical blow. This oversized bat had first broken through the sheetrock to escape the sulfur dioxide fumes building up in the mine's drifts. When Jon and his grandfather had blocked the hole with the bureau, *the creature was already hiding in the basement.* It had been trapped there ever since, and it was undoubtedly very hungry.

Convinced he was about to be torn to pieces and devoured on the spot, Jon screwed his eyes shut. He hoped the end would come quickly. Then he felt a moist, tickling sensation on his cheek.

Opening one eye, he saw the beast's tongue was playing over his face. Resisting the urge to pull away, he held his breath. Surely the monster was "tasting" him before it made him the main course. Instead, its supple tongue rasped gently at the skin around his mouth, much as Jon's mother used to wipe off his face after a messy meal.

Peanut butter. The animal was licking the peanut butter off his face. When the slithery tongue retracted into the tapering beak, Jon slowly backed away from the beast and fled up the stairs.

As he pounded up the steps, his mind flashed back to the "brollachans" that had chased him in the cavern. With their beaks or "gobs" buried beneath their wings, he had mistaken them for cloaked, hook-nosed old men with head-crest hoods. The brollachans, the Lake Lights, and this winged creature were all one and the same!

This discovery also explained the bizarre behavior of Ginny and the other horses at the Equestrian Club. The creature's rancid, fishy smell alone would spook any animal with a nose.

But what *was* this cross between a bat and a lizard? How many others like it were skulking about the passages and caverns beneath Iron Mountain, and how long had they been living down there?

Jon sprinted into the kitchen and climbed onto the counter. He removed a Karl's Kreamy jar from the cabinet holding his mother's stash and jumped down. Then he grabbed his phone from his room.

Returning to the basement, he found the Creature waiting for him by the video-game table, its wings fanned out in a threatening, Draculan posture. Its fathomless eyes followed his every move.

After sending a quick prayer heavenward, Jon pulled out his phone and snapped a photo of the intruder as proof of his encounter.

He noticed the animal's torso was covered with a thin layer of coarse, dark fibers that probably helped insulate its body during cold weather. Raccoon hair, indeed! Then he twisted the cap off the peanut butter jar and peeled away the seal before extending the plastic container toward the long-beaked beast.

The Creature tipped its head from side to side as if examining the jar. Then it hopped forward on clawed feet, and its agile tongue plunged into the peanut butter, darting in and out of the container as rapidly as a cat's tongue lapping up milk from a saucer. In less than five minutes, the jar was completely empty.

The giant bat licked its snout and screeched. Jon flinched. He didn't want his mother to awaken and march downstairs to investigate. She would come apart at the seams if she saw what had been living there. But what was he to do with this animal? He couldn't keep it penned up in the basement. It was meant to fly freely.

He would have to let it return to its home behind the wall. After pushing the bureau away from the hole, he stood aside and waited for the Creature to make its next move.

The "brollachan" watched him unblock the opening. Then it furled its wings and crouched down on all fours. Hobbling along on its short legs and curving wing-claws, it wriggled agilely through the hole. As it vanished into the blackness beyond, Jon felt a pang of loss. Would he ever see this fascinating animal again?

Before racing up to his bedroom, Jon first pushed the bureau back into place to prevent further unpleasant surprises. Once inside his room, he shut the door and flipped open his laptop.

Scouring the internet for "winged dinosaurs," he found images of a short-tailed, bat-winged animal with a long, toothless bill and a prominent head-crest. The pictures were labeled, "Pteranodon."

He had finally identified the Brollachan-Beast. His first attempts at correctly pronouncing *pteranodon* resulted in "repterodon," then "reptanodon" and "neraptodon." In frustration, he at last looked up the proper pronunciation: ter-an´-o-don.

Narrowing his search, he found an informative web page devoted to pteranodons. Based upon the crest size and shape, Jon gathered that his peanut-butter thief was a male. He also learned that this type of *pterosaur* or "winged lizard" wasn't a dinosaur at all but a prehistoric reptile that had supposedly died out sixty-five million years earlier. Jon had stumbled upon a living fossil.

He was not alone. A number of websites documented confirmed sightings of the broad-winged creatures. As far as Jon could tell, though, he was the first modern-day human being ever to see a pterosaur close up, let alone have his face licked by one. He searched the internet for "pterosaurs as pets" but found nothing.

Some of the internet sites suggested pteranodons fed on fish. Jon's lip curled. No wonder his pterosaur loved peanut butter. Raw fish was disgusting. Still, that could explain why the reptiles lived so close to Oswego Lake, which was home to bass, perch, and bluegills.

Grandfather Roberts would be so thrilled with this discovery! Jon might even win a Nobel Prize along with a generous cash reward. Then he could afford to buy a new skateboard and video games.

Zoos all over the world would compete for the privilege of keeping a live pteranodon or two in captivity. On a second thought, Jon wasn't so sure he liked that idea. Still, he would be famous.

Famous. The word had an impressive ring to it. Maybe Renée Doulière would look him up—if she remembered him from school.

On the other hand, fame would also attract news reporters and their cameras along with all sorts of unwelcome attention from would-be dinosaur hunters. It was the same line of reasoning that had convinced Jon to keep his father's anti-gravity belt under wraps.

In any case, he would have to name his newfound pteranodon friend. After some thought, he decided to call the creature, "Ptera."

They're still alive! Dr. Ingersoll was about to break into the Olivers' house when the wife emerged to pick up the morning paper from the front porch. Muffled in a frayed pink bathrobe, she scanned the paper's headlines before returning inside. As the door closed, the shrieks of children's laughter escaped from within the house.

How could anyone have survived such a toxic gas leak? Perhaps the family had spent the night at Kendall Roberts' home—or in some local flea-infested flophouse that passed for a hotel.

A toxic gas leak. The physicist smiled as a fresh idea dawned on him. He wouldn't have to break into the house after all. Those Olivers were so gullible they would invite him inside. Anyone naïve enough to buy into Christianity's fairy tales would fall for the most outrageous lie he could concoct.

Mrs. Oliver was still taking her children to church, no doubt to beg a mythical God for the safe return of her dead husband. He chuckled. As Karl Marx had so aptly put it, "Religion is the opiate of the masses." Only the weak and simple-minded needed religion.

The Christians had gotten one thing right, though: It took a Trinity to make a man happy and whole. Dr. Ingersoll had devoted his entire life to the material trinity of Science, Money and Power (not necessarily ranked in that order). His triune god had never let him down. Now that same god was about to reward him handsomely. He needed only to claim his prize in the form of the Device.

Chapter 25
THE FIREWORKS BEGIN

Jon, have you been getting into my peanut butter again?" Mrs. Oliver demanded. "I'm missing a couple of jars." She had just arrived home from work and was counting her stash. The former basketball standout was tall enough to reach the topmost cupboards without using a step stool. Jon envied her.

"Not lately," he replied truthfully. Ptera was the culprit. For once, Jon was glad to have garbage duty. It meant he could toss out empty peanut butter containers without anyone's being the wiser.

"Did you catch the 'wascawuy waccoon' that's been sneaking into our home?" Mrs. Oliver went on in her best Elmer Fudd imitation. She took down a jar of Karl's Kreamy and opened it up.

Jon laughed nervously. "Not exactly." His mother had an uncanny knack for skewering him with pointed questions. "Grandpa and I blocked up the hole where the coon was getting in, remember?"

Mrs. Oliver grunted her approval. "Just be sure that bandit doesn't show his masked face around here again, understood?"

Jon nodded and swallowed a mouthful of sand. For the past two weeks, he had been sneaking down into the basement to feed Ptera after finishing his chores and homeschool lessons.

To avoid leaving telltale marks on the floor when he shoved the bureau away from the hole in the wall, he had slipped an old throw rug underneath it. The rug also made the bureau easier to slide.

Once the hole was exposed, he would dangle an open jar of Karl's Kreamy in front of it. Presently, Ptera's long, tapering beak would emerge, and his quick tongue would scrape the jar clean. Afterwards, Jon would stroke the pteranodon's head, which the animal seemed to enjoy. Back went the bureau, and no one was the wiser.

The process took little more time than toasting a slice of bread.

Still, since Ptera was consuming a jar of peanut butter every day, Jon's mother was growing suspicious. Jon could switch Ptera's diet to raw fish, but that would raise more red flags. He could try hijacking a Karl's Kreamy delivery truck, but he didn't want to spend the next five years of his life mopping the floors at a boys' reform school. His parents had often described such places in dreadful detail.

That brought him back to peanut butter. Once a week, he would have to sacrifice his allowance to purchase seven jars of Karl's Kreamy at the local market and bicycle home with them.

He hoped he could keep up with Ptera's prodigious appetite. He also hoped he could keep the pteranodon's existence a secret. He was sure that once anyone else learned what was living in the Prosser Mine, all the creatures would be hunted down and captured or killed.

A week later, Jon was bicycling up Twin Fir on a hot afternoon. Sweat drenched his shirt and his peanut butter-filled backpack. For once, he had a perfect excuse to visit the grocery store. Because it was the third of July, his mother had given him a few dollars to purchase packs of firecrackers and sparklers for the family.

Ordinarily, Jon's father bought boatloads of fireworks for the occasion as one expression of his extravagant love for the United States of America. Now that job had fallen to Jon. He wished he could magically make the holiday disappear rather than celebrate it without his father. The Fourth wouldn't be the same without him. No exploding firecrackers, Roman candles, pinwheeling spinners, whistling bottle rockets or aerial starbursts could ease Jon's heartache.

He arrived home on wobbly legs just in time to hear the first firecrackers going off in the neighborhood. Most people purchased only the tamer varieties of fireworks because of the summer fire hazard and the risk of personal injury. After dark on the Fourth, they would camp out where they could view an official fireworks display— usually near Oswego Lake, which offered one of the finest shows.

Jon had just flipped down his bike's kickstand when Jennica shot out of the front door, armed with a long butane lighter. "Mom said we could set off some firecrackers!" she cried, waving the lighter like an unlit sparkler or a baton. Never patient when it came to holidays, Jennica insisted on opening at least two presents on Christmas Eve and eating the ears off a chocolate bunny before Easter.

"Mom also said you're not allowed to light them without my supervision," Jon reminded her. He removed some fireworks from his backpack and closed it up again before his sister could see his other purchases. All those jars of Karl's Kreamy would be hard to explain.

Tearing open a cellophane package of firecrackers, he removed five and handed them to his sister. Then with a pull on the lighter's trigger, he lit the stream of butane. The flickering flame glowed a pale blue in the afternoon sunlight.

"Okay, you can give me a firecracker now," he said.

"What? No way. I wanna light 'em myself."

"It's too dangerous," Jon patiently explained. Taking one of the fireworks from Jennica, he lit it and tossed it onto the driveway behind his mother's car. It blew up with a gratifying "bang" in a flurry of smoke and shredded paper. The next four firecrackers suffered the same fate, leaving black streaks on the concrete.

"That's enough for now," Jon told his sister. "Let's go inside. This morning, Mom said something about baking cookies after work. Maybe if you help her, she'll give you a few."

Slinging on his backpack again, Jon dropped off the packages of firecrackers and sparklers in his bedroom. Then he stowed the jars of Karl's Kreamy in the basement bureau's wooden drawers.

Back upstairs, Jon found his mother and sister shoving pans of peanut butter cookies into the oven. While their backs were turned to him, he sneaked up and pocketed several finished cookies from a plate on the table. He was munching on one of them when Mrs. Oliver spun around and waved him off with her spatula.

"You stay away from those cookies, young man!" she scolded him. "They're for tomorrow, while we're watching the fireworks. Honestly, you must be going through a growth spurt."

Jon couldn't argue with her. He was always hungry. He scurried out of the kitchen and into his room, where he spread out the fireworks on his bed. He would have a grand time setting them off.

The tree-shadows were lengthening when a white utility van pulled up to the Oliver home. "Oregon Natural Gas" was emblazoned across its side. Wearing coveralls and a fully equipped utility belt, the driver remained in his seat, studiously examining the house. Then he opened the door, unfolded his long legs and clambered out.

Striding up the driveway, he kicked aside one of Jon's spent firecrackers. All along the street, more fireworks were sizzling and popping. The technician smiled. The more explosions, the better.

He stepped over to the black Malibu sitting in the driveway. It was just the sort of vehicle a soccer mom like Olivia Oliver might drive. He could never fathom why women wanted to have children. He himself was content to be childless and married to his job.

Kneeling beside the Malibu, he jabbed its tires one after the other with a stiletto he had hidden in his utility belt. Air hissed out, and the car settled lower onto the driveway as if sinking into quicksand. Then he went to the front door and knocked.

When Olivia Oliver answered, the technician said, "Hello, I'm from the natural gas company. I understand you've got a gas leak."

The Olivers would pay for making a mockery of him.

Chapter 26
EQUAL & OPPOSITE REACTIONS

After feeding Ptera his daily ration of peanut butter, Jon had just shoved the bureau back to cover the hole in the wall when he decided to recharge the anti-gravity belt. Several days had passed since he last topped off its battery, and he wanted to make sure the device still worked properly. He would test it for only a minute or two—or so he told himself.

He descended on Captain Gray's chair into the secret laboratory, removed the belt from the ruined refrigerator and plugged it in. When the battery was fully charged, he strapped on the belt and re-turned to the basement, where he pressed the device's power button. Pushing off from the floor, he floated weightlessly into the air. How he wished to leave the room's confines and soar into the sky!

All at once, he heard a noise on the stairs. Someone was coming! He thrashed about, trying to rebound off some solid surface in order to return to earth. He was too far from the floor to turn off the belt. Only an artificial Christmas tree stood within reach, but when he grabbed it, the bristly plastic top came away in his hand.

"I don't know why you came out here," his mother was telling someone. "We didn't have a natural gas leak. It was a different kind of leak—something volcanic, as I understand it. Anyway, the fumes dissipated weeks ago. You can't smell a thing down here now. I'll bet your gas probe won't find any leaks, either." She turned on the lights.

"It's always best to play it safe," said a familiar male voice.

Jon was still hanging helplessly in midair when a lanky figure clad in white coveralls and a cap followed his mother downstairs. Jon instantly recognized Dr. Ingersoll, despite his elaborate disguise. The physicist was munching on a peanut butter cookie while waving his detector to and fro, scanning the room. The device was frantically beeping. Slowly, the man's gaze rose toward Jon. Their eyes locked.

"Good Heavens!" Dr. Ingersoll gasped. He quickly recovered his composure. "It's a gravity-cancelling device, just as I surmised. This invention will fetch a handsome price indeed."

"You!" Mrs. Oliver gasped. "You're not with the gas company!"

"Right you are," said Dr. Ingersoll. "I can see nothing gets past Olivia Oliver. And thank you for the peanut butter cookies. When you weren't looking, I took a few extra. They are surprisingly good."

"I'm reporting you!" cried Jon's mother, fleeing up the stairs.

She was too late. Quick as a striking snake, Ingersoll raced after her, grabbed the neck of her blouse—and yanked. Tumbling backward down the stairs, she sprawled bleeding on the concrete floor.

"Mom!" Jon screamed, flailing in a vain attempt to reach her. "Mom, are you all right? Please speak to me!"

"She can't talk right now," Dr. Ingersoll remarked, as if making women fall down the stairs was routine for him. He brought out his cell phone and glanced at its screen. "Tsk, tsk. What a pity. There's no reception down here. Still, if you cooperate, I could be persuaded to call 911 from upstairs. Otherwise . . ." He let the unspoken threat hang in the air like a poisonous cloud of sulfur dioxide.

The physicist strolled over to Jon and looked up at him. "I see you brought me an early Christmas present. How thoughtful—and how clever of you to hide the device down here, where I couldn't detect its electromagnetic emissions. But I have caught up to you in the end, as I knew I would. Science wins out again, as it always does."

Christmas present? Dr. Ingersoll must have been referring to the Christmas-tree top Jon was still gripping. In utter desperation, he hurled it at the scientist. However, the act of throwing the treetop propelled him backwards into the basement's south wall.

"Help!" he cried. "Somebody help us! Murder! Robbery!"

"Don't you know every action has an equal and opposite reaction?" Dr. Ingersoll sneered up at him. "And don't bother crying for help. Nobody can hear you down here. You're trapped. Now kindly come down from there before I decide to hurt you."

"No!" Jon shouted. "Go away! This belt belongs to me."

"Correction: It now belongs to *me*," grated the physicist. He pulled a pistol out of his utility belt and pointed it at Jon. "I'm running out of patience," he said. "Give me the belt, or I shall pull the trigger—and I'll warn you that I'm an expert marksman."

"You wouldn't dare," Jon blustered. The short-barreled pistol in the man's fist looked as big as a bazooka. "If you fire that gun, you risk hitting the belt and ruining it. If you want my dad's invention, you're gonna have to come up here and take it away from me."

Ingersoll surveyed the jumble of chairs and decorations standing between him and Jon. Then he spotted the boathook on the floor where Jon had left it. He picked it up and put away his pistol, fished a cookie out of his pocket and popped it into his mouth.

"Mmmm," he said, licking his lips. "This peanut butter cookie is delicious. My compliments to your mother. I'm sure she would be grieved to lose you at such a tender age—if she herself survives. This is your last chance, boy. Come down, and I'll let you live. I'm offering you your life for the device. It's a fair trade, don't you agree?"

"No, it's not a trair fade, I mean, a fair trade," Jon stammered.

Ingersoll shrugged. "Very well. Have it your way, my dyslexic little man. First, I'll pull you down with this hook and take the belt off you. Then I will shoot you, but no one will hear it because of the fireworks going off outside. I planned it that way all along."

Jon believed him. The scientist had taken every precaution except one: He had stolen some of Mrs. Oliver's peanut butter cookies. Jon was counting on the man's having plenty more of those cookies in his pockets. In fact, Jon was staking his life on them.

Thump. Thump. Distracted, Dr. Ingersoll turned toward the noise, which seemed to be coming from the wall beside the bureau.

Riiipppp! With a sharp, rending sound, something punched and tore through the stained section of sheetrock, slashing from top to bottom. White dust flew everywhere. Then with a terrific crash, the wall blew apart. Chalky gypsum chunks exploded into the basement like an avalanche thundering down the slopes of nearby Mt. Hood.

Out hobbled Ptera, his clawed wings snowy with plasterboard powder. The ravenous reptile made straight for the goggling scientist and jabbed at him with his thick, tapering beak.

Jon quailed. Though he'd hoped Ptera would show up, he never dreamed his pet would stage such a dramatic entrance. Unable to get past the heavy bureau, it had clawed its way through the wall to reach the source of the peanut butter smell. Thriving on its rich diet of Karl's Kreamy, the pteranodon had nearly doubled in size.

"Stay away from me!" Dr. Ingersoll shouted at the reptile. He dropped the boathook and drew his pistol. The scientist's hands were shaking so badly he couldn't draw a bead on the beast before him.

"Don't shoot it!" Jon cried. "Give it your cookies!"

The physicist frantically emptied his coverall pockets. Coins, rubber bands, paper clips and broken cookies flew everywhere. Ignoring the other items, Ptera snapped up the cookies. Then he shook his wings and let out the same piercing screech Jon had heard while camping on the back deck with his family.

Shrinking before the voracious creature, Dr. Ingersoll unfastened his utility belt and hurled it at the reptile, striking its chest. Ptera hissed and raised his wings in a threatening posture.

While the physicist was distracted, Jon braced his feet against the basement's back wall and launched himself like a missile over Ingersoll's head. Somersaulting in midair to reverse his orientation, he smacked feet-first against the wall above the stairwell. After leveraging himself closer to earth, he punched the belt's power button. No longer weightless, he dropped to the floor beside his mother.

Remembering how he had saved his sister, he removed the belt and fastened it around his mother's waist. She was groaning as he scooped up her now-weightless, limp body under one arm and quietly started up the stairs with her, feeling lighter himself.

Gun still in hand, a pasty-faced Dr. Ingersoll was backing away from Ptera. "You're not going anywhere, boy," he growled at Jon over his shoulder. "One way or another, I'll have that belt."

Jon bounded up the steps—nearly running his mother's head into the door at the top—raced down the hallway, swerved into the kitchen, and darted through the sliding door onto the deck. Buoyed by the belt, he hoped to elude his pursuer by leaping off the deck's far side with his mother and landing softly on the Iron Mountain trail.

Hard on Jon's heels, Dr. Ingersoll followed him onto the deck.

Pow! Pow! Pow!

Jon braced himself, expecting bullets to zip past his head. Instead, he found Jennica kneeling on the deck, looking guilty and alarmed. Matchbox in hand, she had just set off three firecrackers she had evidently taken from Jon's bedroom. He would deal with her later.

Brandishing his pistol, Dr. Ingersoll backed Jon and his mother up against the deck's railing. "Give me the belt!" the physicist ordered Jon. "Give me the belt, or I shoot your mother!"

"All right, you win," Jon said wearily. "She's wearing it."

Mrs. Oliver groaned again and opened her eyes. "Where are we? What happened?" she asked weakly.

Keeping his pistol trained on Jon, Dr. Ingersoll stripped the belt off Mrs. Oliver's waist and awkwardly fastened it around his own. As the weight returned to his mother's body, Jon had to support her with both arms to keep her from falling to the deck.

"At last!" the physicist crowed. "You could have saved us both a great deal of time and trouble by handing this belt over to me earlier, young man. I warned you I would take it from you by force—and then shoot you. Since I am a man of my word, I must follow through on my promise. Your mother and sister will be next. I can't leave any witnesses behind. I'm sure you understand my position."

Jon helplessly looked on as Dr. Ingersoll leveled his pistol at him and squeezed the trigger. Jon flinched. He couldn't believe he was about to die. At least now he would see his grandmother in Heaven.

POW! CRACK! Amidst billowing flames and smoke, Dr. Ingersoll rocketed into the air as if shot out of a circus cannon. The same law of physics that had propelled Jon backward into the basement wall had also sent the scientist corkscrewing into the sky.

More shots rang out as Ingersoll fired his gun overhead to control his ascent, but the pistol's recoil merely sent him careening off in a different direction. His panicked shouts were growing fainter.

Rooted to the deck, Jon continued watching until the man's form dwindled to a dark speck and disappeared into the clouds. In all likelihood, the anti-gravity belt was lost to the scientific world forever.

Prevailing winds would carry the hapless physicist along until the belt's battery ran down and he fell back to earth—or into the ocean. Dr. Matthew Oliver's one-of-a-kind prototype would be destroyed.

"Every action has an equal and opposite reaction," Jon said to himself with grim satisfaction. The scientist was getting what he deserved. Jon tried not to imagine how terrified the man must feel.

"Help me up," said a woozy voice.

In all the confusion, Jon had forgotten he was still hanging onto his mother. Straining, he propped her upright against the deck rail. A patch of dried blood stained her temple.

Jennica rushed up to them. "Mom! Jon! Are you all right?"

"I'm fine," said Mrs. Oliver, slurring her words.

Jon hugged his sister. "Thanks to you, I'm okay, too. You saved my life!" He had just pieced together what had happened from the scraps of burnt paper scattered around the scene.

"What do you mean?" Jennica asked him.

Jon pointed to the burnt match she was still gripping in her fingers. "Didn't you toss a lighted firecracker at Dr. Ingersoll? It threw off his aim and his shot went wild. See, here's where the bullet went."

He knelt and poked his finger into a fresh hole in the deck's cedar planking. It was blackened around the margin.

Jennica stared back at him with large, solemn eyes and shook her head. "I didn't throw any firecrackers at him. I had only three to start with, and I already set 'em all off. I got them from your room."

Perplexed, Jon glanced about. "Then who set off the fourth one?"

"That would be me," came a thick, deep voice. Jon spun around to see Ted, the old man who daily stumped up and down Glen Eagles Road. With Ted's help, Jon eased his mother onto a deck chair.

"I was sure Dr. Ingersoll had shot you," she told Jon, reaching up to caress his face. Tears rolled down her cheeks. "What happened to that awful man, anyway? Did he get the, ah, *belt*? It's all a bit fuzzy."

Feeling chagrined, Jon replied, "I'm afraid he did."

"Well, I'm just glad you're still alive," his mother said.

For her benefit, Jon described her fall down the stairs and the events following. He thought it best not to mention Ptera and the anti-gravity belt in Ted's presence. Instead, he wove a jeweled heirloom belt into the story, claiming Dr. Ingersoll had stolen it from Mrs. Oliver at gunpoint before making good his escape. Surely old Ted hadn't witnessed Ingersoll's spectacular "human rocket launch."

Only Ted's role remained a mystery. "Thank you for distracting Dr. Ingersoll," Jon told him. "Where did you get the firecracker?"

Ted's eyes were watering. Jon assumed he had allergies. "I grabbed the biggest one I could find in your room," Ted confessed.

Jon recoiled. His privacy had been violated twice in one day—first by his sister and then by this senile stranger. "You . . . you went into my room? How did you know which one it was?"

"Never mind that," rasped Ted, wiping his rheumy eyes. "We must get Liv—I mean your mother—to a hospital. She's probably had a concussion and needs medical attention." Leaning over her, he touched her cheek, letting his fingers linger on her skin.

Jon and Jennica exchanged alarmed glances. Ted had never been inside their house before, yet he knew where to find Jon's room. Moreover, he knew their mother's pet family nickname. Was the old man pulling a practical joke, or was he stalking them?

"Nonsense," said Mrs. Oliver defiantly, brushing Ted away. "I'll be fine." She stuck out her hand. "Thank you for helping us, sir. My name is Olivia Oliver. These are my children, Jonathan and Jennica."

The old man ignored her hand. "I know," he said, his eyes watering again. "I'm Ted. This is no time for niceties." His voice sounded oddly strained, as if he were trying to talk with marbles in his mouth. "We have important work to do before—"

Grandfather Roberts' cheery voice interrupted him. "Hullo!" he called, shouldering his way through the kitchen sliding door. "Are you all having a barbecue without me? Say, did you know someone let the air out of your car's tires? They're flat as pancakes."

Jon groaned. "I'll bet that was Dr. Ingersoll's doing."

Dr. Roberts' face paled as he noticed Olivia Oliver's bloody head. "What happened?" he cried, rushing to his daughter.

"She took a fall," Jon explained. He didn't wish to go into greater detail for fear his grandfather would ask too many probing questions.

The paleontologist examined his daughter's scalp and eyes. "Your right temple is slightly swollen, but your pupils are of equal size," he told her. "Do you feel sick? Do you have a headache?"

"I did, but it's gone away," she replied. "I'm feeling much better now. Really, you shouldn't make such a fuss over me."

Dr. Roberts' worried expression softened. "You don't seem to have a concussion," he remarked. "How did you hit your head?"

Jon retold the Ingersoll incident from start to finish, again leaving out Ptera and substituting the heirloom belt for the anti-gravity belt. "And this is Ted," he concluded, gesturing at the old man.

Dr. Roberts shook Ted's hand. "A pleasure," he said. "I'm Ken Roberts. Thanks very much for coming to my family's rescue."

Ted humbly inclined his head. "I just happened to be passing by when I heard a commotion back here on the deck," he said. "Turns out God arranged for me to be in the right place at the right time."

"I should say so," Dr. Roberts agreed as he collapsed into a deck chair. "My, my," he murmured. "This is rather a lot to take in. What an adventure you've all had!" He glanced keenly up at Jon. "It's quite remarkable, to my way of thinking, that you managed to escape Dr. Ingersoll unscathed, while your mother did not. Are you certain you didn't leave out any details I should know about?"

Jon opened his mouth and then closed it again. He desperately wanted to present his grandfather with a genuine living fossil as a show-and-tell for his next lecture—but not in front of Ted.

A cool wind sprang up, and a few scattered raindrops spattered on the deck. Ted squinted up at the darkening sky and grunted, "In Western Oregon, we've got just three types of weather conditions: 'Raining,' 'Just Rained,' and 'About to Rain.'"

A great weight crushed Jon's chest, squeezing all the air out of his lungs and the tears from his eyes. The world turned gray. Had he heard Ted aright? Only one person ever used that expression, a man who had gone missing somewhere in the wilds of Afghanistan.

Reaching into his mouth, Ted pulled out two oval pieces of clear silicone about the size and shape of mango pits. His cheeks shrank, becoming taut like those of a younger man's. Next, he grabbed a shock of his unruly white hair and pulled up. His entire head of hair came off as a one-piece wig. Underneath the wig, his shaved head was as smooth as a nectarine.

After peeling away his beard, moustache and bushy eyebrows, he ripped off the tip of his nose and parts of his ears, removed some padding from under his shirt, and popped out two gray-tinted contact lenses. The man's eyes shone blue under the cloudy July sky.

"That's better," said Ted, shaking himself. "I was beginning to feel as old as I looked. Now you can see the real me."

Already weak from loss of blood, Mrs. Oliver let out a strangled sigh and fainted dead away in her chair.

Chapter 27
THEODORE REMMICK

Dad?" chorused Jon and Jennica. They looked at each other and back at Mr. Oliver. Then they rushed into his waiting arms. Laughing and crying, their father squeezed them before turning them loose. Together, they pulled Mrs. Oliver upright and massaged her limbs until she recovered from her faint.

Afterwards, Jon's parents embraced for so long that he thought they had forgotten the world around them. Finally, Mrs. Oliver held Mr. Oliver by his shoulders at arm's length.

"All this time, I thought you were dead," she said reproachfully. "Now I find out you've been roaming the neighborhood wearing that ridiculous disguise. What have you been up to? Why didn't someone tell us you were alive and were back in the States? We have all suffered terribly without you, Matt."

"I'm sorry, Liv," he said heavily. "Nobody told you because nobody knew—except me. The secrecy couldn't be helped. I didn't dare reveal myself to you for fear Ingersoll would use you to get to me and force me to divulge my private research. I never dreamed he would stoop to robbery and attempted murder."

"But how did you know he was trying to cheat you?" Jon asked.

Dr. Oliver rubbed some beard-glue off his chin. "Just before leaving for Afghanistan, I discovered Ingersoll was passing along some of our company's trade secrets to a shadowy Russian group known as the 'Korporatsiya.' I am reasonably certain he was planning to sell my gravity-cancelling technology to this organization for a tidy sum.

"After learning of his treachery, I took the precaution of carrying a passport, driver's license and credit card issued in the fictitious name of 'Theodore Remmick,' in case I needed to travel incognito. I've been 'Ted' ever since leaving Afghanistan."

"So that's why you encrypted your message to Jon," Dr. Roberts said. "You wanted him to find your secret laboratory before Ingersoll could get his hands on the anti-gravity belt—or should I say, 'jeweled heirloom belt.'" He winked and smiled conspiratorially at Jon.

"Indeed," said Dr. Oliver, grinning broadly at his father-in-law and son. "I'm very impressed, Jon, that you deciphered my riddle and figured out how to use the CL—Compact Laser—for its intended purpose. My Bible code would have stumped most people."

Jon flushed with pride and embarrassment. How he had missed his father's words of encouragement! "But what about the Taliban, Dad?" he asked. "Did they let you go, or did you escape?"

Dr. Oliver's face darkened. "Roughly thirty insurgents attacked our convoy near Kandahar and took me hostage. They were quite surprised to find a Westerner wearing what they thought was a suicide belt. I had brought the belt from Oregon to work on during my spare time. When I activated it, they all scattered like rats.

"After that, I launched myself into the air and let the wind carry me away. My captors took a few potshots at me, but providentially, I floated out of range before they could hit me."

His wife hugged him again. "I can't believe you're alive and back home, safe and sound. How did you find your way to Portland?"

Mr. Oliver drily chuckled. "That's another tale in itself. I had the misfortune of getting caught up in a katabatic wind, a northwesterly summer gale that blows in that region. In a matter of hours, I was swept out of Afghanistan and into Pakistan. When my battery finally gave out, I landed in a mango orchard just outside the city of Multan.

"Once the orchard owner understood I was a lost American, he pointed me toward the Multan International Airport, which is located about ten kilometers out of town. I hitched a ride to the airport with some Pakistani students. From Multan, I flew to Dubai. After a layover, I caught a flight to Seattle and another to Portland."

"God has certainly answered our prayers," murmured Dr. Roberts, his eyes moist. "It's a miracle you survived your ordeal."

Matt Oliver nodded. "It certainly is, considering that one of my friends was killed during the Kandahar ambush. Ironically, those terrorists unintentionally handed me the perfect opportunity to go underground without having to fake my own death. As 'Ted,' I could keep an eye on both my family and Dr. Ingersoll."

"Speaking of Dr. Ingersoll," said Mrs. Oliver with a look of distaste, "what do you suppose has become of that nasty man? The last I saw of him, he was sailing away like a leaf on the wind."

Matthew Oliver sighed. "He's probably halfway to the coast by now. I reckon he has fewer than two hours of power left. We'd better go after him before the belt's battery gives out."

"'Gives out'?" Jon repeated, mystified. "I just recharged that belt this afternoon. The battery should last quite a while."

His father explained, "That model is an earlier prototype with a battery that has a very limited number of charging cycles. With each cycle, the battery weakens until it won't hold a charge any longer."

Jon's mouth went dry as he realized he might easily have ended up like Dr. Ingersoll, lost among the clouds and liable to fall at any moment. Fortunately, he hadn't yet tested the belt outside.

He peevishly kicked at the spent firecrackers. "Why worry about Dr. Stalker? Why not let him suffer for the wrongs he's done? You've always taught Jen and me that bad behavior has consequences."

"A man's life is at stake here, Jon," his father sternly reminded him. "Despite his flaws, Ronald Ingersoll is still a unique creation made in God's image. He has value just because he's a human being."

"That's debatable," Jon muttered. "Anyway, I'll never understand why you teamed up with that guy in the first place."

His father answered, "Dr. Ingersoll was the first physicist to believe in me and my work. At the time, I never suspected he would betray me by stealing my discoveries. At any rate, I want to see him brought to justice for the crimes he's committed. He's also my only link to the Korporatsiya. If we're to prevent more of this industrial espionage from happening, we must cut off the head of the snake."

Mrs. Oliver peered up at the sky, as if Dr. Ingersoll's floating form might still be visible. "I suppose it's possible Ingersoll could make a safe landing, as you did in Pakistan," she told her husband.

She added, "Then he could make off with his prize. If he dies, someone could still steal the belt off his body. Either way, we lose."

Unruffled, Dr. Oliver replied, "I've designed a built-in failsafe for just such a contingency. If anyone tinkers with that belt's mechanisms, the components will harmlessly self-destruct."

Jon was glad he had never tried to take apart his father's invention, or he would have ended up destroying it. He asked, "Then why worry at all about Ingersoll's stealing your invention, if it can't be—what do you call it—reverse-engineered?"

"I didn't say it couldn't be reverse-engineered," his father replied. "I simply meant that most amateur electronics buffs couldn't defeat the self-destruct feature. Unfortunately for us, Dr. Ronald Ingersoll isn't your average 'solder-monkey.' He's a brilliant physicist."

"How do you plan to rescue Ingersoll?" Mrs. Oliver broke in. "You don't have a plane or a helicopter to chase him down with."

"I know of a place that sells hang gliders," suggested Jennica.

"We need another anti-gravity belt," Jon said gloomily.

"Oh, but we already have one," said his father brightly. Pulling up his shirt, he exposed a belt like Jon's wrapped around his midriff.

"This is the selfsame belt that saved my life in Afghanistan. It's equipped with an improved battery. Unfortunately, it won't help us much without a means of propulsion—a way to control our flight.

"Otherwise," Matt Oliver continued, "we'd be no better off than Dr. Ingersoll. The wind would just carry us along willy-nilly until the battery gave out or we ran into something solid, like a tree or a barn."

"'We'?" said Jon. "Do you have a third belt somewhere?"

His father winked at him. "Didn't you know? These devices generate a gravity-cancelling field large enough to contain two people."

Jon's mind whirled with possibilities. He settled upon the wildest idea of the bunch. *I think I'm gonna need a whole lot more peanut butter,* he decided. Then he announced, "C'mon, everybody. I want to show you something in the basement."

Chapter 28
THE SQUATTER

Jon paused at the door leading to the basement stairway. His family bunched up behind him like baby chicks following a hen. On the way past his bedroom, he had ducked inside to grab a jacket against the chill air downstairs—and perhaps even colder temperatures outside, if his plan panned out. His heart hammered like a string of firecrackers going off inside his chest.

"What's so important it couldn't wait till after we take your poor mother to the local hospital?" Dr. Roberts gruffly demanded. "She needs to be checked out by a physician."

"Don't worry about me," said Mrs. Oliver. "A few extra minutes in the basement won't kill me. Besides, how could I deny my son such a simple request, when he bravely risked his life to save mine?" Squeezing his shoulder, she teasingly added, "Are you going to show us where you stashed all the missing peanut butter and cookies?"

"Not exactly, Mom," Jon replied, red faced. "I've been purchasing peanut butter with my allowance money and keeping it down there, but I'm not eating it. It's for a friend of mine."

His mother's eyebrows ominously rose. "A *friend*? Are you telling me we have a squatter living in our basement?"

"Something like that," Jon grunted, his feet rooted to the floor. He couldn't help feeling he was making a serious mistake.

"The boy always did have a soft spot for strays—whether animals or people," Grandfather Roberts diplomatically observed.

Turning to her husband, Mrs. Oliver asked, "While you were 'Ted,' did you invite any homeless people to live down there?"

Mr. Oliver laughed. "No, but at times I was tempted to sneak in and crash on Jon's ratty old sofa and watch some TV."

Olivia Oliver looked horror stricken. "Do you mean you had no place to live? How did you manage to survive all this time?"

Her husband shrugged. "I stayed in character by sleeping under bridges, in haylofts, and in homeless shelters. I even went 'dumpster-diving' a few times. *That* was a truly unpleasant experience. My trials gave me a fresh appreciation for the hardships of the homeless. No one should have to live on the streets as I did."

"Thank the Lord those days are behind you," said Mrs. Oliver, embracing him tightly. "I'm so happy you're home again!"

"What did you wish to show us, Jonathan?" asked Dr. Roberts, his voice dripping with anticipation.

Motioning for his family to follow, Jon swiftly descended the stairs and flicked on the basement lights. The great gash Ptera had torn in the sheetrock still gaped darkly above the white apron of gypsum rubble. Jon saw no sign of the reclusive reptile.

"Now what?" said Jennica, wrinkling her nose against the basement's musty stench. "Mutant raccoons?"

"Raccoons?" Mr. Oliver said with a perplexed look.

Jon hurried to the bureau and removed an unopened jar of Karl's Kreamy from one of the drawers. If Ptera was anywhere nearby, the fragrant nut butter would draw out the reptile. He was unscrewing the jar's lid when he spotted Dr. Ingersoll's discarded utility belt on the floor and handed it to his sister for safekeeping.

Dr. Oliver pointed out a tall, fluted object standing in the shadows. "I see you bought a patio umbrella," he said. "It must come in handy on the back deck during hot summer days."

"I didn't buy any umbrellas," said his wife in a puzzled tone.

"That's not an umbrella," said Jon slyly. Approaching the pleated pillar, he tore off the peanut butter jar's paper seal.

Unfolding like a giant origami figure, the "umbrella" sprouted wings, claws and a spear-like beak. Jon's mother and sister screamed in warbling harmony, sending Ptera into a panic. The creature took flight, sailing around the room like an overgrown fruit bat. Jennica and Olivia screamed even more loudly.

Jon was impressed. He considered asking his sister and mother how they had managed to blend their voices so well but thought the better of it. He didn't want them both turning on him.

"My word!" rasped Jon's father, lapsing into his "Ted" voice. "What on earth is that thing, and what's it doing in our basement?"

Dr. Roberts' face blanched frost-white as the breath caught in his throat. Here was a prehistoric relic come to life, the stuff of nightmares and legends, a horror straight out of a science-fiction film.

"It's a pteranodon," he gasped, "or I'm not a Welshman. It looks just like the fossils I've found! Where did it come from?"

"Meet Ptera, one of our 'brollachans,'" Jon told him. "He and his friends have been hiding out in the Prosser Mine."

"What's a brollachan?" Dr. Oliver asked without taking his eyes off the animal gliding about the basement.

Jon briefly described the history behind the name and how he had discovered the winged reptiles living beneath Iron Mountain.

"This is *incredible!*" cried his father. "Pteranodons are supposed to be extinct, and they're living in tunnels under our house?"

By now, Ptera had returned to Jon and was licking out the peanut butter jar. Mrs. Oliver glared at the batlike animal. "So *this* is what has been eating all our Karl's Kreamy!" she said in disgust. "Shoo! Shoo! Get out of my house, you repulsive *thing!*"

Ptera ignored her. With his beak, he snapped the plastic jar in two like a dry twig and began cleaning out the halves.

Dr. Roberts shook his head. "Who'd have imagined pteranodons loved peanut butter? I assumed such creatures ate only fish."

"What will you do with your 'pet' now?" Jon's father asked him.

"Lend me your belt, and I'll show you," Jon declared.

Matt Oliver removed the belt from around his waist and handed it to Jon, who fastened it around his own middle over his jacket. Then from the bureau he brought out a fresh Karl's Kreamy jar for the pteranodon. While it was busy emptying this second jar, Jon activated the belt and swung himself onto the animal's back.

Ptera turned a red, suspicious eye up at him before returning to his nut-buttery feast. Mrs. Oliver clawed the air with her fingers as if trying to scratch out the pteranodon's eyes. "Jonathan Oliver, you get off that creature *right now!*" she screeched. "Do you hear me?"

"Yes, Mom, I hear you," Jon calmly replied. "Please lower your voice, or you'll upset Ptera. You don't want to do that."

His mother's eyes flashed. "And you don't want to upset *me*, either. Just remember who it is that prepares your meals!"

"Surely you don't expect to ride that beast like a horse," said Jon's father, staring up at him in alarm.

"Come up here with me, and you'll see," Jon told him.

Still distracted with the Karl's Kreamy jar, the pteranodon let Dr. Oliver climb onto its back. When the animal tried to shake him off, he scooted up behind Jon. As the gravity-cancelling field enveloped him, his weight no longer burdened the creature, and Ptera relaxed.

"Hold that tool belt up to its beak," Jon ordered his sister.

For once, Jennica obeyed him without any argument. Bravely confronting the pteranodon, she flapped Dr. Ingersoll's belt in front of it like a matador waving his cape at an enraged bull. Jon hoped Ptera wouldn't react like a bull by charging his defenseless sister.

"Now back away and move up the stairs," he instructed her. "I want you to lead Ptera outside, if he'll follow you."

Slowly, Jennica retreated from the fearsome creature, still dangling the belt in front of her. Ptera stalked after her, snapping his beak and waggling his head. Then Jon felt a tapping on his shoulder.

"What in the world are you up to?" his father demanded.

Jon replied, "If Ptera can sniff out an unopened jar of peanut butter on the kitchen counter, I'm sure he has a good sense of smell. When Dr. Ingersoll first entered the basement, he threw that utility belt at Ptera. I'm betting my pet still remembers Ingersoll's scent on the belt and will take us right to him—wherever he is."

"I hope you're not suggesting we actually fly on this monster!" Dr. Oliver protested, scooting backward.

Glancing over his shoulder, Jon teased his father, saying, "You're not afraid of heights, are you? Besides, rescuing Dr. Ingersoll was your idea, not mine, remember?"

While Jon's sister coaxed the pteranodon up the stairway, Mrs. Oliver collapsed onto Jon's old couch, murmuring, "Oh, no. Please tell me he's not going to let that thing run amok in my house. I'll have to fumigate the place for a week, if not a month."

Helping his daughter up from the sofa, Dr. Roberts told her, "I'm taking you to the hospital, and don't argue with me. I'll have to drive my pickup. Your old car isn't in working order, thanks to Ingersoll."

As Jennica backed up the stairs, Ptera lurched after her, using his foot- and wing-claws for traction. Upon reaching the top of the stairway, Jennica ran screaming down the hall, threw open the front door and tossed Dr. Ingersoll's utility belt into the yard.

The reptile chased the belt outside and launched into the air, still bearing its riders. In taking flight, it left all its ungainliness behind. Jon felt a surge of panic as the Oliver house shrank beneath him.

After his stomach had returned to its proper place, he leaned forward and gripped the pteranodon's bony, backward-curving crest. Fortunately, Ptera was a male. A female's smaller, rounded crest would have offered scant handholds.

"Hang onto my waist!" he called back to his father, and strong arms encircled his middle.

Aided by a brisk east wind, Ptera hurtled westward, his wings rhythmically flapping. Jon prayed that neither his belt's battery nor Dr. Ingersoll's would run down before Ptera could catch up to him.

Jon didn't know for sure whether the pteranodon was following Ingersoll's scent or not. The reptile might simply be seeking food or a new home. He could only hope revenge was driving his pet onward.

By now, Ptera had climbed so high into the sky that the earth appeared as a fuzzy patchwork of greens and browns, while the air had taken on a decidedly frosty bite. Jon was glad he'd worn his jacket.

Looking ahead, he spotted a hawk-like object fluttering among the clouds. As Ptera approached the object, Jon realized it was a human being sailing through the air, stick limbs flailing wildly.

They had found Dr. Ingersoll. Seeing the pteranodon rapidly overtaking him, the physicist shrieked in terror.

Jon's heart flip-flopped. He hadn't thought this far ahead. Now that Ingersoll couldn't defend himself, what would Ptera do to him?

Swooping down, the reptile seized the scientist with its feet and swung around to fly eastward. Clutched in the pteranodon's claws, Dr. Ingersoll trailed behind the beast like the tail on a gigantic kite.

Suddenly, Jon was struck with a sickening certainty. The pteranodon was heading back to its hidden Iron Mountain lair, where it could devour its prey without interruption.

"Help! Let me go, or I will shoot this brute!" Dr. Ingersoll bellowed, waving his gun in the pteranodon's general direction.

Jon's father leaned over Ptera's back to address his former business associate. "I would advise against doing that, Ron. If you shoot our mount, it will drag you down to the ground with it."

Dr. Ronald Ingersoll's eyes grew as large as the pteranodon's. "You're still alive!" he croaked. "How did you—? Never mind. Tell this creature to put me down safely, or I will shoot *you*."

"We cannot control Ptera," Dr. Oliver replied. Still holding onto Jon with one hand, he removed a black box from his pocket with the other. His thumb pressed and held its single button.

"This," he told Dr. Ingersoll, "is the remote control for your belt only. I have already pressed the power button. If you shoot me, I will release the button, your belt will switch off, all your weight will return and the pteranodon will drop you like a hot rock.

"When your battery runs down, you'll be dropped anyway. I've calculated you have only a few minutes of battery power left. The unit you stole is a prototype with a smaller power pack than the one in our model. Just sit tight and be thankful we came looking for you."

Grumbling under his breath, the scientist lowered his pistol. Still, Jon didn't like having a loaded gun at his back. There was no telling what Dr. Scoundrel might do in his desperation.

Before long, Jon thought the treetops looked a little closer. Ptera was losing altitude. *Ding! Ding! Ding!* Ingersoll's belt chimed. As Jon's father had predicted, the thieving physicist's battery was losing its charge, and he was growing heavier by the minute.

Now the treetops were brushing Jon's feet. He was about to pull off his shoes and toss them away to lighten Ptera's load when his father handed him a smooth, flat object resembling a black laptop battery, only shorter and thicker.

"You'll want to replace the power pack in your belt before it runs down," Dr. Oliver said. "I forgot to mention that this newer model has two battery compartments. That way, you don't have to unplug the spent battery before plugging in the charged one. Otherwise, I don't need to tell you what would happen."

Jon knew. Switching out a single-port model's depleted power pack in midair could have fatal results, since that operation would interrupt the belt's electrical supply. He crammed the replacement power pack into his pants pocket, since his jacket lacked any.

He was twisting the anti-gravity belt around so as to access its power pack from the front when the trees opened up, and he saw his neighborhood laid out below him. Abruptly, Ptera furled his wings and landed on the Oliver house's shake roof.

"Oof!" grunted Dr. Ingersoll as he sprawled across the sun-baked cedar shingles. Then he hopped up and pointed his gun at Jon.

"Now that we're back on terra firma, Matt," he told Dr. Oliver, "I have the upper hand again. I'm leaving now with my gravity belt—

and I'm taking your son as insurance. Besides, his belt still works, and I need a quick way down from your roof. Try to stop me or call the police, and your boy will suffer the consequences."

Matt Oliver's jaw tightened and his fists clenched. "Leave my son out of this! He has nothing to do with our quarrel."

"Oh, but he does," said Dr. Ingersoll smoothly. "Who do you think has been experimenting with your belt all this time?"

The scientist grabbed Jon's arm and pulled him off the pteranodon. Before Jon could break free, his captor leapt off the roof. Because Jon's power pack was also nearly depleted, the two landed solidly on the front lawn. Then Dr. Ingersoll dragged Jon across the street to his utility van and tossed him onto the front passenger seat.

After slamming Jon's door, Ingersoll slid into the driver's seat, engaged the power door locks and sped off, tires squealing. Jon tried to unlock his door using its control switch, but the physicist foiled his escape attempt by pressing the master override switch.

Jon was trapped. Helplessly he watched his father through the rear window as he climbed down a tree from the roof and sprinted toward the Malibu, which was squatting low to the ground. The car's tires were all flat, as Grandfather Roberts had already discovered.

Jon groaned in despair as the van barreled around a corner, and the Oliver house disappeared behind some fir trees. Nobody could help him now. Dr. Ingersoll had cleverly covered his getaway.

Chapter 29
THE FLYING VAN

D r. Ingersoll pointed his pistol at Jon. "If you try to escape again or refuse to cooperate," he snarled, "I'll make you 'holier' than a slab of Swiss cheese."

The physicist snickered at his own sick joke. Then he slapped the power button on Jon's anti-gravity belt. As his full weight returned, Jon sank into the cushioned seat like a sack of lead.

"You're not going to get away with this!" he screamed at his captor. "My father will call the police on you. You'll go to jail for kidnapping and robbery, and attempted murder, too."

Dr. Ingersoll smirked over at Jon. "What would your father tell the authorities? 'A nasty bad man stole my anti-gravity belt'? Who would believe such an absurd accusation? As for the kidnapping charge, I'm merely taking my business partner's son to GyroSensors in my utility van. What could be the harm in that?"

Jon slumped in his seat. The scientist was right. Jon's father would probably never make that vital 911 call, knowing he would be endangering his son's life. No police car would pull up behind the white van, lights flashing and siren wailing.

Nobody was coming to rescue Jon. He was on his own.

"Thanks to your naive, Christian do-gooder sentimentality," Dr. Ingersoll went on mockingly, "I have come out on top again. You should have let me float away until my power pack ran down. Now hand over that belt, or I'll shoot you where you sit."

Reluctantly, Jon took off his father's gravity-cancelling belt and laid it on the console between him and Dr. Ingersoll. The physicist then pulled out his cell phone and speed-dialed a number.

When someone answered, he growled, "*Oo menya etot apparat. Vstreteet'sya som noy na stoyankye.*" Then he disconnected the call.

Curious despite his apprehension, Jon asked, "What was that you just said? It sounded like Chinese to me."

Dr. Ingersoll snorted. "That just goes to show what a moron you are. I was speaking Russian, a language you will never learn, first because you are dyslexic and second because I plan to dispose of you. Now I have one device to keep, and one to sell to my friends."

Jon shuddered, remembering his father's mention of the Russian *Korporatsiya*. It was true: Dr. Ronald Ingersoll was a traitor not only to GyroSensors but also to his own country.

Thunk. Something struck the van's roof with the force of a falling tree limb. Tires screeching, the vehicle swerved into oncoming traffic and back again as Dr. Ingersoll wrestled with the steering wheel.

"What was that?" he shouted, regaining control of the van.

"I don't know—" Jon began, when he spotted a telltale shadow wheeling above the van. Ptera! The reptile dove again on the vehicle, passing right in front. Ingersoll veered and slammed on the brakes.

While the physicist was busy dodging Ptera, Jon snatched the belt from off the console and strapped it on under his coat. Just as the van crested a high hill, he punched the power button. He could only hope the battery had rested long enough to regain some of its power.

Jon's gamble paid off. The vehicle's wheels left the pavement, and the van sailed off the wooded hilltop. Its momentum carried it through the air about a hundred feet above the road before the belt's field weakened and the van began to sink.

Dr. Ingersoll frowned as the speedometer needle dropped to zero. He gunned the engine and twisted the steering wheel, but the van maintained its course. Ingersoll glanced out his side window, and his face blanched. The van was floating sixty feet off the ground.

As if rubber-band powered, the man's head spun toward the empty console. Then he reached with clawed fingers to throttle his passenger. "You!" he howled. "What have you done with my belt?"

Recoiling, Jon slipped a hand under his jacket and found the belt's power button. "Touch me, and I'll turn off this belt," he warned the scientist. "Then your van will drop like a rock—with us in it."

Dr. Ingersoll drew his pistol again. "I'm not going to touch you!" he growled. "I'm going to shoot you and take the belt, as I should have done before. Then I'll kick you out of my van and *you* can drop like a rock. See, I don't need you as a hostage any longer."

Fear shot through Jon like a lightning bolt. He lunged across Ingersoll to jab the door-lock override switch while pinning down his foe's gun hand. Then he flung open his door and leapt out.

At the last second, Dr. Ingersoll grabbed the back of his jacket. However, Jon wriggled out of the coat, leaving it behind.

No longer buoyed by Jon's belt, the van plummeted to earth and spectacularly pancaked onto the road. All its windows blew out, but miraculously, the cargo vehicle still ran. Belching clouds of blue smoke, it rattled along the road, its engine clanking and grinding like a garbage disposal full of rocks.

Only then did Jon notice his right arm was bleeding. When bailing out of the van, he must have cut himself on the metal door frame. Meanwhile, his anti-gravity belt was losing energy—and he was losing altitude. *Ding! Ding! Ding!* The belt's low-battery warning began chiming, and its power button's light blinked.

"Help!" he cried as the ground rushed up to meet him. If only he had stayed safely inside the van!

Chapter 30
THE KORPORATSIYA

Bracing himself for the impact, Jon felt something seize the back of his shirt, bringing him to a sudden stop. It was Ptera. Flapping mightily, the pteranodon bore down on Ingersoll's fleeing van. As he dangled helplessly from the creature's claws, Jon remembered the spare power pack in his pants pocket and plugged in the charged unit, ensuring Ptera wouldn't drop him.

The world rolled by beneath him as if in a chase scene shot from a helicopter. But this was no film. The wind was whistling all too realistically past his ears, and he felt dizzy from Ptera's bobbing flight.

Even though he was weightless, the wind's resistance still tugged at his body. Suddenly, his shirt's top button popped off and fell away. If the rest of his buttons followed suit, Jon would slide right out of his shirt and would end up like Dr. Ingersoll—drifting aimlessly above the earth until his battery ran down.

Ptera swooped down on the smoking van. "Pull up! Pull up!" Jon screamed as the vehicle's white roof filled his field of vision.

Whoomp! Jon's body struck the van's flat roof a glancing blow, bruising his ribs and driving the air from his lungs. He wheezed and gasped as more buttons popped off his torn shirt.

Ptera jerked him back into the air, leaving the van to swerve from side to side. A shallow, boy-size dent marred its roof.

Jon raised his eyes in time to see a lamp-lit overpass approaching. He cried out as the pteranodon pulled up at the last possible moment, scraping his shins on the overpass's side railing. Startled drivers and passengers goggled at him as he shot over their vehicles.

Briefly, he entertained the notion of grabbing a car antenna to break free of the pteranodon, but the overpass flashed past before he could carry out his plan. It was just as well; at such a speed, the jolt would have ripped his arms from their sockets.

By now, an orange sun was sinking behind the Coast Range. Early fireworks displays were already blossoming and dying across the landscape like varicolored chrysanthemums. In the thickening gloom below Jon, a long line of cars was snaking behind Dr. Ingersoll's sluggish van. Passengers and drivers alike were hanging out of their windows, craning their necks toward the sky and pointing upward.

At first, Jon assumed the gawkers were gazing at the evening fireworks. Then he realized they were staring at *him*—or rather, at the alien form winging through the dusky heavens. He could only hope the onlookers had mistaken Ptera for a patriotic kite or perhaps for a stealth bomber on its way to join the holiday festivities.

However, no aircraft glowed as Ptera did. After sunset, the animal gave off an unearthly light, reminding Jon of his first encounter with the reptile. No wonder the people below were rubbernecking! Jon hoped none of them would attempt to shoot Ptera out of the sky.

Onward the long-necked beast flew through the canopied night. Wings tirelessly whipping up and down, Ptera blazed through the blackness. Below the sleek pteranodon, countless pairs of headlights speared the darkness as cars wound along invisible traffic lanes like so many glow-worms going mindlessly about their business.

Jon wondered which of those glow-worms was Ingersoll's van. At such a height, it was difficult to distinguish one vehicle from another.

Ptera, though, was unfazed. Guided by his sense of smell, by his eerily luminescent eyes or by a combination of the two, the vengeful reptile unflinchingly followed the streams of traffic westward.

Cushioned in velvety darkness, Jonathan Oliver forgot his fear of heights. He was flying free, a ptera-boy wearing borrowed wings, un-disputed master of the sky, inspiring awe and terror in human hearts as his body obscured the moon and stars.

Pop! Pop! Jon felt two more buttons leave his straining shirt, and he remembered who he really was—a wingless, earth-bound boy with nothing but his bottommost button standing between him and a short flight followed by a long drop. His stomach lurched.

Suddenly, Ptera veered over an access road, where a lone vehicle was crawling toward a sprawling complex of buildings ringed by fir trees and security lights. *GyroSensors.*

The vehicle backed into a parking space, and its lights snapped off. Ptera followed. As the pteranodon swung low over the GyroSensors administration building, *Zing!*—Jon's last button flew off, and he slipped out of his shirt. Ptera carried the shirt away without him.

Rather than drift off into the night, Jon took his chances on the nearest solid surface and punched the green power button. With a bone-jarring *thud*, he dropped six feet onto the building's gravel-covered, asphalt roof. He made a mental note to ask his father to build a belt prototype that would let the wearer down more gently.

After picking bits of gravel out of his skin, he crawled to the edge of the roof and peered over the parapet. Dr. Ingersoll's still-smoking van sat almost directly below him, its front end facing away from the building. Jon saw no sign of the physicist or of Ptera.

Just then, two black SUVs pulled into the spacious parking lot, their headlights swinging wildly to and fro. At the same time, the van's headlamps flashed on and off twice.

The SUVs swerved toward Ingersoll's vehicle and pulled up beside it, one on either side. The two drivers climbed out, both wearing heavy overcoats despite the evening's lingering summer heat. In turn, the van's door creaked open, and Dr. Ingersoll emerged, still wearing Jon's original anti-gravity belt around his waist.

The three men exchanged words in the Russian language. Then they switched to English.

"You have device?" the taller of the Russians asked in an accent thicker than his coat. Jon dubbed him, "Ivan" and his ham-handed partner, "Igor." They looked capable of twisting the spindly Ronald Ingersoll into a human pretzel. Jon hoped it wouldn't come to that.

"Of course I do," Ingersoll answered, pointing at the gravity-cancelling belt. "Did you transfer the money to my account?"

"Nyet!" said Ivan. He laughed unpleasantly as he and Igor produced two assault rifles from under their overcoats. Jon recognized the weapons as AK-47s from photos he had seen on the internet.

"Hey!" Dr. Ingersoll protested. "We had a deal! The device for one hundred fifty billion dollars—and that's a bargain."

"We don't bargain," said Igor. Reversing his rifle, he thrust the butt end into Dr. Ingersoll's midsection above the anti-gravity belt. As the scientist grunted and doubled over in pain, Ivan stripped the belt from the traitor's waist and took the pistol from his pocket.

After conferring in their own language, the Russians fastened a handcuff to Ingersoll's right wrist and tossed him into the cargo bay of Ivan's SUV. Then Ivan crawled into the cargo space behind him.

"What is this thing in here with me?" bellowed Dr. Ingersoll.

Ivan muttered something in Russian before exiting the vehicle. "Let me out of here!" Ingersoll demanded even more loudly.

Igor growled, "Be happy we not kill you now, annoying little man. We enjoy—how you Americans say?—to *whack* you on this spot. But better you sweat first before *phhhht*." With a malicious grin, the Russian drew a forefinger across his own throat.

"We don't like competition," Ivan explained. "We fix two problems same time—you and your GyroSensors *kompaniya*."

"Wait! You don't know how to disarm that belt!" cried Dr. Ingersoll. "If you don't enter a code, it will explode when you try to use it."

The Russians pointed their guns at him. "Then give us code, or we shoot you," they told him bluntly.

Jon could hear the physicist hemming and hawing. For once, the man couldn't talk his way out of his dilemma. In spite of himself, Jon actually felt sorry for his former kidnapper.

The pair of foreign agents guffawed. "We not stupid," Igor said. "Our engineers can figure out belt. *Do svidaniya*, soo-ker!"

He slammed the cargo hatch shut. Igor and Ivan were heading for the other SUV when a shadow fell over them. Suddenly, Igor shot into the air. Moments later, a long, wailing scream echoed into the night, ending abruptly in a sickening *crunch*. The hapless Russian had plummeted onto the parking lot beside one of the security lights.

Searching for an unseen foe, Ivan frantically spun this way and that, AK-47 at the ready. A bat darted by, looping as it chased insects, and the Russian emptied his magazine at it. The bat escaped unscathed, but Igor's light pole did not. Bullet-riddled, it tipped over with a creaking groan and collapsed onto his broken body.

The shadow swooped again, and Ivan crumpled, headless. Jon retched. Ptera must have taken a dislike for guns—and the people packing them—after Ingersoll had brandished his in the basement.

Now that the double-crossing (and double-crossed) physicist was out of commission—along with the Korporatsiya's hired thugs—Jon decided it was safe to come down from the roof.

But how? He didn't have a rope or a ladder. If he activated his belt and jumped off the building, the slightest breeze would carry him away before he could land. He pulled out his cell phone to call for help, but the battery was dead. Ptera was nowhere to be seen.

Exploring the rooftop, he came across a zig-zagging fire-escape ladder attached to the side of the building. After scrambling down the ladder, he cautiously approached Ivan's body. To his relief, he found the anti-gravity belt still in the headless Russian's grip. Had Igor been holding it, the device would have been destroyed in his fall.

A strong wind was kicking up dust clouds in the parking lot as Jon snatched his old belt from Ivan's grasp and fastened it around his waist above the newer prototype. Then he went to the SUV where Dr. Ingersoll was still cooped up in the cargo bay. Muffled cries for help pierced the cargo hatch.

Knowing the scientist's cold, calculating methods, Jon was reluctant even to speak with the devious man. Grimacing, he popped the hatch and found Dr. Ingersoll curled up in a corner of the cargo space, handcuffed by his wrist to a sturdy steel strut. Behind him, a cigar-shaped metal cylinder was strapped to the floor. Jon's spine tingled. He had seen such a device somewhere before.

"Eh, I'm afraid you have me at a disadvantage, Master Oliver," Ingersoll said weakly. "This time, we may need to work together to survive. I assume our Russian friends have left."

Jon snorted at the formal title. "Master Oliver," indeed! A short time ago, Ingersoll had called him a "moron." The cunning fellow had to be desperate to resort to such flattery.

"I may be young, but I'm not stupid," Jon said flatly. "I will never work with you. Not now, not ever. As for *your* Russian friends: They are both dead, and good riddance, too."

Dr. Ingersoll licked his dry lips. "Dead, you say?" A new but misplaced respect for Jon shone in his eyes. "That is good news. But I'm afraid you don't apprehend the seriousness of our predicament. You may wish to examine this apparatus here more thoroughly."

Assuming Ingersoll was referring to the cylinder, Jon leaned in to give it a second look. Constructed of brushed stainless steel, it bore indecipherable markings in the Russian Cyrillic alphabet—and a stylized, clover-leaf design arranged within a yellow circle.

Being Dr. Matthew Oliver's son, Jon immediately recognized the dreaded trefoil universal warning symbol. *Radiation.*

Sticking his head farther into the cargo space, he saw a small, rectangular window set in the cylinder's far side, just above a black numerical keypad. Red digital numerals were counting down in the window. *02:35:15*, read the numbers. Horrified, Jon backed away from the SUV so hastily he struck the back of his head on the hatch.

Dr. Ingersoll remarked in a despairing tone, "According to my *former* business associates, this object is a '*Taktichyeskoye yadyernoye oostroystvo*'—a tactical nuclear device with a full fifty-kiloton yield. Though not particularly powerful by modern nuclear standards, a fifty-kiloton blast would level all of Portland."

A nuclear weapon! Jon went weak at the knees.

We fix two problems same time, Ivan had said. The nuke would obliterate both Dr. Ingersoll and GyroSensors, thus eliminating any and all potential anti-gravity belt competitors. When it came to tying up loose ends, the Russians were nothing if not thorough.

"Can't you defuse it or take it apart?" Jon breathily asked.

"We would need to disarm the bomb first, but our Russian friends inconsiderately neglected to give me the access code," said Dr. Ingersoll heavily. "I suggest we vacate the premises immediately."

Just over two and a half hours remained on the timer. That would have given "Igor" and "Ivan" plenty of time to escape the blast zone—but not enough time for Jon to safely dispose of the device in an unpopulated area. Perhaps he could drive the SUV into Central Oregon's desert with scant time to spare—but then what?

"Are you going to release me, or do you plan on leaving me here to be vaporized?" Dr. Ingersoll demanded.

"I don't have the handcuff key," Jon snapped. He needed time to think, but time was a luxury he could ill afford. He couldn't bring himself to rummage through the dead Russians' pockets, yet even if he had the key, releasing Ingersoll was a spectacularly poor idea.

The scientist rattled his handcuff chain. "If you free me, maybe I can disarm the device and save us both," he said.

Jon ignored him. Instead, he prayed aloud, "Lord, please tell me what to do. I need Your wisdom here. Without the code, I can't disarm this bomb, and I doubt Dr. Ingersoll can, either."

"Talking to your imaginary sky-god again, are you?" the physicist taunted him. "Does he ever answer you back?"

Jon was beginning to sweat. "Yes, He does."

"Well then, did he tell you the disarming code?"

"Not exactly," Jon replied, "but I may not need it."

A last-ditch option had intruded on Jon's thoughts. Wetting his finger, he tested the wind. It was blowing from the east. He would have to act swiftly and decisively if his plan was to work.

From his neck, he removed the lanyard with his GyroSensors key card. Hoping it would still work, he raced around to the administration building's glass front door and swiped the card through the magnetic lock. The door opened to a dimly lit, unoccupied lobby.

After a brief search, he found an electrical outlet and plugged both anti-gravity belts into it. Then he snatched up a sheet of blank printer paper and a GyroSensors pen on his way out the door.

Returning to the SUV, he placed the sheet of paper on the hood and scrawled: *The man handcuffed in the back is Dr. Ingersoll. You should arrest him for espionage, kidnapping, assault, robbery, attempted murder, stalking, and being an all-around crook. Please call my parents and tell them I love them. I have both belts, and I'm using them to save Portland from a nuclear disaster. They'll understand what I mean. Dr. Ingersoll can tell you more about it.*

After jotting down his name and home phone number on the note, Jon slipped it under the SUV's left windshield wiper. Then he returned to Dr. Ingersoll. Sweat droplets beaded the scientist's ashen face as he repeatedly glanced at the compact bomb's shiny casing.

"Are you setting me free," he whined, "or am I about to become part of a radioactive mushroom cloud?"

"Neither," said Jon. Crawling into the cargo compartment, he released the strap-clamps securing the nuclear device to the floor.

Next, he rolled the cylinder backwards to make the countdown display easier to see. While Dr. Ingersoll mopped the sweat from his forehead, Jon watched the timer until it showed ten precious minutes had elapsed. Then he dashed off to check on the belts.

"Where's your Christian charity now?" shouted the physicist after him. "You've left me to watch my life ticking down to zero!"

Ignoring him, Jon swiped his key card to re-enter the administration building, unplugged the recharged anti-gravity belts and strapped them both on. After that, he ran back to the SUV, where he powered up his original belt. Finally, embracing the tactical nuclear weapon with both arms, he lifted it effortlessly out of the cargo space.

Dr. Ingersoll stared up at him. "What are you doing with that? Are you insane, do you have a death wish—or both?"

Choking on his own fear, Jon couldn't answer. He flexed his knees and sprang straight up into the sweltering night sky.

Chapter 31
ON THE EAST WIND

Jon was sailing straight toward a grove of tall fir trees on the parking lot's west side when a wind gust barely boosted him and his deadly cargo over the trees. Fortunately, a waxing moon had risen, helping to illuminate the slumbering landscape.

Originating east of the mighty Cascade Range, the Gorge wind was howling through Portland in all its scorching strength. As the main gap through the Cascades, the Columbia River Gorge acted as an air-pressure relief valve between the mountains' east and west sides. Carved chiefly by the churning waters of the Missoula Flood, the roughly eighty-mile-long, scenic canyon regularly funneled fierce winds between its high cliffs.

Harnessing those winds, an endless procession of statuesque, three-bladed turbines snaked along the barren bluffs above the Gorge's eastern reaches. From a distance, the turbines resembled spiky toy jacks set atop elegant white saltshakers.

Jon was counting on that ferocious easterly wind to carry him west out of prosperous Lake Oswego and the Willamette Valley, across the Coast Range and eventually over the Pacific Ocean—if the wind and his partially recharged power packs held out.

Speeding along, he scrambled atop the bomb, sitting astride it like a cowpoke riding a barrel-chested pony. The nuclear weapon's electronic counter continued relentlessly ticking off the seconds and minutes until detonation. *02:03:29*, the timer now read.

He did the math: At best, assuming sustained winds of forty miles per hour (which was unlikely), he might just reach Tillamook—but not beyond—before the clock ran out. Having enjoyed many pleasant vacations in that coastal town with his family, he knew the distance from GyroSensors to Tillamook was seventy-five to eighty miles.

And this would definitely be a one-way trip, both for the ticking time bomb and for him. Since the nuclear device would most likely explode before he could drop it into the Pacific Ocean, he decided instead to cut it loose over the Coast Range in order to spare Tillamook. After all, a ground burst anywhere near the resort city would flatten it, unless the wind shifted and carried boy and bomb farther south or north into more sparsely populated areas.

Of course, if his power packs died before he reached the coastal mountains, he wouldn't have much choice in the matter.

Regardless of the outcome, nobody would ever know for certain what became of Jonathan Oliver. If he escaped the bomb blast and his belt batteries lasted long enough, the wind would blow him out to sea, along with most of the nuclear fallout. He would prefer that fate to being caught in a fifty-kiloton explosion.

He wondered whether anyone had discovered his note yet and sounded the alarm, or whether the residents of Tillamook were still blissfully unaware that death was riding the wind toward them. Not for the first time Jon wished his cell phone battery was fully charged.

Below him, galaxies of lights marked the sprawling suburbs west of Oswego. As the lights thinned out, they gave way to dark, unbroken forests marching toward the mountains beneath the moon.

While Jon silently sailed along, an aching loneliness gripped his heart. He longed for a glimpse of his parents or even of his sister. For too long he had ridiculed and resented Jennica. If he survived his ordeal, he promised himself—and God—to be a better brother to her. He might even let her handle his Fruitadens dinosaur fossil.

And what of his father? To be reunited with him so briefly only to be torn away from him again was more than Jon could bear.

Soon he was passing among craggy, fir-clad peaks. Having lost both his jacket and his overshirt, he shivered in his thin, short-sleeved undershirt. According to the timer, over an hour had passed, though it felt as if he had been bomb-riding forever.

The breeze shifted, driving him closer to the forest below. He winced as the wobbling weapon grazed the tips of moonlit trees. All at once, the bomb lodged itself between two hemlocks. Jon tried to shake it loose, but to no avail. He would be forced to abandon the device and take his chances with the wind and his anti-gravity belts.

He was about to launch himself away from the steel cylinder when a strong gust lifted bomb and rider back into the air. Once he had gained more altitude, Jon noticed a glow on the western horizon. It wasn't the dawn, since the sun rose in the east, not the west.

Was he seeing a forest fire sparked by illegal fireworks? He recalled the Tillamook Burn disaster from his Oregon history studies. Between 1933 and 1951, hundreds of thousands of acres in the Tillamook State Forest below him had repeatedly gone up in smoke.

As the wind carried him closer to the glow, he realized with growing horror that he was approaching a conglomeration of artificial lights. What *was* this place? Had he nearly ditched the Russian nuclear device just east of a major town or city?

The lights rapidly slid by beneath him, followed by dark forests. Then a few more lights appeared, and Jon heard a distant, drumming rumble like the roar of a crowd in a football stadium. Beyond all hope, he had reached the Pacific Ocean with its crashing breakers.

Not far from shore, a cluster of huge, conical rocks caught his eye. Jon recognized them as the Three Arch Rocks, a famous natural feature just offshore from the town of Oceanside.

That meant he had just overflown Oceanside as well as Tillamook. But how had he reached the coast so quickly? He was sure of his calculations, unless the Gorge wind had been blowing more strongly than he had originally estimated.

Whatever the reason, God had granted him an extra thirty-one minutes. If the wind held, he hoped in that half-hour to travel far enough to dispose of the bomb safely at sea.

Like a wisp of thistle down, he rode the winds alone above that vast expanse of thundering ocean waves. All the while, the Russian weapon's electronic timer continued its inexorable countdown.

Chapter 32
THE LOST BOY

W e interrupt this program to bring you some breaking news," announced the grim-faced newscaster. "This evening, numerous callers in southwest Portland have reported sighting a large flying creature unlike any known bird.

"Some commentators have dismissed the sightings as an early Fourth of July hoax, while others have suggested the unknown object was nothing more than an ordinary hang-glider, since a human figure was observed dangling beneath the craft. However, most of the witnesses maintain the entity was flapping its wings, while modern hang-gliders are equipped with rigid airfoils."

Jon's parents, sister and grandfather sat spellbound in front of the living-room television. Earlier that evening, Dr. Roberts had brought his daughter home from the Tualatin hospital with a mild concussion, a sprained wrist and a colorful contusion or two.

Meanwhile, Jon's father had called the authorities, despite Dr. Ingersoll's threats. However, a search of the local area had turned up no sign of Jonathan Oliver, Dr. Ronald Ingersoll or of the utility van. While awaiting further word from the police, the family gathered in the living room to monitor the news and to pray.

"We have just received a cell-phone video clip of the mystery object from motorist Cameron James," the serious newscaster droned on. "Please message us on our website with your comments about this video. We will keep you updated as more reports come in."

The newscast segued to a blurry shot of the dusky sky. The phone camera wobbled before settling on a dark, fuzzy blob sailing overhead. As the blob came into focus, it took on the form of a crane-necked creature flapping its wings. The photographer followed the flying beast until it vanished into the falling night.

Matt Oliver aimed a remote at the television and shut it off. "I think we would all agree what *that* thing was," he said. His father-in-law, wife and daughter all shared knowing glances.

"It *looked* like Jon's ptera-whatever," Mrs. Oliver declared.

"Maybe it was a griffin or a dragon," offered Jennica. "I thought I saw flames shooting out of its mouth."

"You've been reading too many fantasy books," said her mother reprovingly. "Dragons and griffins don't really exist."

"Those pterodactyl thingies aren't supposed to, either, but we're living on top of a bunch of them," Jennica shot back.

Her grandfather nervously paced about the room. "They're *pteranodons*," he corrected her. "You were probably seeing reflections in the sky from fireworks displays, not actual flames. It's like the water-mirages people sometimes see in the desert."

Olivia Oliver waved her long arms as if she were guarding an opponent in a basketball game. "Who cares about mirages?" she cried.

"I just want my son back. And what are the authorities doing to find him? Not enough. Why, they haven't even issued an AMBER Alert yet. A missing pet turtle would garner more attention than Jon has."

"Tomorrow's the Fourth, Liv," her father reminded her. "Many of our law-enforcement personnel are taking some well-deserved time off. Speaking of time off, I thought the doctor instructed you to get some rest. You mustn't upset yourself."

Mrs. Oliver waved her arms again even more vigorously. "Why shouldn't I be upset, when my son is missing and probably about to be eaten by that flying creature? Heaven only knows what's become of the poor boy. I just wish we knew where he was."

Her husband replied, "The Lord of Heaven does know where Jon is and what has happened to him. That's why we needn't fret, since our son is in God's hands. Besides, the police should be calling any minute now to update us on the search progress."

As if on cue, the inventor's cell phone jingled "Amazing Grace" in his hand, and he jabbed the answer key. "This is Matt Oliver," he said tersely. He listened for several minutes, his face slowly turning to a granite mask.

"Yes, sir," he said, nodding. "I understand. Thank you for calling. You'll let me know as soon as you hear anything further, won't you? Good. Thank you again, and God bless you."

Mrs. Oliver's face blanched as tears ran down her cheeks. "Who was that?" she whispered. "What's happened? It's Jon, isn't it? Please tell me! Don't hold back anything."

"That was a Sergeant Jameson," Dr. Oliver replied. "The police have found Dr. Ingersoll lying handcuffed inside the back end of an SUV in the GyroSensors parking lot. Ingersoll's badly damaged cargo van was sitting nearby, along with another SUV."

Mrs. Oliver put a hand to her mouth. "Was Ingersoll *dead*?"

"Far from it," Mr. Oliver told her. "Apparently my ex-business partner is threatening to sue the police for not rescuing him sooner. The authorities did find a couple of AK-47s lying in the lot beside two dead men. One of them was missing his head."

"Ewww, gross!" Jennica commented.

Her father hastened to add, "Neither of them was Jon. The police found no sign of him, though it seems he left a short note tucked under the first SUV's windshield wiper."

"What did it say?" asked his wife eagerly.

Dr. Oliver rubbed his stubbly chin. "Our son wrote that Ingersoll should be arrested for his misdeeds—which he was. Jon also wrote that he loves us, and that—get this—he is using both gravity-cancelling belts to protect Portland from a 'nuclear disaster.'"

"A nuclear disaster!" chorused his listeners skeptically.

"That's right," said Dr. Oliver. "It sounded farfetched to me, too, except that forensics investigators detected radioactivity in the SUV's cargo space where Ingersoll insisted a nuclear device had lain."

"Who would want to level Portland with a nuclear bomb?" exclaimed Mrs. Oliver. "And how could Jon have gotten mixed up in such a dangerous business? It's inconceivable."

Under his breath, Dr. Roberts murmured, "It sounds to me as if the poor boy doesn't expect to see his family again, bless his heart."

Dr. Oliver's phone rang again. When he answered it this time, his face turned ashen. "Yes . . . yes . . . I see. All right. Thank you for calling. Good-bye." He pressed the disconnect button.

His wife, daughter, and father-in-law gazed up at him expectantly. "The police found traces of blood inside Dr. Ingersoll's vehicle," he said. "They need to run more tests to determine whose it is."

Mrs. Oliver wilted like a leaf of day-old lettuce. "If Ingersoll had a car accident, Jon could have been hurt! Maybe you should call Sergeant Jameson back and ask him to check the local hospital emergency rooms. Jon could be in any one of them."

Matt Oliver patted his wife's shoulder. "Jameson assured me he and his men are doing all they can to find our boy. However, I doubt they will know where to look. I haven't yet told the police what kind of 'belts' Jon has, so they don't realize how far he could have traveled just by hitchhiking on the air currents, as I did in Afghanistan."

Mrs. Oliver shivered. "I hope he hasn't 'hitchhiked' very far."

"In the meantime," her husband continued, "we had best pray for our lost boy. Since only God knows where he is right now, only God can bring him back to us safely."

Jennica burst into tears. "Am I ever gonna see my brother again?"

Her father lovingly embraced her. "You mustn't worry about Jon. Think of God as having a GPS tracker for everyone on the planet. He is looking out for all of us every second of every day."

A startled look came over Dr. Roberts' face. "A GPS tracker?" he repeated. "Maybe that idea isn't so farfetched."

"What do you mean?" his son-in-law asked him with a half-smile. "You know God doesn't need GPS devices to find people."

The paleontologist looked embarrassed. "No, but I do. You see, I forgot to mention that as a precaution against theft, I attached a miniature GPS unit inside the belt Jon found in your laboratory. It had escaped my mind until you brought up the subject."

Dr. Roberts put on his reading glasses and took out his cell phone. After tapping on the screen, he excitedly announced, "The tracker is still active! I was afraid it had been damaged."

"Where is Jon?" the others asked, gathering around him.

Kendall Roberts owlishly gazed down at the phone through his glasses. More taps. "Oh, dear," he said. "If this information is accurate, Jon is currently located about eight miles due west of Lake Oswego—and he's moving along at a rapid rate."

Chapter 33
COUNTDOWN TO ETERNITY

Ding! Ding! Ding! Jon's gravity-cancelling belt sounded its dreaded warning. He had hoped the older model's power pack would last a while longer, but the nuclear weapon's added mass had probably drained the battery more quickly.

Still gripping the bomb with his legs, Jon switched on the newer belt and shut off the earlier model. He was on his last battery pack.

As dawn frosted the restless waves with a weary gray light, he glanced down at the counter. It read, "00:25:37." Anxious to release the bomb as far as possible from the mainland, he waited until the coastline had shrunk out of sight. With just over ten minutes left on the timer, he shoved the cylinder away from him with his feet. In actuality, because the device possessed a much larger mass than his own, he was pushing himself away from it.

As soon as a few feet separated Jon from the weapon, it escaped the belt's gravity-cancelling field and began to free-fall toward the water. Jon watched it shrink to a speck and plunge into the Pacific, raising a white spout of spray. Having viewed an educational video of an underwater nuclear explosion, he knew that in ten minutes, a second, much mightier water eruption would burst from the ocean.

Jon hoped he'd allowed the bomb enough time to sink to a safe ocean depth. However, he also suspected that when it came to undersea nuclear detonations, no depth was truly safe. The explosion would still produce a shock wave and plenty of radiation—and ten minutes would leave him well within the blast zone.

He had to get away—and quickly.

But how? The wind was still gusting fiercely, but it kept changing direction. Without the bomb's stabilizing effect, Jon began tumbling through the air, much as he had seen happen earlier to Dr. Ingersoll.

Whump! Something sandbagged Jon with the force of a runaway locomotive. Had the device already exploded? Was he dead? If so, why did his shoulders burn so badly?

Against the wind, he was traveling rapidly eastward toward the rising sun and the mainland. An enormous shadow loomed above him. Wings vigorously flapping in impossibly wide, graceful arcs, a pteranodon had seized him by the shoulders in its claws.

Ptera. Jon wept for joy. The reptile must have doggedly followed him all the way from the GyroSensors complex to the coast. For once, his pet had come to help him instead of hunting down Dr. Ingersoll or smelling out a pocketful of peanut butter cookies.

But could the pteranodon fly swiftly enough to escape the blast zone? Since releasing the bomb, Jon had lost track of the time. Glancing behind him, he saw nothing unusual. Waves and their following troughs unhurriedly advanced across the heaving ocean like regular ranks of green-helmeted soldiers.

He stared ahead, trying to ignore the pain where Ptera's claws were digging into him. When Oregon's rugged coastline swam into view, he estimated five minutes remained until detonation. But would exposure to salt water and the pressures of the ocean depths disable the bomb before it unleashed Armageddon on Tillamook?

Soon, Jon could make out people moving about on the beach. Arms raised and fingers pointed as startled beachcombers noticed the bat-winged creature hurtling toward them like a jet plane. Only fifty yards remained . . . forty . . . thirty . . .

Ding! Ding! Ding! The anti-gravity belt sounded its death knell—and Jon's. He groaned. The device had picked a fine time to give out on him. He felt heaviness returning to his body.

Ptera faltered before plowing into the blessed beach like a base-ball player sliding into home plate. Dog-walkers and beachcombers alike scattered. Jon rolled out of the pteranodon's grasp and brushed himself off. He shakily stood on solid ground for the first time since leaving the GyroSensors parking lot with the nuclear device.

A moment later, he felt a vibration in the soles of his feet as if an earth tremor had struck. He knew the Cascadia Subduction Zone off Oregon's coast was long overdue for a severe earthquake, but this was different. The ground was trembling, but the ocean was swelling.

Far from shore, the Pacific bulged. The bulge quickly grew, expanding into an immense white globe of churning steam and water. The globe ruptured as boiling brown clouds burst through its crown. A mighty thunderclap sounded, followed by a rumbling roar.

In just seconds, the cloud had taken on a flattened mushroom shape. "Get off the beach!" Jon yelled at the dumbstruck onlookers. Shutting down his failing belt, he ran for higher ground. Ptera wisely took to the air and disappeared over some shore pines.

Jon slogged across the sand and raced up a rickety flight of stairs that clung to a crumbling seaside cliff. After climbing the stairway, he staggered onto a parking lot laid out on the clifftop. Behind him, a wave-ring was expanding from the mushroom cloud's base.

Jon braced himself for the towering tsunami he was sure the explosion had spawned. Instead, only a few large waves swamped the shore, producing minor flooding.

He was puzzling over this turn of events when a sheriff's patrol car pulled into the parking lot, lights flashing. Realizing he was a prime suspect in the first hostile nuclear detonation in U.S. territorial waters, Jon ducked behind a wind-sculpted pine at the lot's edge.

A beefy deputy climbed out of the vehicle. Seeing the misshapen mushroom cloud, he let out a low whistle and reverently removed his service hat. "Holy Moses!" he exclaimed. "We've got a front-row seat. We'd better evacuate this whole area. Can't risk people getting radiation sickness from the fallout."

"You needn't worry about fallout," said a familiar voice. "Seawater will dampen much of the harmful radiation."

Dr. Roberts was exiting the patrol car, followed by Jon's father, mother and sister. They all stood gaping at the dying remnants of the massive underwater nuclear explosion.

"My poor, dear, brave Jonathan," murmured Mrs. Oliver, tears streaming down her face. "What have you done? What has become of you? Will I ever see you again here on this earth?"

"From what I understand of the situation, your son is a bona-fide hero," declared the sheriff's deputy, replacing his hat.

Jon's mother huskily replied, "That may be, but the fact is I just want him *back*—and preferably in one piece."

The deputy mournfully shook his head. "Nobody could have survived that explosion. I am truly sorry for your loss, but you can take comfort knowing your boy saved a lot of lives."

"Ours included," said Matt Oliver reverently.

"Homeland Security has been trying to track that nuke, but it disappeared off their radar," the deputy went on. "The thing could have wiped out all of Lake Oswego and Portland, too. How did it end up so far out in the ocean, anyway? I'm pretty sure your boy didn't have time to drive it through the mountains. Besides, he was too young to have a driver's license—or own a boat."

Mrs. Oliver sniffled, "Jon wouldn't have let that stop him."

"I have a pretty good idea how that bomb was transported out here," Mr. Oliver told the sheriff's deputy. "Unfortunately, I can't divulge the details for ah, security reasons."

Dr. Roberts fiddled with his cell phone. "According to my phone application," he said, "Jon's GPS tracker is still working. However, the app shows him standing practically on top of us. Maybe I'm just seeing our location instead, and his GPS really is disabled."

Jon's father choked back a sob. "Why couldn't he have waited for help instead of escorting that weapon all the way out here? He could have strapped a belt onto it and let the wind do the rest."

"Maybe that's just what he did," said Dr. Roberts, lowering his voice to prevent the sheriff's deputy from overhearing the conversation. "I never thought of that possibility. The GPS device would work whether Jon was with the anti-gravity belt or not."

"Except that the belt—and your GPS locator—would have been destroyed when the bomb exploded," Dr. Oliver pointed out.

Mrs. Oliver brushed away a tear. "If I know my son, he wouldn't have set the nuke loose like that, not knowing where it would land. He would have stuck with that thing until it was safely over water and then let it go, even if it meant losing his own life."

She sighed. "If I had known he would pull such a foolhardy stunt, I would have let him eat all the peanut butter cookies he wanted."

"Really?" Jon blurted out. He covered his mouth as his family and the sheriff's deputy turned toward his hiding place.

"Who's there?" barked the deputy, drawing his gun. "Show yourself, but don't make any sudden moves, understood?"

Jon crept out from behind the pine. "It's just me," he said.

Pure bedlam ensued. Jon's family rushed over to surround him, peppering him with hugs, kisses and questions. "Where have you been? How did you get here? Are you all right?" they asked.

"I'm fine—I think," he replied. "But what's this about a GPS tracker? Is that how you found me?"

While the sheriff's deputy was busy talking on his radio, Grandfather Roberts told Jon about the GPS locater he had planted in the original gravity-cancelling belt when Jon was asleep one night. Then everyone made Jon go over his hair-raising adventures—twice.

When he had finished, his father observed, "You couldn't have picked a better spot to release that nuclear weapon."

"Why is that?" Jon asked him.

"The continental shelf is relatively narrow off this stretch of coastline. When you gave that bomb the heave-ho, you had already passed the drop-off point where the shelf falls away into much deeper water. By the time your nuke detonated, it had sunk far enough that the ocean absorbed most of the explosion's energy."

"It's not my nuke," Jon weakly protested.

"The shelf itself dampened some of the shock, too," his father went on. "Otherwise, this section of the Oregon coast would have been completely devastated, with the loss of countless human lives."

"I was gonna drop it in the mountains," Jon said, "but I got here a lot faster than when our family used to drive to Tillamook."

His father joyfully laughed. "Of course you did! If you look at a map of the highway route from GyroSensors to Tillamook, you'll see it describes a wide arc of seventy-five miles or more, but as the crow flies—or the boy glides—it's only about fifty-seven miles.

"Now, if you had just attached your gravity-cancelling belts to the weapon and launched it into the air by itself, that nuke probably would have detonated right over Tillamook's cheese factory."

"Just what Oregon needs: a ton of radioactive cheese," Mrs. Oliver quipped. "But why would Jon's riding that awful bomb have made any difference in the distance or speed it traveled?"

"Simple," said her husband. "Based on Jon's description, I'd say the Russian device was aerodynamically shaped. That is, it offered little wind resistance, which would have kept it in the slow lane, so to speak. Jon's body, on the other hand, acted as a sail that caught the wind and propelled him and the bomb along at a good clip."

By this time, more police cars had screamed into the parking lot. Next arrived some sinister-looking, black SUVs that Jon feared belonged to the Korporatsiya until he noticed the official United States government license plates.

He and his father were whisked back to Portland for several days of interrogations, which included demonstrating the remarkable capabilities of the anti-gravity belts. However, neither Jon nor Dr. Oliver revealed the role Ptera had played in the whole affair.

As far as the interrogators knew, Jon had outwitted Dr. Ingersoll on his own, and a change of wind direction had blown him back to the mainland after the bomb's release. Suggesting that live pterosaurs were roaming the night skies of Lake Oswego would have made the Olivers sound like a couple of crackpots. As Jon saw it, Dr. Ingersoll had already cornered the market in the crackpot department.

Chapter 34
REUNIONS

When the police, the FBI and Homeland Security finally released father and son from custody, Olivia Oliver picked them up in her trusty Malibu. Earlier, Dr. Roberts had called a mobile service to replace the car's tires. Wearing coveralls, he met the Malibu as it pulled into the driveway. He was cradling a caulking gun like a baby in the crook of his arm.

"Welcome back!" he called out. "I just fixed that bullet hole in your deck. It looks as good as new now."

Enormously excited to arrive home, Jon was the first to exit the car. He was about to hug his grandfather when he spotted a droopy, forlorn form perched on the rooftop. "Ptera!" he shouted.

The bedraggled pteranodon swooped down to alight on the driveway. Furling its wings, it nuzzled its wedge-shaped head against Jon and probed his pockets with its beak. The reptile squawked its displeasure at finding no cookies, peanut butter or otherwise.

Jon looked over at his mother questioningly and mimed scooping up a spoonful of peanut butter from a jar.

"Oh, all right," she sighed, throwing up her hands. "I'm sure I've still got a few Karl's Kreamy jars in the cupboard."

While his mother went in search of peanut butter, Jon inspected his pet. Ptera seemed thinner but otherwise healthy.

"What's this?" Jennica asked. She pointed to a bloody furrow marring the pteranodon's sleek torso.

Jon gasped, "Ptera is hurt!" Suddenly, nothing else mattered to him except helping his friend get well.

"I suppose we'll never know what caused that injury," Jon's father mused. "If only the poor beast could talk!"

"I think I can tell you what happened," Jon remarked, examining the shallow gash. "When Ptera dove on Dr. Ingersoll's van, its radio antenna must have raked his chest. I was so busy trying to protect myself that I didn't even notice it at the time."

Jennica ran into the house, returning with bandages and a tube of antiseptic ointment. Ptera didn't protest as she smeared some of the salve on his wound and applied the bandages. Afterwards, he tested his wings and let out a screech that echoed down the mountainside.

"Where did you learn how to do that?" Jon asked his sister.

Jennica affectionately smiled at him. "From working with horses, silly. Underneath their skins, most animals are pretty much alike."

Just then, their mother appeared with a jar of Karl's Kreamy. After she removed the lid and offered it to Ptera, the reptile polished off the contents in record time, to everyone's delight and amazement.

Mrs. Oliver peered into the empty jar. "Well!" she remarked with a thoughtful look. "That was just like watching a stray dog lick out a bowl. I think this creature might come in handy after all."

As the Olivers trooped into their home, Ptera trailed after them. Mrs. Oliver pretended not to notice. While the pteranodon sniffed around the kitchen, everyone took a seat at the dining-room table and joined hands. Jon's father gazed pointedly at him.

"Will you pray?" he asked.

Jon bowed his head. "Dear Lord," he began, "we can't thank You enough for saving us from Dr. Ingersoll and the nuclear bomb. You have watched over our family while Dad was gone and brought him home safely from Afstanigan—I mean *Afghanistan.*"

Pray for Dr. Ingersoll.

Jon stopped mid-prayer. *No, Lord. I can't pray for that man.*

I will give you the words to speak and the will to pray for him.

Jon collected himself. "Speaking of Dr. Ingersoll, Lord, uh, please keep him from causing any more trouble and . . . and guide him into the truth. Oh, and I thank You, Lord, for making pteranodons and letting them live under our house. They're an awful lot of fun."

Jon's mother made a gurgling sound, and the family broke into gales of laughter. Afterwards, Jennica helped the lady of the house prepare her specialty—a deep-dish chicken pot pie. As the family ate, Jon once again recounted his narrow escapes from Dr. Ingersoll, the Korporatsiya, and the nuclear weapon that nearly destroyed Oswego.

When the pot pie was gone, Mrs. Oliver placed the empty glass dish on the floor for Ptera to lick clean, much to Jon's astonishment. "I've seen how this ptera-thingy can scour out a peanut butter jar," she explained. "I hope it can do the same for my casserole dishes."

Dr. Roberts pushed his chair back from the table. "Thank you for another lovely meal, Liv," he told her. "I'd better be going now. I'm looking forward to a good night's sleep for a change."

Jon jumped up to see his grandfather out. As soon as he had cracked the front door, it was shoved open the rest of the way. A forest of microphones, expensive cameras and yammering faces pressed through the doorway, driving him back. Then the questions began.

"Are you Jonathan Oliver, young man?"

"You can't hide in your house forever, you know."

"Is it true you have discovered a living dinosaur?"

"May we see it?"

"Did your father actually invent an anti-gravity device?"

"Could you demonstrate it for us?"

"We've heard Dr. Oliver was kidnapped by insurgents in Afghanistan. Has he been found yet?"

"What about your sister and your mother? Are they here?"

"SHOW US THE DINOSAUR!"

Jon was completely flustered and tongue tied. "Yes, I am. Yes, I have—I mean no, it's not really a dinosaur. Er, that is, I don't know what you're talking about. No, you can't see it! No, he didn't! No! No! No! Now get out, all of you! Help! Help!"

With that, Ptera himself howled down the hallway, scattering the nosy news reporters like a flock of frightened sparrows. After Jon slammed and bolted the door against the intruders, Ptera sniffed at him as if to make sure he was unharmed.

It was Dr. Ingersoll all over again. Jon resisted the urge to race around the house locking the doors and windows.

"It looks as if I'll be spending the night with you folks after all," Grandfather Roberts told him with a rueful grin. "I'll ask your mother to put on another pot of coffee. I have a feeling we're in for a long siege. Reporters are a persistent lot, once they've caught the scent of a sensational news story."

"What was all that uproar?" Mrs. Oliver called out. She and her husband were hurrying down the hall with Jennica.

"Your pet just tore out of the kitchen like a runaway kite on steroids," Jon's father added, glancing around suspiciously.

"Ptera was just trying to protect me," Jon said. He pointed to the living-room window, where goggling faces and long-lensed cameras pressed against the glass. Jennica ran in and closed the drapes.

"Who are all those people?" Mrs. Oliver gasped. "Should we be calling the police or the fire department?"

"They're just news reporters, Mom," Jon told her.

"Unfortunately, we can't deny that these pteranodons exist," Grandfather Roberts said. "Too many people have seen Ptera flying about, and just now, he sent a whole gaggle of journalists packing."

Matthew Oliver laughed, a sound Jon had missed for months. "Who would have guessed a reptile could make such a fine watchdog?" the scientist said. His expression sobered. "We still have much to learn about Ptera and his kin. More importantly, we must protect them from curiosity-seekers and the like."

"How can we do that?" Jon asked his father.

"First of all," Dr. Oliver began, "we won't be selling these creatures to any zoos. They should remain wild and free, while allowing for strictly controlled scientific observation. We'll also want to ensure the population continues to thrive, even if it means buying out all the local stocks of Karl's Kreamy." He smiled and winked at Jon.

Everyone nodded in agreement.

"What I don't understand, though," Dr. Oliver went on, "is how these supposedly extinct creatures could suddenly show up on our doorstep. Did someone clone them from fossil DNA?"

Dr. Roberts brightened as he warmed to his favorite subject. "No, they weren't cloned. These pterosaurs have survived here not only because Oswego Lake offers plenty of fish and frogs, but also because Iron Mountain's geothermally heated caverns and mine drifts make a perfect habitat. Like other reptiles, pteranodons undoubtedly require consistently warm temperatures to remain active year 'round.

"They're similar to Florida's manatees, which congregate around hot springs and power-plant outflows to stay warm. I also suspect the extra heat helps the pteranodon eggs to incubate and hatch."

Pteranodon eggs! Jon thought. *Now that's something I'd like to see.* Neither VORCATS nor CORVATS had come across any eggs in their subterranean explorations—at least not that Jon had noticed.

"But what about the sulfur dioxide in the mine tunnels?" he asked his grandfather. "Wouldn't the pteranodons die from all those stinky fumes building up inside their lair?"

"Good question. It's possible these creatures have developed a slight tolerance for the gas. This evening, I also noticed Ptera fanning his wings when smoke from the oven filled the kitchen. It's a habit acquired over many generations that would help reduce the concentration of sulfur dioxide underground and improve ventilation."

Jon pictured Ptera and his friends lined up in a tunnel, wings flapping to bring in fresh air and to drive out the sulfur dioxide vapors. But where was Ptera now? The reptile had disappeared after scaring off the reporters, and Jon hadn't seen a beak or a tail since.

Then he heard a faint rasping noise coming from the basement doorway. He crept down the stairs and turned on the lights to find Ptera masquerading again as a patio umbrella. The pteranodon was perched on the threadbare back of Jon's broken-down sofa, head tucked under one wing, snoring softly.

Ptera had finally made himself at home.

Smiling at the sight, Jonathan Oliver turned off the lights and quietly tiptoed up the stairs. At the top, he left the door ajar. This time, he had nothing to fear from what was lurking in his basement. This time, he had nothing to fear at all.

EPILOGUE

S ince the authorities could hardly deny the fact that a nuclear blast had occurred off the Oregon coast (making for quite a memorable Fourth of July in Tillamook), they elected to reveal only the main details surrounding the explosion. Before long, word got around that a Jonathan Oliver had single-handedly averted a nuclear disaster in Oswego and the surrounding communities.

A few weeks after the blast, the City of Lake Oswego held a lavish parade in Jon's honor. Much to his chagrin, he and his family were seated in a convertible and had to toss handfuls of candy at the crowds of spectators. Complete with wailing fire engines and police cars, the procession traveled north along State Street and turned up "A" Avenue to stop at City Hall, where the mayor presented Jon with the keys to the city. To avoid tripping over his dyslexic tongue, Jon restricted his remarks to a stilted, "Thank you very much."

Jon's former school also got into the act with an assembly held in his honor. He was wishing he could use an invisibility cloak to escape all the attention when he spotted Renée Doulière at the back of the gymnasium, which had been renamed for him. When she smiled at him, he forgot all about gravity-cancelling devices, nuclear bombs and pteranodons, peanut butter cookies and even Dr. Ingersoll.

Unfortunately, since Jon had witnessed so many of Ingersoll's criminal acts, the day came when he was forced to testify against the scientist in court. Facing his nemesis again triggered traumatic flashbacks: Ingersoll scuttling through the pteranodons' tunnel, Ingersoll sending Jon's mother tumbling down the stairs and later threatening to shoot her, Ingersoll stealing the anti-gravity belt, Ingersoll firing his pistol into the deck and rocketing skyward, Ingersoll kidnapping Jon and trying to kill him. Plotting, scheming, sneering and screaming, the treasonous physicist haunted Jon's dreams on many a night.

Throughout the court proceedings, the accused was unrepentant, refusing to testify on his own behalf. Every time Jon was called to take the stand, Ingersoll mouthed at him, "I will get you, little man!"

Thanks to Jon's testimony, Dr. Ronald Ingersoll was convicted of attempting to sell sensitive technology to a foreign power and was sentenced to fifty years in a federal maximum-security prison. Though the physicist was about to trade his lab coat for an orange prison jumpsuit, Jon couldn't shake the nagging fear that prison bars could not long confine the cunning and unscrupulous Dr. Ingersoll.

Shortly after Matthew Oliver began full-scale production of his patented gravity-cancelling device, GyroSensors became the most profitable—and generous—business in the world. Proceeds from the sale of Dr. Oliver's inventions helped fund schools, libraries, churches, hospitals, universities and overseas humanitarian missions.

A small portion of those profits eventually enabled Mrs. Oliver to replace her ancient, earth-hugging Malibu with a gravity-cancelling,

Levitational Personal Transportation Vehicle (LEPTVEE). With its streamlined, teardrop shape and powerful propulsion and steering fans, the LEPTVEE could take off and land on a postage stamp.

Daredevils preferred to get around with an anti-gravity belt and a gas thruster. They usually carried backup batteries, just in case.

Before long, roads, streets, highways, bridges, overpasses and train tracks became obsolete and disused as people chose to move themselves and their freight using gravity-disrupting machines. A thriving industry sprang up to dismantle the old transportation network and recycle the asphalt, steel and concrete.

Streets in the Glen Eagles neighborhood were among the first to be torn up, making way for more houses, bike paths and park-like greenbelts. Most driveways were also phased out, except those used as basketball courts—as at the Oliver home.

Brick chimneys became a liability as burglars and would-be Santa Clauses learned to descend into them from overhead. The Olivers capped theirs, at Mr. Oliver's insistence. By then, Jon and Jennica had learned the truth about Santa, anyway.

Trucks, airplanes, ships and trains gave way to passenger-saucers and freight-barges. Some shippers slapped a gravity-cancelling device on each pallet of goods, roped the pallets together and towed the whole lot through the air using a sky-sled, a glorified airboat with an anti-gravity generator and an oversized propulsion fan.

Tethered to the ground or sea-bed, floating buildings became commonplace, freeing up more space for farms, homes and forests.

Equipped with industrial-size, gravity-cancelling generators, massive battery banks and solar panels, these weightless structures could remain aloft for years, safe from floods, fires, tsunamis and earthquakes. GyroSensors now occupies one such floating edifice.

Speaking of natural disasters, Dr. Oliver installed some powerful exhaust fans in the house to remove volcanic gases in case further "magma burps" occurred. He also converted the basement into a pteranodon observatory and feeding station, with free access for the public through a side door cut into the foundation's west wall.

After the inventor had opened up the lower half of the wall where Ptera had broken through, the reptiles could come and go as they pleased, which they often did. Jon and his father kept the spacious observatory stocked with Karl's Kreamy and a motley assortment of broken-down couches—the pteranodons' favorite perch.

Once the Olivers began their peanut butter feeding program, fewer local pets went missing. That meant fewer placards plastering the neighborhood power poles—and fewer unhappy children.

Hugging the observatory's south wall, an illuminated glass case displayed the mementos of Jon's adventures: his anti-gravity belts and gas mask, the pteranodon claw, his father's encoded message, the NAS Bible Jon had used to decipher it—and CORVATS. This mini-museum became a shrine for pterosaur-lovers the world over.

For those wishing to observe the pteranodons in their natural habitat (without building their own CORVATS), Jon's father helped him install night-vision cameras inside the creatures' main cavern.

While seated before computer monitors in the temperature-controlled comfort of the basement observatory, viewers can watch the reptiles go about their daily underground activities.

Though it turned out the "brollachans" possessed no hoarded treasure, Jon wasn't disappointed in the least. By his reckoning, he had found something of greater value during his many adventures—the knowledge that God would look after him and his family even when all hope seemed lost.

When they aren't putting on free exhibitions at schools, summer camps, churches and universities, Jon and Ptera enjoy taking long, leisurely flights over Oswego Lake and the scenic mountains and valleys of the Pacific Northwest. Ptera eventually grew to become the largest pteranodon in Oregon—or anywhere else, for that matter.

Drs. Roberts and MacKenzie turned down many job offers at prestigious universities and other institutions to devote themselves to the Young Earth Geological Society. They frequently tour the world together, conducting lectures and seminars at churches, colleges and universities. Their seminars are especially well attended at New Hope Church, where Reverend and Mrs. Sanford continue to minister.

Dr. Roberts homeschooled Jon and Jennica until they enrolled in an accelerated online program. Powered by his mother's prayers and her delicious cooking, Jonathan Oliver distinguished himself as a scientist and inventor in his own right, with many patents to his name.

Not to be outdone, his impish sister went on to earn a Ph.D. in reptile biology. As the official pteranodon veterinarian-in-residence, she has introduced those incredible flying cryptids to many fellow biologists and veterinarians.

Jennica's pterosaur paintings have become recognized the world over, while her exquisitely lifelike pteranodon murals grace many a wall in downtown Lake Oswego. In her spare time, she helps look after the horses at the Equestrian Club.

Never again did Jennica call dinosaurs "boring."

After learning of the reptiles' fondness for peanut butter, Karl's Kreamy, Inc. adopted a pteranodon as their product logo (courtesy of Jennica's artistic talent). In a goodwill gesture, the company awarded Ptera a lifetime supply of peanut butter, which Mrs. Oliver occasionally dips into when she bakes her delicious cookies.

These days, however, Jon and Jennica's mother spends more time on the basketball court than she does in the kitchen. As the coach of the "Amazons"—Lake Oswego's homeschooled girls' team—she has led her studious players to several league championships.

If you're wondering what became of Dr. Oliver's office key, it never did turn up after Jennica dropped it in the basement. However, to this day, Ptera sets off metal detectors wherever he goes.

This book details only the first of the Oliver family's exploits. The Olivers invented more scientific marvels and enjoyed further adventures, which I shall chronicle if time, pen and paper do not fail me.

ORDERING INFORMATION

Readers may contact the author at: WilliamBurt@Greencloaks.com.

Available from Amazon.com and other online stores
Available for Kindle and other devices

OTHER TITLES BY WILLIAM D. BURT

Titles in the "King of the Trees" series (listed in order):

The King of the Trees
Torsils in Time
The Golden Wood
The Greenstones
The Downs
Kyleah's Mirrors
The Birthing Tree

Made in the USA
San Bernardino, CA
14 June 2017